"Captain, were you never in love?"

Nana's breath was warm on his cheek. He thought of all
the cold winds from the Channel to the Bering Sea that had
scoured his face. He prided himself on knowing how to
keep his ship aright and sail close to the wind. How could
he explain that Nana's breath on his cheek gave him more
heart than any breeze from any point of the compass?

"Yes, as a matter of fact, I was in love once," he whispered
back. "What about you, Nana? Lost your heart yet?"

"Yes," she answered, her voice so soft. "It's a dreadful
business, isn't it?"

"There will be another one along someday, Nana," he said,
and hated himself.

"I doubt it," she replied. She looked at him, and he could
not help seeing the tears in her eyes. "How…how did you
get over her?"

I can't, he thought. *I won't.*

* * *

Marrying the Captain
Harlequin® Historical #928—January 2009

MARRYING the CAPTAIN

Carla Kelly

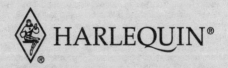

HARLEQUIN®

TORONTO • NEW YORK • LONDON
AMSTERDAM • PARIS • SYDNEY • HAMBURG
STOCKHOLM • ATHENS • TOKYO • MILAN • MADRID
PRAGUE • WARSAW • BUDAPEST • AUCKLAND

Recycling programs
for this product may
not exist in your area.

ISBN-13: 978-0-373-29528-9
ISBN-10:   0-373-29528-6

MARRYING THE CAPTAIN

www.eHarlequin.com

Printed in U.S.A.

To my dear sisters, Karen Deo and Wanda Lynn Turner,
who showed me Plymouth.

Said the sailor to his true love, "Well, I must be on my way,
For our topsails they are hoisted and the anchor's aweigh;
And our good ship she lies awaiting for the next flowing tide,
And if ever I return again, I will make you my bride."

—"Pleasant and Delightful"
English folksong

Prologue

After five years in Plymouth following her 1803 expulsion from Miss Pym's Female Academy in Bath, it still burned Nana Massie to be an Object of Charity.

She closed the door to the Mulberry Inn behind her and looked down at the hand-lettered placards in her hand. In these hard times of war, made harder for Plymouth by the blockade of the French coast, the innkeeps at the bigger inns closer to the harbor still had no objection to the placards, even though everyone knew there was no need for them, because there was no overflow of clientele.

We Massies are engaged in a great deception, Nana told herself as she hurried toward the harbor, blown along by the stiff November wind. She glanced back at the Mulberry, knowing Gran would be watching her from an upstairs window. Nana waved and blew her grandmother a kiss. *This grand deception is for my benefit entirely,* she thought, *and I am hungry.*

She was cold, too, even though she wore Pete's cut-down boat cloak and two petticoats under a wool dress. She knew Gran was knitting her a cap to cover her short hair, and it wouldn't be done a moment too soon. After a look of deep worry when Nana returned from the wigmaker last week with short hair and a handful of coins for the more pressing bills, Gran had turned straight to her knitting.

Even though Nana could see one small frigate bobbing in anchor at the harbor below, Gran and Pete both had insisted it was time to take placards to the large inns. Time meant noon, when the inns would be serving dinner. Those two old conspirators knew the keeps and cooks would see that their darling Nana ate.

The sailors were seldom allowed off the warships, but the officers and petty officers were usually free to go ashore and stay in Plymouth's inns. Many ships meant more officers. If the larger inns were full, some could be persuaded to stay at the Mulberry on far-distant Gibbon Street, if there was a placard announcing the little inn's existence.

Nana almost turned around after she passed St. Andrews Church. The matter was hopeless because the admiral of the Channel Fleet, in his wisdom, had decreed that his warships would not leave their watery stations for anything except dire emergency. They were to be revictualed at sea—with food and water—and remain there, because of Boney and his threats.

One frigate in the harbor. Nana stopped and nearly crammed her signs in a bin, then reconsidered. Gran would be devastated if she returned from the harbor unfed, and would see right through a lie to the contrary.

Besides, the wind carried the fragrance of sausages from the Navy Inn, her first stop. Nana wiped her mouth with the back of her hand and let the wind coax her along.

There was a sausage for her at the Navy Inn, with a crunch when she bit into it that nearly brought tears to her eyes. She went through the charade of protesting when the keep insisted on wrapping an extra one in oiled paper, then hurried to the

Drury Inn, where she left another placard and sat down to potato soup with hunks of ham and onion, bubbling in the broth of cream flecked with butter.

The keep even handed her a pot of it to take along, declaring the soup would just sit around, uneaten and unappreciated, if she didn't take it back to the Mulberry. Maybe Gran or Pete could have it, if Nana was full. She accepted it with a smile, even as her face burned from shame.

At Drake's Inn, the bill of fare was pasties, as she had hoped. Mrs. Fillion, the keep, insisted she eat one quickly, before it went bad, then packaged two more for her, all the while complaining about an admiral so mean-spirited as to keep his ships from Plymouth and make life a trial for the quayside merchants.

"Well, we *are* at war, Mrs. Fillion," Nana ventured.

Mrs. Fillion sighed. "You'd think in the year of our Lord 1808 we could have figured out some way to abolish such stupidity."

She took a placard, but gently informed Nana that the Drake had already received the frigate's surgeon, both lieutenants and captain.

She slid another pasty on Nana's plate. "At least we'll have Captain Worthy when he returns from Admiralty House in London in a day or two. His sea chest is already here."

"That's his frigate in the Cattewater?" Nana asked.

"Aye. The *Tireless,* a thirty-four, and bound for dry docks," the keep said. She snorted. "Not even an admiral can figure out how to repair a frigate in the Channel."

Nana glanced out the window and let Mrs. Fillion run on, declaring how she would run the war and the Royal Navy, if put in charge. Maybe the rain would stop by the time the keep ran out of words.

It didn't. Mrs. Fillion handed her a bag to hold the pasties and the other food Nana had accumulated. "Just return it next time you're in the Barbican, dearie," she said. She shook her head. "I wish I could send you Captain Worth, but we need the trade. He's not a bad-looking man, if you could get him to smile. 'Course, nobody's smiling much."

At least I never ask for anything, Nana thought as she excused herself and started for the Mulberry. There was food enough for supper now. She paused to look at the *Tireless,* noting the listing main mast, and what looked like canvas draped across the stern. "Dry docks for you, Captain Worthy."

And who knows what for me? she considered. She couldn't help but think of her father, William Stokes, Viscount Ratliffe, and his devil's bargain, which had sent her fleeing back to the safety of Plymouth, Gran's protection and more uncertainty.

"I may be hungry now," she whispered, "but if you think I ever intend to change my mind, *dear* Father, you're as wrong now as you were five years ago."

Her anger—or was it fear?—made her speak louder than she intended. As a child of Plymouth, she knew the prevailing winds were speeding her words to the French coast. No one could hear her. Beyond Gran and Pete, she knew no one cared.

Chapter One

Twelve hours into the return journey from Admiralty House, Captain Oliver Worthy felt the familiar but unwelcome scratchiness in his throat and ache in his ears. "Oh, damn," he whispered. This was no time to be afflicted with the deep-water sailor's commonest complaint—putrid ear and throat.

He tried to get comfortable in the chaise, mentally ticking off a long list of duties upon arrival in Plymouth, all of which trumped any ailments. The dockmaster was waiting for his final appraisal and list of repairs to the *Tireless*. The warped mast—the result of patching two splintered ones together—was bad enough. Even worse, the inept captain of the *Wellspring,* who had crashed his bow into the *Tireless*'s stern, caused more damage to a vulnerable part of the ship. Welcome to life on the blockade.

He had to make arrangements with the purser to complete the laborious resupply lists that ran on for mind-numbing pages. The chances of receiving all requested stores were slight, but he had to apply anyway. He also intended to release his crew, a few at a time, for shore leave. Oh, Lord, details and paperwork.

Right now—nauseated from the post chaise's motion, his head pounding and his throat as painful as sandpaper grating on bruised knuckles—all he wanted was a bed in a quiet room, with the guarantee not to be disturbed for at least a week.

Even more than that, all he wanted was a glass of water, and then another one, until he no longer felt that his insides were coated with slimy water stored months in a keg.

No landsman who took a drink of water for granted would understand the feeling of thirst beyond belief, as he stared long and hard at a cup of water, green and odorous. After a month or two, the water would even begin to clump together, until swallowing the offending mass was like choking down someone else's spittle. After only a few years at sea, he developed the habit of closing his eyes when he drank water more than two months old.

Then there were the days of thirst, especially in winter, when the water hoys from Plymouth were delayed because of stormy weather. Days when even a drop from the malodorous kegs—now empty—would have been welcome relief. Like all the others on the *Tireless,* he tried hard not to think of water, but surrounded by water as they always were, such a wish was not possible.

Past Exeter, where the view of the ocean usually made his heart quicken, he began to reconsider his impulsive agreement with Lord Ratliffe. The whole thing was odd. At Admiralty House, he had made his report of Channel activity, this time to William Stokes, Viscount Ratliffe, an undersecretary more than usually puffed up with his own consequence, and someone he generally tried to avoid.

Oliver had been irritated enough when Lord Ratliffe tried to pry into his Spanish sources, something no captain—even under Admiralty Orders—would ever reveal. And then the damned nincompoop had asked for a favor.

Maybe it was Oliver's own fault. He shouldn't have admitted the *Tireless* would be in dry docks for at least a month. But the undersecretary had picked up on it like a bird dog.

"A month?"

"Aye, my lord."

"Not going home to your family?"

"I have no family." Too true, although why a country vicar and his wife should succumb to typhoid fever in dull-as-dishwater Eastbourne, when their only child had survived all manner of exotic ailments from around the world, was still beyond him. No family. A wife was out of the question. He seldom met women, and he was too cautious to trouble any with a seafaring mate. In these times of war, he might as well hand over a death warrant with the marriage lines.

"I want to show you something."

Ratliffe had picked up a miniature from his untidy desk and handed it to Oliver, who couldn't help but smile.

It was the face of a young lady approaching—or smack on the edge of—womanhood. Her hair was the same shade as Ratliffe's, but he could see no other resemblance. The miniaturist had dotted tiny freckles across the bridge of her nose.

Her eyes had caught and held him: brown pools of melting chocolate. He glanced at the viscount's eyes. Blue.

"She resembles her mother."

After another look, Oliver handed back the miniature.

"Pretty, isn't she?"

More than pretty, Oliver thought.

"She's old now. Twenty-one. This was painted when she was sixteen." Ratliffe sighed heavily, almost theatrically, to Oliver's ears. "She lives in Plymouth in a run-down inn owned by her grandmother, Nancy Massie, a regular shrew. Twenty-two years ago, I was in Plymouth. I made the mistake of dallying with the shrew's daughter. Eleanor is the result."

Oliver couldn't think of anything to say. "So you fathered a bastard?" hardly seemed appropriate, and to offer his condolences seemed even less palatable. He knew the viscount would continue, however.

"I did the right thing by Eleanor," Lord Ratliffe said, putting down the miniature. "As soon as she was five, I had her sent to a female academy in Bath, where she was raised and educated."

Oliver hoped he covered up his surprise. The country must be full of by-blows, and his superficial acquaintance with the viscount gave him no inkling Lord Ratliffe was one to own up to his responsibility. Imagine, he thought, bracing himself for whatever favor Lord Ratliffe had in mind.

Ratliffe threw up his hands. "When the child was sixteen, she suddenly bolted from Miss Pym's school and returned to Plymouth! I had made her an excellent offer regarding her future, and she thanked me by leaving my care and bolting to that wretched seaport!" He glanced at Oliver. "You're a man of the world. You know what Plymouth is like. Imagine my distress."

Oliver could, even as he could also feel his suspicion growing. Although he had only been a post captain for two years, he had commanded men for many more. Something in Ratliffe's tone did not ring true.

"Would you do me the favor of staying at the Mulberry Inn—that's the name of it—during your time in Plymouth? Look things over and let me know how things are with Eleanor." He leaned closer. "I am certain a few days would suffice to get the drift of matters. I could not bear it if Eleanor has fallen on hard times."

"I usually stay at the Drake, my Lord," Oliver temporized. "My sea chest is there already."

Ratliffe sighed again, which only irritated Oliver. He was ready to say no, when the viscount shifted his position, and there was Eleanor Massie smiling up at him from the desk. Captivated in spite of himself, he wondered how an artist could capture such youthful promise in so small a space. A moment earlier, he might have just felt old. Now he felt something close to joy. For all he knew, the earth's axis had suddenly shifted under Admiralty House. Was the Astronomer Royal aware?

What harm would it do to stay a week at the Mulberry? He could look over the situation, make sure the shrew wasn't beating her granddaughter twice a day before breakfast, pen a report to the viscount and retreat to the Drake.

"I'll do it, my lord," Oliver said.

The viscount looked for a moment as if he were going to take Oliver by the hand, but he refrained. "Thank you, Captain Worthy. You'd probably understand my concern better if you had a daughter."

That will never happen, Oliver thought, as he returned his attention to the November scenery outside the post chaise window. Only a crazy woman would marry a captain on the blockade. And only a crazier captain would ever offer.

He closed his eyes after Exeter, deciding to abandon Miss Eleanor Massie to her fate. But as the post chaise stopped in front of the Drake later that afternoon, he knew he couldn't go back on his word, no matter how much he wanted to.

If Mrs. Fillion had been standing inside with a pitcher of water, he would have changed his mind again, but she was busy arguing with a tradesman. Oliver had quite forgotten into what octaves her voice could rise when she was on a tirade, and it made him wince. He came inside the inn and looked into the Den of Thieves. Sure enough, the perpetual whist game was in progress. Whist anywhere but the Drake tended to be a polite game, but he knew how noisy poor losers could be, and the room he usually rented was right overhead.

Mrs. Fillion drew breath from her rant concerning greengrocers in general, and this one in particular, and glanced his way. She came over immediately, which gratified him, but did not change his sudden resolve.

He held up his hand before she could even begin, trying to look apologetic and adamant at the same time. "Mrs. Fillion, I know my sea chest is already here, but I believe I will stay at the Mulberry this time. Can you direct me to it?"

You would have thought he had requested her to strip naked and turn somersaults through the Barbican, so great was her surprise at his request. Then a funny thing happened. She got an interesting look in her eyes, one he couldn't quite read.

"Captain, that is probably an excellent choice right now," she said. "It's only a mile away and not fancy, but you look like someone who could use some solitude."

I look that bad? he asked himself, amused, in spite of how dreadful he felt. "I think you're right," he said. "Let me send in the coachman and you can give him directions. And if Lieutenant Proudy is here, could you summon him? I'll just wait for a moment."

After letting his lieutenant know of his change in plans, Oliver struggled to his feet and walked slowly to the post chaise, hating the thought of getting inside again, but desperate to lie down, no matter how horrible the Mulberry Inn was.

If that was a mile, it was a longer one than found most places, Oliver decided, as the post chaise finally stopped in front of a narrow building of three stories. It was covered mostly with ivy that continued to cling stubbornly to the stonework, even though the November wind was trying its best to dislodge it. Paint flaked on the windowsills and door, but the little yard was as neat as a pin. He looked back toward the harbor. *It's a wonder anyone stays so far away,* he thought.

The post boy shouldered his sea chest and leather satchel and took it to the front door, which was opened by an old man with a wooden leg.

"Have you room?" he asked, as the old fellow—he had to be a seafaring man—took the chest from the post boy.

"Captain, you're our first lodger in at least six months."

Oliver stared at him. "I'll be damned! I thought this was an inn. How on earth do you manage to stay open?"

"We've been asking ourselves that lately," the sailor said and shook his head.

Oliver came toward him, trying to walk in a straight line. "Maybe I shouldn't even ask this," he began, "but is lodging just room, or does it include board?"

"Just room right now, sir," the old sailor said uncertainly. Oliver watched him glance at the post chaise, which had only gone a little way down Gibbon Street. "If you want, I'll call 'im back, sir. We won't deceive ye."

Oliver stood there on the front walk, undecided, when he heard someone else at the front door. He turned his head, even though he ached from the neck up.

It must be Eleanor Massie, even though her hair was cut quite short, in contrast to the miniature Lord Radcliffe had shown him. Her eyes were the same, though: pools of brown, and round like a child's. She wore an apron over a nondescript stuff dress, but Oliver couldn't think of a time when he had ever seen a lovelier sight. Even more to the point, she was looking straight at him, her brow wrinkling in what appeared to be deep concern for someone she didn't even know.

"I'll be staying," he heard himself say.

Maybe it was the combination of little food, no sleep, the swaying motion of the post chaise, the roaring in his ears, his throbbing head and the ill humors lodged in his throat. Before he could even warn anyone, he turned away and was sick in a pot of pansies that had got through a long summer and had probably wanted to survive—hardy things—beyond late fall. Too bad for them.

"Pete cleaned him up. He's tucked in bed now, and all he wants is water," Gran said, as Nana came up the narrow stairs with her tray.

Eyes closed, Captain Worthy lay propped up in bed, the picture of misery, with red spots burning in his cheeks. He opened his eyes, and almost smiled at what she carried. He indicated the table by the bed. "Set it there and pour me a glass."

She did as he said, and handed it to him. He drained the glass and held it out for more. Only a little water remained in the pitcher when he closed his eyes.

"Can…can I get you anything else, sir?" she asked. "Is there someone we can write who can be here to nurse you?"

"There isn't anyone."

"Oh, dear. There should be."

"No, Miss Massie," he said. "The blockade is the devil's own business and I'd never share it with another living soul. That old salt…"

"Pete Carter? He works for Gran."

"…tells me there is no board here."

"With the blockade and general shortages, Captain, we don't have the clientele or the resources to provide food anymore. I'm truly sorry." She hesitated. His eyes never left her face. "Perhaps you will want to reconsider and return to the Drake tomorrow."

"No. I am here to stay until my ship is out of dry dock."

"You really want to stay at the Mulberry?" she asked in frank surprise.

She could tell he felt miserable, and he was having a hard time keeping his eyes open. "Well, yes," he replied, even smiling a little. "Am I, er…allowed?"

He sounded so much like a small schoolboy in that moment that she had to laugh. "Of course you are! We're delighted to have you. It's just that meals…"

He pointed to the bureau. "Pete said he stowed my purse in the top drawer. Get it out, please, Miss Massie, and take what you need to provide me with three meals a day. Right now I favor porridge with lots of cream and sugar, mainly because I do not think anything else will stay down."

She had never rustled about in someone else's possessions before, but the captain appeared to expect it, so she did, pulling out his purse. She closed the drawer quickly and brought the purse to his bed. He opened it and she tried not to stare at the coins.

He counted out a generous handful. "When this is gone, just ask for more. Miss Massie, I like to eat well when I am in port." He looked at her with that frank gaze that should have embarrassed her, but didn't. "I expect the people who run the inn to eat well, too."

"Certainly, sir. Can I get you anything now?"

"What are you having for dinner?"

"A little tea and toast," she replied, then wished she had said nothing, or lied, because it was starvation food. "I mean, I ate a large meal at noon and wasn't…"

He took her by the wrist. "Miss Massie, I intend to stay at the Mulberry for a month, but if you tell me another lie, I'll be gone tomorrow."

"Yes, Captain," she replied, her voice no more than a whisper. "T-toast."

"And breakfast?"

She shook her head, too embarrassed to look at him. He was still holding her wrist, but his grip was easy.

He let go of her then, and relaxed against the pillows again. "All I need tonight is another pitcher of water. Would you do me a favor?"

"Anything, Captain," she said and meant it.

"Ask Pete if he knows a good remedy for sailor's throat."

"He has a thousand cures, almost as many as Scheherazade had tales."

Her answer made him smile. "I'll wager he has. And might your…your grandmama know of a poultice for my throat?"

That is odd, she thought. *How does he know about Gran?* "Have you stayed here before?" she asked. "I don't believe I mentioned Gran."

It was his turn to look confused. "Pete must have said something," he replied.

"That's a whopper," she said candidly, looking him in the eyes.

He looked at her in exasperation. "I do believe an older woman was in here when Pete relieved me of my uniform and bared me to the skin, but I didn't want to be so indelicate!"

She left the room, smiling to herself.

Gran put the money in the strongbox she kept in the drawer under the bread box. Only a few coins remained from Nana's haircut, and the sound of Captain Worthy's money made Nana sigh with relief.

"I wonder why he's doing this?" she asked her grandmother.

"Who knows?" Gran said. She turned to the nearly bare shelves and put her hands on her hips. "Nana, get on the stool and hand me that sack on the left. I can make the captain a poultice for his neck. I'll send Pete to the apothecary's for some oil and cotton wadding."

"And food, too, Gran, food," Nana said. "He wants porridge and cream for breakfast."

Gran rested her hand on Nana's shoulder. "You've been hungry." It was a simple statement. "Maybe our luck is turning."

And hour later, Nana carried the poultice upstairs. It was made of wheat, simply heated and packed into a clean stocking someone had left behind, back when the Mulberry had lodgers. Gran had wrapped it in a dish towel so she could carry it. "We may leave it wrapped in that, too," she said as Nana knocked on the door. "It wouldn't do to cause him bodily harm, not after he's paid so much for our help."

Gran carried the oil Pete had brought from the apothecary before he left again to convince a grocer to open his shop. She warmed the vial in her hands.

The captain was asleep, but he rolled over as soon as she tiptoed into the room. He was half out of bed before he realized who it was.

"Lie down, Captain. You're not on the blockade now," Gran ordered. "Turn over. I'll put some oil in your ears."

He did as she demanded. Gran dropped oil in each ear and plugged it with cotton. She motioned Nana forward.

"Just drape it around his neck. That's the way," she said, as Nana lifted the poultice over the captain's head. "Settle it around his ears, too."

The captain was silent as she followed Gran's instructions. She leaned close to him, wrinkling her nose to discover that Captain Worthy smelled of brine. Trying not to be obvious, she sniffed his shabby nightshirt. Salt again. Surely they didn't wash their clothes in salt water.

When she finished, Gran settled the captain back against the raised pillows. "That should do," she said. "Come, Nana, let us leave this man in peace."

Gran left the room. Nana made to follow, but the captain cleared his throat and she turned back to the bed, a question in her eyes.

"Make sure I am up by seven," he said. "I'll eat breakfast downstairs and then go to the dry docks."

"I don't think so, Captain," she replied. "You're a sick man."

"All the same, Miss Massie, that's an order."

"Aye, sir," she said, amused, "though I doubt you'll be going anywhere for at least a week."

"Try me." There was no amusement in his voice. "I'll be at the dry docks tomorrow if Pete has to push me in a wheelbarrow."

After she left, he lay in bed, trying to think about the *Tireless,* and not about Nana Massie. He thought of Lord Ratliffe's concern for her, and wanted to know why on earth she had decided to return to Plymouth, rather than continue to receive the comforts her father seemed ready to offer. It was not his business, though.

Chapter Two

Drat her pretty hide, Nana Massie was right; he was a sick man.

Oliver woke before it was light. His throat ached and his ears throbbed, but at least the pain in his shoulders was less, thanks to the wheat poultice still strung around his neck. It had ceased to give off warmth hours ago, but the smell of wheat had set him dreaming of bread—loaves unbelievably tall from yeast, soft, slathered in melting butter, and nary a weevil in sight.

He was cold. Through the fog of last night's humiliation at vomiting on the pansies, then crawling into bed and shutting out the world, he remembered Gran or Nana saying something about extra blankets in the bottom drawer of the clothespress. He thought about getting up to retrieve another blanket, but he was disinclined to so much exertion.

As he lay there, thinking about the merits of another blanket, the door opened. *The 'tween-stairs maid,* he thought, *has come to rescue me from the cold.* He lay there, peaceful, in spite of his pain, and thankful for the prospect of more coal on the fire.

She laid a quiet fire—how many inns had he frequented

where the opposite was true. In another minute the room would be his again, and warmer. Maybe he wouldn't need another blanket, after all.

She didn't leave. He heard her opening the lower drawer of the clothespress; in another minute, she covered him with a welcome blanket. Even that wasn't enough. She tucked it high on his shoulders, bending close enough in the low light until he saw it was Nana Massie, and no 'tween-stairs maid.

"I could have done that," he told her, sounding gruffer than he meant to, maybe because his throat seemed filled with foreign substances.

"I know," she whispered, apparently not in the least deterred by his tone. "You're not the only human on the planet who sometimes lies in bed because he—or she—is too indecisive to get up for another blanket."

He couldn't help chuckling at her observation on human nature, even as he wished there was a 'tween-stairs maid at the Mulberry. He hated to think the daughter of a viscount had to work so hard, even if she was illegitimate.

What an uncharitable man you are, he told himself sourly. Who on earth has a say in the pedigree of her birth?

She tugged the blanket higher around his shoulder. "Go back to sleep, Captain. I'll bring your breakfast in an hour, and then Pete has a foul concoction to try on you."

"I told you I'd get up for breakfast," he reminded her.

"I have decreed otherwise," she replied in complete serenity.

To his surprise, he did precisely as she ordered and went back to sleep. When he woke again, the sun was up. At least, watery dawn seeped around the curtains. He heard a shutter banging somewhere across the street from the force of the wind outside, but the Mulberry itself seemed sound as a roast. Somewhat like its inhabitants, he concluded, as he sat up slowly.

He eased himself out of bed, found the chamber pot under the bed and used it, hoping Nana wasn't the one to dump it. He slid the chamber pot out of sight and crawled back into his warm nest, loath to leave it again, but knowing today he must visit the *Tireless* in the dockyard, and conduct all manner of shoreside business for the good of his crew and ship. Sometimes he wondered why he had not chosen the serene life of a country parson, like his father.

He lay there, going over everything he had to do that day, and realized he needed Mr. Proudy, his number one, close at hand. He knew he could summon the man and he would eventually appear, but why bother a fellow busily engaged in refreshing his wife? He had another idea. He didn't know much about female academies in Bath, but Miss Massie could probably write. Of course, this meant he would have to succumb to breakfast in bed to placate her. The blockade had taught him a great deal about flexibility, however.

She knocked on the door a little later, when the wind had settled down and rain pattered against the windowpane.

"Come."

She opened the door, carrying a tray of food and concentrating on keeping it level. Pete Carter stood behind her. It was all he could do to keep from sighing out loud. Nana Massie was beautiful. Thank God he had decided years ago that he would never be troubled by a wife. His personal pledge had only been strengthened in recent years by seeing too many distraught wives meeting ships in the harbor, hoping for news. He'd be damned if he'd do that to anyone.

He knew there was no ordinance against admiring a pretty woman, but his glimpse at Lord Ratliffe's miniature and his own wretched state yesterday had not fully prepared him for Nana Massie.

Thank God I am too old for her and too kind—despite what my crew thinks—to punish a woman by loving her and leaving her for war on the ocean, he told himself. Those eyes. He had never noticed such round eyes on an adult. Or maybe it was her high-arched eyebrows that gave her a wide-eyed gaze. Whatever it was, he wanted to study the matter during some leisure time he knew he would never have.

And why shouldn't I have that opportunity? he asked himself. *Other men do. They must, or Adam and Eve would have had no offspring.* He decided to indulge himself, and kept looking.

He thought her cheeks were too thin, but he knew that look could be cured with more food. He couldn't properly assess her figure, because she wore the same stuff gown and apron. It was on the thin side, but that could be rectified, until she was softer and more rounded in all the right places.

Nana appeared to be one who could develop soft edges, if given the opportunity. *What am I doing?* he thought, as he admired her. *She would thrash me across the chops, if she could read my mind.*

All this reckoning had taken place in just a few seconds. Nana seemed to be unaware of his assessment because she was concentrating on placing the tray on his lap now, and adjusting the legs around him. On the other hand, Pete Carter didn't look like someone who would allow much scrutiny of his little charge.

But here she was, bending over him. Oliver couldn't help himself. He looked her square in the face, and smiled to see those freckles across the bridge of her nose, probably destined to fade as she aged, but there now to entertain him. And he was entertained, hugely so. He liked everything he saw.

He could have cried when Nana stepped back and folded

her hands in front of her. "Porridge and cream, Captain, just what you ordered," she told him. "I didn't know how much sugar you liked, so I brought up the whole bowl. Gran stewed some apples, too, but we decided against any toast. Your throat, you know."

He nodded, wishing she were still bending over him. She smelled faintly of roses, not a fragrance he chanced upon much, but far more appealing than tar, bilge and gunpowder.

He looked at her again. "Miss Massie, could you prop up these pillows? I'd hate to dribble porridge across my chest like a hospital pensioner, since you're so determined I am to eat in bed."

She did as he asked, plumping up the pillows behind him, then getting out another from the lower drawer of the clothes-press. As she put that one behind his head, her arm brushed his temple. He was in heaven.

Then it was Pete Carter's turn. As Nana stepped back, the old sailor set down a vile-looking compound on the bedside table. "For what ails you, Captain Worthy," he said. "Drink all of that after you finish breakfast."

Oliver eyed it suspiciously, wishing that Pete did not look so pleased with himself at the punishment he was inflicting. "All of it? Shouldn't I spread it out over the day?"

"All of it, sir," Pete insisted. "And when you're done, I'll bring up more." He smiled then. "It'll work, Captain. It always does. I guarantee the remedy."

For one disconcerting moment, Oliver felt that he had returned to his midshipmen days, under the scrutiny of a sailing master. *You old rascal,* he thought to himself, as the former sailor whisked away the chamber pot, not giving Oliver a single moment to feel embarrassed.

He was struck with a moment of shyness after Pete left his

chamber, then reminded himself of the business at hand. Even the *Tireless* could wait; Nana Massie was going to eat more.

"Miss Massie, have you had breakfast yet?"

He could tell his curt question came at her out of the blue. She blinked her eyes, and then thought about an answer. Oliver leveled her with a stare generally reserved for midshipmen contemplating prevarication.

"You promised me last night you would tell the truth," he reminded her as he picked up his spoon.

"That was for last night," she said quickly, then laughed at his expression. "Aye, sir, I did promise," she amended. "The answer is no."

He set down the spoon. "I'll wait until you come back with a bowl and spoon. If there's porridge left…"

"There is," she said hurriedly, interrupting him. "We kept it back in case you wanted more."

"I don't." Oliver looked down at the tray in his lap. "This is quite enough. Please take what you want from the pot and come back."

Without a word, she left the room, closing the door behind her. He stared down at the porridge, certain he had offended her and wondering if his next step now was to dress and go in search of her. To apologize? To bully her further? He asked himself why it was suddenly his problem.

The porridge tasted like ambrosia. It was sugared precisely right and needed no more. It even went down smoothly, causing his raw throat no further indignity. Too bad he wasn't enjoying it, feeling sorry for himself and pining for company.

To his relief, she came back into his room with a full bowl and spoon. She pulled up a chair to the bed and helped herself to the sugar in the bowl on his tray. "All the sugar is up here," she explained.

He smiled into his porridge, surprised at how much better it tasted. He glanced at Nana, who was spooning down a mouthful, a beatific expression on her face. He looked away quickly, so she wouldn't think he was spying on her. *I probably dare not do this with every meal, but I can try,* he told himself.

When he finished, he eyed Pete Carter's concoction.

"Do you *know* this elixir?" he asked, his voice cautious.

"I've had it a time or two myself," she said. "I recommend you drink it first, and then follow it with the applesauce."

"Does it work?"

"You're stalling, Captain," she teased, and he knew she wasn't angry with him about the porridge.

"I am indeed. Facing the French fleet is one thing." He picked up the glass. "This is quite another."

"Cowardice will land you onshore permanently, and at half pay."

Well, Miss Massie, you seem to know something of the navy, he thought. "So you are appealing to my patriotism now?" he asked, then took a deep breath and drank down the brew, reasoning it couldn't be any more vile than old water in rotten kegs.

It was more pleasant than he had any reason to hope, with a strong aftertaste of molasses and just a hint of rum. There were other ingredients he could not name, and had no desire to find out. Following it with applesauce proved to be good advice, and so he told Nana. She beamed with pleasure.

"I'll bring you another pitcher of water," she said, rising to leave.

"Bring a tablet and pencil when you return," he ordered. "What time is it?"

"Half-past seven, Captain."

He rubbed his hands together and lay back against the

pillows again as she picked up the tray. "I intend to be dockside staring up at the *Tireless* by two bells in the forenoon watch. Oh. Nine o'clock." She began to protest, but he overrode it. "I need to prepare some lists before I go. Will you help me?"

"I suppose," she said, her expressive eyes a little wary.

He watched her face, noting her wariness, and put it down to reluctance to spend more time in his chamber. *So that's how it is?* he thought. *Gran must have warned you about officers, too. Well, good for Gran, if bad for me.*

"I must establish a list of priorities," he told her. "If my number one—my first mate—were here, I would order him to help me. He, alas for me, is in the arms of his wife of less than a year. Although my men will tell you I am a hard task-master, I am not without feeling. Miss Massie, plain and simple—will you help me?"

That was blunt enough, he thought, observing the blush that rose to her cheeks, rendering her even sweeter to look at than before. "I would ask Pete Carter, but I doubt he can write," he continued.

"His name only," she said. "He didn't need anything else in the fleet." She looked at him, as if weighing the matter against her usual duties. "I can help," she told him.

"Good! Have Pete summon me a hackney for half-past eight o'clock."

"You should stay in bed," she said, but without much conviction in her voice.

"I should, but I can't," he told her, trying to sound reasonable and less like a captain. "Boney doesn't much care about my putrid throat, and probably less about my ears."

She didn't seem to have an argument prepared for Napoleon. "Especially your ears," she echoed, as she closed the door behind her.

* * *

Nana went down the stairs quietly. She had gone upstairs, mostly afraid of Captain Worthy, and come down with a revised opinion. He was blunt and plainspoken, but surely no more than any other seaman she had encountered in the years since her return to Plymouth. His apparent concern for her was a surprise; she did not know why he should feel any obligation to make sure she had something to eat.

"You don't know anything about me," she whispered, looking back up the stairs.

She passed into the sitting room at the foot of the stairs, and then to the equally small dining room that adjoined it. Gran had told her to prepare a table setting for Captain Worthy—one table among eight. It looked faintly ludicrous in the empty room. She sat down, thinking of their only other tenant at the inn, who had died last spring.

Miss Edgar—Nana never knew her Christian name—had been a governess, a lady somewhat down on her luck whose last position had been with the harbormaster's family. When the two daughters had outgrown Miss Edgar's services, she had not the funds to relocate anywhere else, nor the energy, at her advanced age, to try for another post. It seemed no one was interested in hiring an old lady whose French was getting rusty, and who had difficulty remembering the capitals of Europe.

She had come to the Mulberry because it was cheap and clean, and stayed there five years before her money ran out. From Nana's fifteenth birthday on, when she visited Plymouth during holidays, she had observed Miss Edgar sitting by herself in the otherwise empty dining room, and spending her evenings alone in the sitting room.

Gran had tried to get Miss Edgar to join them in their own tidy quarters through the green baize door into the back of the inn. "All I ever wanted to do was invite her to share our company," Gran had told Nana, and there was no disguising the hurt in her voice. "She won't hear of it. We're not quality."

After Miss Edgar outlived all her savings, there was nowhere to go but the street. When she returned to Plymouth for good, Nana had been surprised to see Miss Edgar still in residence.

"I couldn't throw her out," Gran had told Nana later, after Miss Edgar had gone upstairs to her room. "She has never spoken of the fact that her money is gone, and she still refuses to share our low society, even while she eats our food and lives here for free."

Nana gathered up the place setting meant for Captain Worthy, but she did not get up. Two months ago, Gran had nursed Miss Edgar through her final illness, closed the woman's eyes in death and prepared the body for the grave before summoning the parish cemetery society, which ushered paupers into pine boxes and unmarked graves.

Together they had cleaned out Miss Edgar's room, finding nothing of any value beyond yards of tatting, a few old books and a handful of letters. Nana was cleaning out the clothes-press and its threadbare garments when Gran suddenly took her by the arm. "Miss Edgar and I could have been friends!" she had lamented, as her eyes filled with tears. "What's even worse, I had thought your stay at Miss Pym's would prepare you for a career such as hers."

Nana had kissed Gran then, not telling her that Miss Pym had delicately informed her several years before that she would never be able to get such a position, because no family would countenance a governess with questionable parentage. But Gran didn't need to know that. She had assured Gran she had no plans to ever leave the Mulberry.

Nana sat for a few more moments in the empty dining room. The rain drummed down outside as she contemplated class, rank and general stupidity. She wondered if Captain Worthy preferred an empty dining room to low company at the back of the inn.

Pete was out, but Gran and the scullery maid, Sal, were finishing the last of the porridge. "Captain Worthy wants me to take some dictation." She found a tablet and pencil in the drawer where Gran kept her records. "He wants more drinking water." She smiled at Sal. "If you would bring up some shaving water after a while, he means to visit the dry docks."

"I doubt he can stand up," Gran said.

"But he will," Nana replied.

She thought Gran might offer an objection to her returning upstairs, but she did not. Muttering something about "catching his death in this rain," Gran reached for the rest of the wheat, prepared to make a new poultice.

Tucking the pencil in her hair, the tablet under one arm and the pitcher in the other, Nana went back to Captain Worthy's chamber. She tapped softly on the door. There was no answer. She tapped again, no louder, then looked inside the room.

He was asleep. She thought about going downstairs, but remembered what he had said about going to the dry docks. She set down the pitcher quietly and sat again beside his bed.

She was struck by the way he slept—directly in the middle of the bed, with his hands folded across his stomach. She couldn't help but think of a man in a coffin, and the notion sent a ripple down her spine. She considered the man, and understood. Flailing about in a hammock or sleeping cot would probably have meant a quick trip to the deck below.

I wonder, does he ever turn over? she asked herself, curious. No matter. He was sleeping peacefully, his face

probably as relaxed as it ever got. Captain Worthy had a
sharp and straight nose set above thin lips. His hair was
dark brown, with wisps of gray in it by his temples, as well
as a faint, curved scar, circling below his cheekbone and
nearly touching his right nostril. Pirates on the Barbary
Coast? she thought. Or a grappling hook swung by a desperate Frenchman?

He shouldn't be so concerned about her own paucity of
meals, she decided, considering that he was on the thin side
himself. His hands, so peacefully folded, were deeply veined.
Her eyes went back to his face, toasted by coastal Spanish sun
to a pleasant mahogany that probably turned sallow during the
winter. Nothing would change the weather lines around his
eyes. She had lived enough of her life in Plymouth to know
the mark of a deep water man.

He coughed, then tried to swallow, which marred his repose
as he flinched from the pain in his throat, and uttered some small
protest. Then he opened his eyes, looking directly overhead for
a long moment, until he seemed to recall where he was.

He must have sensed her presence, because he addressed
her, even as he continued to stare overhead.

"It's like this, Miss Massie. When I wake up, I always look
at the compass over my head first. Maybe you would induce
more captains to visit the Mulberry if you hung compasses
on the overhead deck beam."

"I think you have been too long at sea, Captain," she
replied, laughing.

"Doubtless."

"It is probably safe enough to turn on your side, sir," she
continued, feeling bold enough to tease him. "We may not be
on the first tier of elegance here, but no bed at the Mulberry
will pitch you onto the floor."

"Old habits are nigh impossible to break," he told her, then turned onto his side and faced her. "Before we begin, go to the clothespress, please, and take out the tar bag."

That was what she had been smelling in the room. She did as he said.

"The log's in there, but I'm looking for the ship roster. It's rolled and tied with twine. Open it. Read the names, and mark a number in the margin where I say."

She found the roster, removed the twine and unrolled it. Before she started to read, she poured him a drink of water, which he downed immediately, and then another.

He handed back the cup, and lay back with his hands behind his head, as though he felt he could relax in her presence. The gesture touched her, even as she was amused at the slow, careful way he moved his hands.

She knew he had business to attend to, and soon, but she couldn't help asking, "Captain, I was wondering about that scar on your face."

He smiled. "Looks like a grappling hook from pirates on the Spanish Main, doesn't it?"

She sucked in her breath, her eyes wide.

"Sorry to disappoint you. I fell out of a tree when I was a little boy and came in contact with a diabolical branch at a vicarage in Eastbourne."

She tried not to look disappointed, but he must have caught her expression. "The grappling-hook scar is under my left armpit," he told her in mock seriousness. He winked. "Right beside the bullet hole."

"You're quizzing me," she accused him.

"Never! Now where were we?"

I don't know where you are, sir, but I must inhabit another realm, Nana thought, as she spread the roster on her lap. *What an ordinary life I lead.* She looked over at the captain, who, to her surprise, appeared almost to be memorizing her face.

"Captain, may I ask you a question?"

"Aye."

"Are you ever afraid?" She regretted the question the moment she asked it. *He'll think I am an idiot,* she thought, her face red.

"I am afraid all the time, Miss Massie," he told her, after a long pause. "I fear for my ship, I fear for my men, I fear for myself." He looked at the ceiling again. "I suppose it's in about that order, too."

"I…I should never have asked such a stupid question," she stammered.

"It's an honest one, and I gave you an honest answer," he told her, then looked her directly in the eyes. "Ships like mine are the only thing standing between England and ruin. I know times are hard here, but they are infinitely worse on the blockade. And in Spain and Portugal? I doubt Oporto will hold out much longer against the French, damn Boney and Marshal Soult to hell. If Sir John Moore's army survives to fight another day, I will be amazed. Yes, I am afraid, Miss Massie. Don't cross me when I say I need to be at the dock-yards at two bells in the forenoon watch, even if I have one foot in the grave. I do."

Nana stared at him, shocked. He stared back, just as surprised, as though amazed at what just came out of his mouth. She watched him in silence, watched as the astonishment on his own face changed into irritation, and then mellowed into a rueful expression she couldn't quite fathom. Maybe it was chagrin.

When he spoke, he sounded apologetic. "Miss Massie, I…I almost don't know what to say. I just told you things no one knows except officials at Admiralty House."

"Maybe you needed to tell someone," she said, after a long pause of her own, remembering the great relief she had felt after she finally confessed to Gran the terrible future her own father had planned for her. "Sometimes it feels better to share bad news." She lowered her voice. "Are things as bad as all that?"

"They are worse." He put his hand over his eyes. "I have to go to the dock now, listen to the master shipwright tell me he needs at least two months for repairs and then bully him into doing it in three weeks. Then I must cajole the victuallers to move really fast to resupply my ship."

"I wish I could help you."

She knew there was nothing she could do, no strings she could pull, no advice she could give. If there was a more powerless person in all of Great Britain, she had no idea who it would be.

Perhaps the captain saw it differently, although she couldn't think why. He looked at her again, that same, searching look. "You already have," he said simply. "You are listening."

"Anyone would," she assured him.

"No, they would not. I have observed that when most people are afraid or bewildered, they just change the subject." He took a deep breath. "People at the highest levels of our government do it."

She had nothing to say to that. *This man would never lie to me,* she told herself. *I suppose it doesn't matter, because when he finally realizes life is more comfortable at Drake's Inn, he will be gone and I will never see him again. I can at least be as honest.*

Chapter Three

Nana looked down at the list in her lap. "Shall I begin?"

He nodded, and stared at the ceiling above, as though wishing for a compass there to tell him which way the wind blew off Spain.

There were two hundred names on the roster, not quite a full complement of crew for a 34-gun frigate. As she read each name, he had her write in a one, two, three or four in the margin.

"What was that for?" she asked, when he finished.

"I'm assigning them to shore leave," he told her. "The fifty ones will go first, for five days, and so on." He chuckled. "My brother officers on other ships think I am insane for allowing any leave at all, but I have not had much trouble with desertion."

It struck her as strange—even after his earlier plain speaking—that he seemed to want to talk to her. She decided it was her very powerlessness that made him garrulous. He seemed to sense—rightly so—that there was nothing he could tell her that would ever be repeated. Obviously she knew no one who could profit by any of his conversation, and he was aware of that.

Or so Nana reasoned. She looked at him, but not as minutely as he had observed her earlier, deciding she had nothing to fear from this stern-looking man who was probably braver than lions, even if he did say he was afraid.

She wanted him to smile. "Do they not desert because you see that their bedding is turned down nicely at night and there is a fire laid in the grate?"

He rewarded her with a laugh, which pleased her beyond all expectation. "I rather think it is the bedtime story, lullaby and gentle rocking of the hammock."

It was her turn to laugh. She looked into his eyes and saw good humor mirrored there. "And hot milk before lights out," she added.

"You've hit upon it. Actually, it's wrapped up in money, as most things are, I must confess," he said. "Although the *Tireless* is part of the Channel Fleet, we operate under Admiralty Orders." He looked at her. "Are you bored yet?"

She was far from bored. She could have listened to him for hours. "I don't think you could bore me," she told him. "We live a quiet life here in Plymouth."

"Admiralty Orders are more onerous because my ship is at the beck and call of Admiralty House for special missions."

He must have thought that sounded ostentatious, so he made a face. "Someone has to do it, Miss Massie. When we take the occasional prize ship, we needn't share it with the fleet, so our shares are larger, from captain right down to the lowest-rated landsman. They love me for the money."

She didn't believe that for a minute. He must have noticed the skepticism on her face. "What other reason can you use to explain my low desertion rate?"

"You are fair."

"You don't even know me," he countered.

"No, I don't," she agreed. The room seemed suddenly too warm. "Is that all, sir? Should I ask Pete to find a hackney?"

He sat up carefully. "Not yet. Look in the tar bag again. I think there is a folded sheet with the heading of Repairs. I have a few more you need to add."

She sat down again and picked up the bag, wrinkling her nose at the smell, but rummaging until she found the sheet.

"That's my copy. I left the original with my sailing master, so the shipwright could see it when the *Tireless* went to dry docks."

Under his direction, she added two more items to check, then handed him the list. He looked it over, then directed his gaze at her again. "If you would have Pete find a hackney now, I can dress and be ready. Also, I am going to write a note for my number one at Drake's Inn. I'm sorry to ask this, but could you please deliver it? I truly hate to bother him, but I still need him in dry docks." He smiled more to himself than to her. "He'll still have to pry himself off Mrs. Proudy."

She knew she should pretend she hadn't heard that remark, so she bit her lip to keep from laughing.

He observed her anyway. "Miss Massie, I feel confident that your grandmother, and certainly Pete, have sufficiently warned you to have nothing to do with members of the Royal Navy. They are vulgar, lewd and single-minded to the point of mania."

She had to laugh then.

"By God, it's good to hear a woman laugh," the captain said, and she could tell he was utterly serious now. Or was he? "But do have a care in your dealings with the sailing fraternity, Miss Massie. I'll see you belowdeck—downstairs."

"Aye, Captain," she teased.

She went to the door, but he called her back, almost as though he didn't wish to be alone. He gestured toward the rain-polished window. "I must confess I am concerned about sending you outside into this Plymouth drizzle to deliver a message." He cleared his throat, as though stalling for time and trying to figure out how to proceed. "I can't help but notice how short your hair is. If you have been recently ill, surely someone else can deliver the message to Mr. Proudy."

She touched her hair. Now it was her turn to figure out how to proceed. She could make light of the matter, and laugh about her hair weighing so much it was uncomfortable on her neck. Or she could just tell the truth, since that seemed to be coin of the realm with Captain Worthy.

"I sold it to the wigmaker," she told him, looking him in the eye. "We needed the money." She opened the door, eager to escape the room now, especially when she saw the sadness come into his eyes. "I'm in fine health, Captain, and can deliver any message in any weather."

Nana closed the door, and leaned against it. She felt out of breath, even light-headed. She wanted to go back into Captain Worthy's chamber and pour out all her worries: no money, no possible prospect of marriage, a shameless father who saw her as a tool, the real and gathering threat of the Mulberry's ruin with its accompanying fear and humiliation of having to throw themselves onto the dubious mercies of the parish.

He has enough worries, and some to spare, she thought, as she went downstairs. *I can at least run his errands. There must be other ways we can make his stay a good one, even if this is the shabbiest inn on the entire Devon coast.*

Oliver Worthy dressed carefully, lying down a few times when his troublesome ears made the room spin around. He felt wretched, and with little prodding would have gladly crawled between the covers again. Maybe he could be ill later, when the work had begun on the *Tireless* and the ship-wright was weary of having him around.

That would be good. He could lie around the Mulberry, reading when he fancied it, eating, and writing letters. He had seen people doing that in London hotels, when orders from the Admiralty dictated he remain in the City. He couldn't really imagine such leisure, ranking it somewhere with the seven wonders of the world.

As for writing letters, there was no one to write to. His parents were dead, and so were some of his earlier comrades in the deep-water trade, those unlucky enough to come up against enemies or storms on the ocean, or lee shores in bad weather. His other friends were at sea, and had no more time than he did. Several years ago, he had written a time or two to a lady he had met in Naples, the widow of a customs official. Three years later, when he was back in that plague-ridden city, he had paid her a call, only to discover she was married again, a mother, and widowed once more. He must have had a sailor's natural superstition, because that sounded like too much bad luck for him; he didn't return.

It had been five years ago, when he was twenty-five and still optimistic. He left Naples harbor with a firm resolve to never even contemplate matrimony again. So far, he had not, which meant that someone as charming as Nana Massie was completely safe from him. He had declared himself immune to women, and he meant it.

This was not something the men of the fleet discussed, but he knew what happened when husbands were too long at sea. Some took to drink, many turned inward and others became soured by long-term separation and took it out on their crew.

He thought it was worse for the wives. He remembered, as clear as yesterday, the *Retribution*'s return from a two-year voyage, to see a row of wives lining the quay, and to watch some scream and others faint when the captain had to tell them their husbands had died and were buried in distant ports, or had been dropped into watery graves midocean. It was easily his own worst duty as a captain. He would never inflict such punishment on a wife.

Still, there was Nana. He couldn't help but think of her, when all was quiet and he was far less busy than usual. He looked himself over while he shaved, or at least what little he could see of himself in the tiny mirror, and saw nothing there to tempt her. It wasn't that he meant to look stern all the time. He liked to laugh as well as the next fellow, but there hadn't been much occasion for frivolity lately, and he suspected the ladies liked to be charmed and entertained.

And what do I do but tell that winsome creature how frightening things are in the Channel? he berated himself. In more peaceful times—Naples had been one—he had attended grand levies and routs and listened to other officers entertain the ladies with romantic tales of life at sea. Couldn't he have found *something* cheerful to tickle Nana's fancy?

Well, no, he couldn't, especially since he had committed himself to the truth, with all its ugly barnacles and whiskers. From the looks of things, Nana probably wouldn't have minded a little lie or two here and there, to make her own problems seem less fraught.

He buttoned his last clean waistcoat and tied his neckcloth. Maybe if he looked stern enough, he wouldn't have to grovel before the shipwright in the hopes of getting those repairs done fast. There was probably no point; desperate captains were a penny a pound at every dry docks in England. Scotland, too.

He sat at the little desk by the fire and wrote a quick note to Mr. Proudy, stating his needs and hoping for the best. As second mate and low man among the three of them, Mr. Ramseur was already at the dry docks. Maybe they could threaten to break the shipwright's legs, ravish his wife and daughters and plunder the man's bank account, if he did not produce instant results.

Oliver signed his note. *Maybe my mind is unhinged at last,* he thought. He heard a horse outside. He opened the window and leaned out. "I'm coming," he called down, then wished he hadn't, because his throat felt as if it were belching fire.

Nana was dusting the mantelpiece in the empty sitting room when he came downstairs. She smiled at him, and he felt grateful for his immunity. My God, she was lovely. He had never seen such luminous skin before. Maybe there was some truth to the rumor that the damp on England's south-west coast gave ladies the clearest hides in all of Europe.

He held out the note to her. "I would deliver it myself, but I'm going directly west to the dockyards."

"I don't mind at all, Captain," she said, taking the note and just barely grazing his fingers with her own. "Gran is sending me out for revictualing, as you would probably call it."

"I would indeed." He put on his hat, then took it off, when the top of it brushed the low ceiling. "Go light on the weevily biscuit. I fancy white bread with no boarders."

She laughed. "I'll insist on nothing in the bread except…well…bread."

She went ahead of him into the hallway, taking off her apron as she walked, which gave him an especially nice view of the swaying motion of her skirts. He thought he could probably span her waist with his hands. She swung her cloak around her shoulders, tucked the note up her sleeve and left him standing there, hat in hand.

The jehu took him to the dockyards, located on the east bank of the Tamar River, some three miles from Plymouth. There was the *Tireless,* looking forlorn now with main sails and rigging gone, and that damned crooked mast marring her otherwise clean lines like a snaggletooth in the mouth of a pretty woman. Standing dockside was Mr. Ramseur and the shipwright.

It begins, Oliver thought. He paid the jehu, sent him on his way and prepared to do whatever battle was necessary to get his ship healthy and back to sea inside of three weeks. He was walking toward the two men when he thought of Nana Massie, and the lovely way she had smiled at him in the Mulberry, dust cloth in hand. Thank God he was immune to females.

If he could wrestle down the shipwright from his standard two months to three weeks, that would be heaven. If he could only manage four weeks, that would be heaven on earth, because then he might find more ways to get Nana Massie to smile on him. Since he was immune, that would be enough.

By the time she arrived at the Drake, Nana had thought the matter through and decided to give the note to Mrs. Fillion to deliver. Heaven knew she didn't want to knock on the Proudys' door and rouse them from whatever they were doing. That was delicacy better left to the innkeeper.

Not that Mrs. Fillion had too many delicate bones in her body, not after twenty years of innkeeping. She took the note and laughed, leaning closer to Nana. "They didn't even come down for breakfast this morning, Nana. Considering that breakfast is included in the bill, the newly married ones are such an economy!"

Mercy, thought Nana. *All I am here for is to deliver a message.* She made some noncommittal reply and started for the door again, even though the rain was coming down harder.

After thinking about it, she waited until Mrs. Fillion came back downstairs. Gran would want her to thank the keep for sending much-needed custom to the Mulberry. She hung her sodden cloak on the rack in the hall.

Mrs. Fillion didn't return immediately. When she did come down, she gestured for Nana to follow her into the kitchen, where she ladled a bowl of yesterday's soup. Nana started to say that she wasn't really hungry, but reconsidered. No telling how long Captain Worthy would stay at the Mulberry.

The soup was wonderful, even a day old. She ate all she could hold, then put down her spoon. "Mrs. Fillion, thank you so much for sending Captain Worthy our way," she said. "I know you had room for him here, but we so appreciate your consideration."

Mrs. Fillion cocked her head to one side. "That's the odd thing, dearie—I didn't send Captain Worthy your way. When Mr. Proudy and Mr. Ramseur and the surgeon hauled up here, the captain told his officers to put his sea trunk in the room I usually reserve for him, before he took a post chaise to London."

"I wonder what made him change his mind," Nana said.

Mrs. Fillion shrugged, obviously not too concerned about the issue. "I've been wondering if I should apologize to you for sending him!"

This is a mystery indeed, Nana thought. *What can Mrs. Fillion mean?* "I don't quite understand," she said.

There was a loud knock at the back door. Mrs. Fillion looked over and motioned in the porter with a quarter of beef slung over his shoulder and unplucked chickens belted around his waist. She sighed and got up. "No rest for me." She turned back to Nana. "You can't precisely call Captain Worthy a little ray of sunshine, can you? Come to think of it, I disbelieve I've ever seen that thin-lipped cadaver even smile. He barely talks."

"Oh, he does," Nana said. "He's quite droll, too."

Mrs. Fillion forgot the porter and stared at her kitchen guest. "Oliver *Worthy?*"

"Why…y-yes, if that's his first name. He *is* rather thin, isn't he?" Nana replied, suddenly unsure of herself. "He told me…"

She stopped. *He told me all kinds of things,* she thought, *and I'll not repeat any of them.* "Maybe he was a little stern," she amended, hoping Mrs. Fillion, who liked to carry a tale, had better things to do in her kitchen at that moment than press her for more information.

Mrs. Fillion did. With a comment that sounded like, "The Second Coming must be the devil of a lot closer than we know," the innkeep opened the door wider for the porter, her attention elsewhere. Nana bobbed a curtsey and quickly left the kitchen.

A decidedly forlorn Mr. Proudy came slowly down the stairs, the picture of reluctance. For one brief moment, Nana wanted to remind him that poor Lord Nelson had inspired a nation-full of sitting room samplers that read, England Expects Every Man To Do His Duty. She didn't know Mr. Proudy at all; quizzing him was quite out of the question.

Although Miss Pym would have gone into utter spasms at her total lack of manners, Nana introduced herself. "Are you Mr. Proudy?"

He owned that he was.

"Your captain is staying at our inn, sir," she said. "I was wondering—does he have a favorite meal that you know of?"

The first mate returned her curtsey with a nod: no more, she observed, than would be expected from a gentleman to a servant. "He does like a good steak and ale pie," he told her, "and nearly any dish with cod. God help us, cod and leeks." He nodded again and went out to hail a hackney.

˙ Nana added leeks to her list for the greengrocers. When she showed the grocer the money in her hand, he went to great lengths to fill her list, and agreed, without any cajoling, to deliver it after noon to the Mulberry. Minding her steps on the rain-slickened cobbles, she went to the wharf next and selected a promising-looking cod.

"I don't like the way it looks at me," she told the fishmonger, who whacked off the head with one stroke of his cleaver. Wrapped in brown paper and trussed up with string, the beast didn't overhang her basket by much.

The rain stopped, only to be followed by a great rainbow that stretched from the Cattewater to the dry docks. *I hope that is a good omen,* she thought, as she started back toward the Mulberry. *I know Captain Worthy is anxious to be back on the blockade.*

There wasn't any harm in putting a little muscle behind her wish, considering that she was just skeptical enough not to put her whole trust in rainbows. She stopped in front of St. Andrews.

The door was open and she went inside, not sure of the protocol of carrying a cod, no matter how neatly wrapped, into the Lord's house. There wasn't any question about leaving it outside. Her faith in man didn't extend to tempting anyone with an easy catch of the day, especially not in Plymouth.

She set the cod by the back bench and took a coin from her reticule. Strictly speaking, she was spending the captain's money, but she didn't think he would mind. It took her only a moment to drop it in the box and light a candle. Determined to keep the cod in sight, she stood there, her hands folded, and implored the Lord and St. Andrew, a fisherman himself, to speed the repairs on the *Tireless.*

"But not too fast, Gracious Lord," she amended. "Captain

Worthy has a putrid throat and clogged ears and he hasn't had Gran's cod and leeks yet."

She opened her eyes to make sure no one was close by. "Besides that, Lord, I like his company."

Chapter Four

O liver knew he was not the most subtle of men—what captain was?—but he had to discover a diplomatic way to find out more about Nana Massie. It was becoming increasingly obvious to him that Lord Ratliffe knew nothing about his daughter.

His first order of business was the *Tireless,* which occupied him the moment he stepped onto the dry docks on the River Tamar and met the master shipwright. Indeed, he would have been hard to overlook. Oliver had never dealt with Roger Childers before, but he had heard stories, mainly about the bald spots here and there on his head. The rumor was that he pulled his hair out in little clumps, with each demand by impatient captains.

Before Childers could begin, Oliver handed him his copy of the survey, with the few items Nana had added. The shipwright read down the list, then began to worry a small patch of hair by his left ear. Oliver could hardly keep from bursting into laughter. He knew he didn't dare look at his mates, who had heard the same rumors.

With a deep sigh, Childers jabbed at the survey with a

finger fringed about with wispy hair. "She'll not be ready before two months, and then we're stretching it, Captain."

"It must be three weeks."

Back went Childers's fingers to his hair. This war had better end soon, Oliver thought, or this man will have snatched himself bald. He turned away briefly to stare into the middle distance and force down a laugh.

During the tirade that followed, Oliver resolutely set his face toward the *Tireless,* and his crew that lined the ship's waist. From bosun to the small gunners' helpers, they watched the whole exchange with interest. There appeared to be money changing hands by the few who had any coins left. Oliver wondered if the wager was how many more bald spots, or the length of time for repairs.

"Six weeks, and not a minute less, Captain," Childers pronounced finally.

"One month."

The same routine followed, but it appeared to Oliver that the shipwright was weakening.

Finally they agreed upon three and a half weeks. Oliver found himself of two minds about the matter. Three weeks would have been better, but that extra few days meant more time admiring Nana Massie. He wasn't even thinking of her as Miss Massie anymore, although he knew he daren't call her by her nickname.

I have so little time, he protested silently. *Almost none, and then I am back at sea.* But there was Childers at his elbow, looking like a broken man, and holding out the revised survey for his signature. He signed.

"You're a hard man, Captain Worthy."

"This is a hard war, Mr. Childers."

He turned his attention to the dry docks. There was a

schooner in one way, and his own frigate next to it. The other four dry docks were empty. He looked to the ways in the distance, and only one showed a ship in progress. "It appears you can use the work."

"We can indeed," the shipwright said, the light back in his eyes, and his voice friendly again. If anything, he looked peppier than before his hair-pulling session. He frowned then. "I know Admiral Lord Gardner has his reasons for keeping the Channel Fleet at its station, but—" he gestured toward the frigate's stern "—you can only defer maintenance so long. When the water's up to your ass, it's a bit late, wouldn't you say?"

It was typical navy graveyard humor. "A bit," he agreed. He held out his hand to the shipwright, who shook it. They parted friends.

Oliver handed his roster to Mr. Proudy. "We'll follow our usual pattern. Number ones go first for five days, and so on in rotation. Remind the crew that if all the number ones don't return, there will be no two, three or four. You might also remind them that their share of the prize money from our last cruise is at Brustein and Carter's, matched against my roster and their identification."

"Aye, aye, sir," Proudy said, as he took the roster. He turned toward the *Tireless* and held it up, to cheers from all on deck.

Oliver turned to Mr. Ramseur. "Is my purser still on board?"

"Aye, sir."

Oliver took some coins from his waistcoat pocket and handed them to his second mate. "Give him my compliments, Mr. Ramseur, and ask him to have a quarter beef and a package of good lamb chops—maybe a dozen—delivered to the Mulberry. He knows the victuallers better than I do."

"Aye, sir."

"And, Mr. Ramseur…"

"Sir?"

"How about you and I watch the shipwright's progress for the first two weeks and allow Mr. Proudy to escort his lady home to Exeter for some peace and quiet?"

Ramseur blushed, as Oliver knew he would. He grinned then and nodded. "Aye, sir. Shall I tell him?"

"Do. And tell him once he finishes the crew's assignments, he can leave for Exeter."

Oliver looked at Ramseur, really looked at him, and saw him for what he was: young, loyal, relatively untried. "Mr. Ramseur, I don't think anything will happen in dry docks that you and I cannot handle."

"Really, sir?"

For a moment, his number two sounded like a schoolboy. *Was I ever that young?* Oliver asked himself. *Of course I was.*

"Absolutely." No point in stopping there. "Mr. Ramseur, I never fully thanked you for the clearheaded way you acted when the *Wellspring* rammed our stern. I'm glad you were on watch then, and not one of the midshipmen, or it might have been a different story."

Oliver touched his forefinger to his hat and turned away to answer another question from Childers. When he turned back, Ramseur, his back straight and his step dignified, was crossing the plank to the *Tireless,* the picture of confidence.

I need to remember to do that more often, Oliver thought, as he watched his number two. Sometimes a kind word is more valuable than prize money. He thought of Nana Massie then, wondering if women could be treated the same way. He concluded they could.

With a look of gratitude worth more than speech, Mr. Proudy left the *Tireless* a few minutes later, saluted his captain and promised to return in two weeks.

"See that you do, Mr. Proudy," Oliver said. "That'll give Mr. Ramseur a week home in Lyme Regis. Didn't he say something about a vicar's daughter?"

"She's the daughter of a solicitor, sir," Mr. Proudy answered. "Dorie, I believe. Thank you again, sir."

Oliver watched him go. *Dorie, eh?* he thought. *Why on earth did I let all the Dories of the world pass me by?* Ordinarily, he wouldn't have given his mates' personal lives a second thought. He blamed his new frame of reference on Lord Ratliffe's miniature, and that curious axis shift at Admiralty House.

He nooned with Childers over a bowl of soup, then realized he had to return to his bed at the Mulberry. "I'll be back tomorrow," he told the shipwright. "If you have any questions, ask Mr. Ramseur."

Even though his ears throbbed and his throat felt as though it was trapped in a vise, Oliver directed the hackney to Drake's Inn first. *All I want is information,* he excused himself. *I've known Mrs. Fillion for enough years to appreciate how much she likes to gossip. I will have to question her carefully, though.*

He told the hackney driver to wait for him. He found Mrs. Fillion in the kitchen, staring glumly at her account book. She brightened when she saw him.

"Is the Mulberry not to your liking?" she asked. "They do need the trade."

"So do you, madam," he replied, sitting down. "Tough times ahead."

She turned worried eyes on him. "We'll fare all right, sir. Are you comfortable enough at the Mulberry?"

"I am," he replied. "The Massies are seeing to my needs." He leaned closer, pleased to see Mrs. Fillion do the same. "Pete Carter has fixed me a wicked brew for my throat, and

Miss Massie seemed determined to keep the fire stoked to healing levels." He shook his head. "It's Gran that fair terrifies me."

Mrs. Fillion laughed. "She's an ogre, is Nancy Massie." She leaned closer again. "If it weren't for her, I can't imagine what would have happened to Nana."

Oliver didn't have to say anything. He just raised his eyebrows.

"Nancy's daughter, Rachel, was a flighty piece. She caught the fancy of a lieutenant. What happened to Rachel has happened to women in port the world over." She looked at him knowingly.

"Ah, yes" was all he needed to say to restart Mrs. Fillion.

The innkeep lowered her voice. "Rachel had the bad fortune to die in childbirth. I don't know how Nancy did it, but she held that lieutenant to some level of accountability."

"That's rare."

"It is." Mrs. Fillion shrugged. "I wouldn't care to stand in front of Nancy Massie when she has an ax to grind. Somehow, a deal was struck. The baby's father would see to her education, and then provide her with a meaningful opportunity."

"Which didn't happen, obviously, because she's back in Plymouth."

Mrs. Fillion nodded. "Five years ago, Nana came home on the mail coach from Bath. No one has said why."

And you can't worm it out of Gran, Oliver thought. *This must be a tight secret indeed. And you don't appear to know who that lieutenant was.* He couldn't deny his own disappointment at Mrs. Fillion's news, which enlightened him no more than Lord Ratliffe had. He still didn't know why Nana had bolted for Plymouth.

"At least Miss Massie has her grandmama," he said, leaning back so he felt less like a co-conspirator.

"Gran's a fierce protector," the innkeep said. "So's that old Pete."

"A regular Scylla and Charybdis," Oliver murmured.

"Are they Frogs?" Mrs. Fillion asked.

"Even worse. Greeks."

"So Nana has returned to Plymouth. Lord knows if she will ever leave it."

"No dowry, I gather?"

"Heavens, no!" Mrs. Fillion sighed, then gave him a knowing look. "A pretty face can get a woman a career in Plymouth, eh, Captain? But not Nana—a rich man's by-blow, and not quite a lady."

"She's very much a lady," Oliver said firmly. He couldn't overlook the calculating look that suddenly came into Mrs. Fillion's eyes, and hastened to neutralize it. "But it's a pity, I agree. What can she hope for?"

"Not much. And what a pity! Such a pretty child. She always came with her gran to the market. I can still see her hurrying to keep up. Even the fishmongers gave her little treats, and you know what a rough lot they are!"

He could imagine Nana Massie captivating her Plymouth audience. For the tiniest moment, he wondered how nice it would be to take a little daughter or son on board the *Tireless* and introduce them to his watery world. He could hold a small son up to the wheel and let him think he was helmsman.

His mind was wandering; it was time to leave the Drake and go to bed. "Times are tough," he repeated. He stood up. "Gran still calls her Nana?"

"We all do. When she was a baby, she couldn't say 'Eleanor.' I suppose she was Eleanor at that la-di-dah school in Bath, but what good did that do?"

What good, indeed. He returned to the waiting hackney.

As they traveled up South Hoe, he noticed the wigmaker's shop on the corner of Lambhay. Surely a town the size of Plymouth only had one such business, especially now that men were inclined to exhibit their own hair, and not rely on someone else's.

He told the driver to wait, and went inside. A bell announced his presence and a bald man came out from the back room. Oliver had to suppress a smile when the man's eyes went right to his hair, studied it, then glanced away, disappointed.

"I'm not a customer," Oliver said.

Here was the dilemma. He wasn't a man to lie, but he was curious about something. "My…my father is sensitive about hair loss, and I thought I would inquire into wigs."

The proprietor launched into a rhapsodic description of all he could do. Oliver felt uncomfortable for his lie, but he had ventured this far, so he might as well continue.

He listened and asked a few questions about the wigmaking process itself. "And where does the hair come from? Do you…do you have any hair here I could look at?"

He did. The man reached under the counter and brought out two long hanks of hair—one blond and the other Nana's. He had to resist the urge to run his hand down the length of it, auburn hair more brown than red, but with deep copper tones. It nearly took his breath away. Or maybe that was his putrid throat; hard to say.

"Go ahead," the wigmaker urged. "Touch it."

Oliver ran his hand over the hair, then combed his fingers through it, unable to resist. He suddenly wondered what it would look like, spread upon a pillow, still attached to its former owner. He had to remind himself his damned occupation had rendered him immune to females.

"That's beautiful," he said at last, reluctantly removing his hands from the dark mass. "What do you pay for hair like that?"

The wigmaker ran his own fingers through the slightly curling locks. "Usually I give eight to ten shillings for hair this length." His eyes looked troubled then.

"And?" Oliver prompted.

"I paid a pound." The wigmaker shook his head. "I tried to talk her out of cutting it. Imagine that. She told me to go ahead, they needed the money." He returned the hair to his drawer. "She cried when I finished."

"I can imagine," Oliver murmured. He had to leave, not so much because of his throat this time, but because he couldn't stand the sadness. "Let me ask my father what he thinks about a wig. Good day, sir."

The thing is, she seemed so proud to be able to help her Gran, Oliver thought as the hackney delivered him to the Mulberry. He paid the jehu and walked up the path, pausing to note that the pansies had been resuscitated and given clean earth. He stood there a moment, looking down. Maybe everyone got a second chance at the Mulberry.

Nana met him in the hallway. "I thought I heard a hackney, Captain."

He wanted to tell her his name was Oliver, but he didn't. "Ah, yes, returning from the docks. Looks like you're stuck with me for three and a half weeks, until my ship heals," he joked.

He must have been more ill than he thought, because her eyes filled with tears. Should he ignore it, or comment? "It's a tough ship," he said.

Bless her heart. She dabbed at her eyes, and looked him square in his. "I was thinking *you* need more time, Captain," she said, with only the slightest quaver in her voice. "If you don't take care of yourself, who will?"

It was a good question, but not one of great concern to either Admiralty House or anyone except captains junior to him who would rise higher on the rolls, if he should suddenly slough off his mortal coil.

"I'll be fit by then, too. Probably even sooner, Miss Massie."

She seemed to have recovered herself. "Yes, certainly," she agreed. She traded concern for belligerence, and he wasn't sure which emotion touched him more. "See here, Captain, you forgot to drink another of Pete's draughts before you left this morning. I intend to see that you do."

"You and who else?" he asked, amused.

"Just me, I suppose," she said in confusion, then looked at him more closely. "You're quizzing me."

"And stalling, too. That's a rough brew." He looked toward the stairs. "But right now I admit to being weary beyond belief. Please excuse me, Miss Massie. I think I want to lie down and die."

"You aren't allowed to die at the Mulberry," she said, teasing him back.

He crawled into bed and slept the afternoon away, after drinking down another remedy, administered by Pete Carter himself. He found himself dreaming of Nana, which only left him embarrassed, and thinking he had left behind such dreams in his midshipman days.

He was aware later of someone adding more coal to the fire, and then tucking a hot brick, wrapped in a towel, at his feet. When he started to sweat, someone applied a cool cloth to his face. Another wheat poultice went around his neck and crossed over his throat, which made him dream of bread this time. He could have sworn then that Nana Massie rested her hand on his forehead, because it was cool and soft and he thought there was a hint of roses. He didn't think Pete had much to do with roses.

When he woke finally, the room was dark, except for a glow from the fireplace. It was too much to hope that Nana would be in his room, but she was. She sat in the chair by his bed, and she appeared to be asleep. He needed to use the chamber pot, but not badly enough to disturb her slumber. He wanted to watch her.

She had leaned her head back and to one side against the high back of the straight chair, sitting somewhat in profile. The light was low, but he was impressed by the length of her eyelashes. She had even propped up her stockinged feet at the foot of his bed.

He slowly moved his right foot until it rested close to hers. He knew better than to touch her foot, but he felt her warmth, and that was enough to send him back to sleep.

When he woke later, he could have cried to see Nana gone and Pete there instead, holding a urinal in his lap. Oliver sighed. *I go from the sublime to the embarrassing,* he thought, wondering if Nana had vacated the room when he began to move around restlessly and finger his member, like a little boy with the urge to piss.

"I think you're needing this," Pete said, his voice gruff, but not unkind.

"My blushes," Oliver said. "I hope I didn't embarrass Miss Massie."

Pete put the urinal under the covers. "She's tended me when I've been too ill to get out of bed. Gran cut up stiff, but Nana's not a shrinking violet. If I hadn't been available just now, she'd have done for you, too."

Horrors, he thought, *horrors.* "I could get up and use the chamber pot," he protested, but only feebly.

"And have you tumbling arse over teakettle because you're

too sick?" Pete scolded. "I'm not in your navy now, sir, so I can speak plainly."

"Indeed you can," Oliver agreed, chastened. "And you're right." He finished and handed back the urinal. *I can be matter-of-fact if you can,* he thought. *I just hope I don't have to see Nana Massie again for the next three and a half weeks.*

She was at the door and knocking, only moments after Pete left. She had a tray in her hands, and it occurred to him that he was more hungry than embarrassed. So much for the delicacies.

She came close to the bed and set the tray at the foot, then picked up the extra pillow from the side table by the window. He sat up so she could place it behind his head, and then adjust the table over his lap.

"It's cod and leeks, cooked in cream. Mr. Proudy said you liked it, and Gran said it will go down easy."

He was almost afraid to look at her, but he had to. He knew he would always have to. There was nothing missish about her expression. *Well, if she doesn't mind I am human, I suppose I shouldn't, either,* he decided, as he picked up a spoon.

It was delicious, and flowed easily around the boulder in his throat. "My compliments to the chef," he told her, pleased to see her smile.

"Gran made it, but I watched. I think I can do it now."

She sat down, then got up again to tuck a napkin in the front of his nightshirt. She pulled the tray a little closer, then picked up another bowl and spoon. He hadn't realized she was planning to eat with him.

"This is so you'll know I'm eating, too," she said. "So are Gran and Pete and Sal. We made plenty for us all."

So the inmates of the Mulberry had come to an understanding. Good. "Who is Sal?" he asked between mouthfuls.

"Our scullery maid." She looked at him, and seemed to know what he was thinking. "We couldn't let her go when times got tough, Captain. She said she'd rather take her chances with us than return to the workhouse."

"Wise choice."

He knew she would leave when he finished, so he ate slowly, savoring the company as much as the cod. She cleaned her bowl, which had been as full as his. He decided he liked a woman with a good appetite.

When he finished, she took the tray from his lap, but stood there, indecisive. He could tell she had something more to say, and allowed her time to work up to it. Her sentence came out in a rush.

"You absolutely cannot go to the dry docks tomorrow, Captain. I forbid it."

He would have laughed, except that the serious look on her face touched him as nothing else could have. He noted how tight together her lips were, and how she gripped the tray, as if ready to spring into all kinds of defiance, if he argued.

"I won't then," he assured her. "You're right. I'll never get better if I don't stay in bed."

"You're worrying me, Captain," she said, her voice no louder than a whisper. "I…we want you to get well."

"I promise I will. Cross my heart."

She relaxed then. "Sir, if you need anything in the night…anything. Pete and I will take turns sleeping on a cot by your door."

He started to protest at that, and the look he got in return was nearly mutinous. He nodded instead.

"Good night, sir," she said, and left the room.

He woke up once in the night, stirring about enough to wake Pete, who came in with the urinal, and another dose of his patented draught, good enough to raise the dead and cure the world.

Toward morning, he woke again. His throat felt moderately better; the boulder in his throat had shrunk to a rock. He thought he could even manage the chamber pot this time. He got up quietly and used it, pleased with himself. Before he got back in bed, he went to the door and opened it, just to see who was on duty in the corridor.

Nana slept on the cot this time, balled up tightly enough to tell him that she was cold. He went to the clothespress in his room and pulled out a blanket, returning to the hall and covering her with it. She stirred, but did not open her eyes. He watched her, and in a few moments, she straightened out her legs and returned to a deeper sleep. Impulsively, he touched her head.

He could have watched her the rest of his life.

Chapter Five

Her years in Bath notwithstanding, Nana was a true daughter of Plymouth. Since she was a small girl, she had known almost by instinct to hold officers in awe.

One of her earliest Plymouth memories—she must have been all of four—centered on a post captain staying at the Mulberry, when post captains used to do that. He had been talking in the hall with Gran, who held her hand. From her viewpoint much closer to the floor, Nana had looked up and up, and burst into tears before getting much beyond the gilt buttons. It was all too much.

Her first glimpse of Captain Oliver Worthy—tall beyond tall from his high fore and aft hat, and majestic down past his boat cloak to his buckled shoes—had given her no reason to change her mind. There was an aura well-nigh impenetrable about the navy. These were hard men in a hard service, deserving of her respect.

Maybe it was the matter of the pansies. It could have been when she put the wheat poultice around his neck that first night. Possibly even—blushes—when she knew he needed some help with a urinal. At some point in only a very few days, she fell in love.

She didn't know what to call it at first. She had fancied herself in love when the brother of a fellow student at Miss Pym's had sent her a ridiculous poem about eyes that eventually rhymed "brown" with "crown," then took a tortuous leap to "drown." The infatuation had passed with his bad spelling, but not before she had allowed him to kiss her on the cheek during a supposed visit to his sister.

She had admired a hemp vendor a few years ago when he spent a week at the Mulberry, extolling the virtues of his product at the rope walk near the dry docks. She had laughed at his humor, and he seemed to like her company, but he had never returned to the Mulberry. She had moped about for a week, but a month later when she couldn't even recall his name, she decided it wasn't love.

Captain Worthy was different. Maybe it had happened when she woke up in the corridor, covered with the blanket she knew was from the clothespress in his room. She lay there in her sleep fog, wondering if he had actually touched her head last night, or if she imagined it. She put it down to imagination, but the touch seemed to linger in her heart.

She tried to put the matter out of her mind and nearly succeeded. Gran would never countenance any connection with a navy man, not after what had happened to her own daughter. There was no way she could casually ask, "Gran, what does it feel like to be in love?" without arousing suspicions of the most dire sort. She had to work through the matter on her own.

There was so much she wanted to know about him, and no way to find out. It was impossible even to know how old the captain was, because men of the sea didn't age well. For all she knew, he could have been twenty-five, except she had enough knowledge of the fleet to know that men didn't often become post captains at such an age. She reckoned he might be thirty; he could have been much older. She decided she didn't care.

Even setting aside her own mother's disastrous ruin, she was fully acquainted with the folly of loving a navy man. From earlier, more prosperous days at the Mulberry, she remembered the wives of naval officers who had gathered in port when portions of the Channel Fleet were due.

She had never forgotten the night a message came to one of the waiting wives. Her screams echoed and reechoed through the inn at the news her husband had died of ship's fever miles away in Portsmouth, where his ship had put in, instead of Plymouth. The new widow's hysteria so terrified Nana that she had to sleep with Gran until she returned to Bath.

As she lay on the cot that morning, she remembered the incident, but it didn't seem to matter. All she really wanted to do was get up, walk into Captain Worthy's room and climb in bed with him.

Thanks to Gran's blunt education, she had a good idea of what men and women did in bed; the urge she felt was more than intimate physical comfort. She wanted Captain Worthy to wrap his arms around her and keep her safe from a world at war. She was too much of a realist to think blockade, hunger, cold, uncertainty and doubt would disappear, just because she was in the arms of someone stronger than she was. She just knew vicissitude would be easier to bear. That was all, but it was more than she had ever dared hope for, until his arrival at the Mulberry.

There was a greater issue, one that cast her own needs into a shadow and made her come to a right understanding about love: more than anything else, she wanted to protect him from the horrors of his own duty.

That she could protect *anything* was ludicrous in the extreme. She was just a woman, poorer than many, more vulnerable than most because of her questionable lineage. Laying all that aside, she knew she had within her the power to help that man—to love him whenever his duty let her; bear and nurture his children, even if he was far away or dead; make him laugh; keep him safe in her arms.

Think it through, she ordered herself, and stayed where she was. She knew nothing about the captain's background, except that he had no family living. She also knew that officers in the Royal Navy usually arrived at their posts through diligence *and* influence. Like other navy men—Lord Nelson's father may have been a clergyman, but his uncle was comptroller of the navy—Captain Worthy was probably well-educated and well-connected. Men like that didn't take illegitimate brides.

Funny that a quirk of fate could render her unfit for the kind of company that her Bath education had taught her to believe was her right and privilege. Too bad she should have to feel less worthy than even a fishmonger's child, dirty and speckled with scales from life on the dock, but possessing parents married to each other.

She knew any connection with Captain Worthy was out of the question, so the matter of making sure she really was in love took on moot qualities. In the cold morning light, Nana resolved no one would ever know. The *Tireless* would be at sea again in three and a half weeks. If she could not survive such a paltry amount of time, considering the whole history of the world, then she was a fool.

Nana decided not to think about life at the Mulberry, or even life in general, after the *Tireless* sailed back to the blockade of the Spanish coast. She knew a huge emptiness would be her purgatory for loving someone out of her reach, both by birth and by the terrible times they lived in.

Nana got up quietly and folded the blankets before tiptoeing down the stairs and into the family quarters. Gran was humming and stirring porridge on the Rumford. Nana went to her silently and just leaned against her arm. Gran inclined her head toward Nana.

"Did you get any sleep, dearie?"

"Yes. I think Captain Worthy is still asleep."

There now; that was easy. She didn't give his name any more inflection than she would have had he been one of twenty lodgers, and more than unusually critical. Nana knew that although Gran had no great skill with books or writing, she was shrewd and wise concerning life's labyrinths. Nana also knew by some instinct that speaking of Captain Worthy too much would invite suspicion. Better to say next to nothing, beyond what her conversation should contain about any Mulberry lodger.

Easier said than done, she decided, especially when Gran insisted on talking about the man.

"Listen for him, Nana," Gran instructed. "When you hear him moving about, ask him if porridge will do again for breakfast, or if he wants anything else."

"Do we have anything else?" Nana asked, surprised.

"Indeed we do. Just this morning, the butcher delivered a dozen lamb chops, some bacon and a quarter of beef. I have made muffins, and there are eggs, too." Gran moved the porridge onto the warming shelf. "The butcher said the meat was compliments of Captain Worthy. Nana, what a kind man he is."

"Yes," she responded. She could tell from the look on Gran's face that she expected more of a favorable reaction. *Gran, you're going to make forgetting him difficult,* she thought. "What a kind man."

Nana dressed quickly, looking in the mirror long enough to wish her hair would grow back overnight, and wondering what cruel fate had decreed freckles on her nose. Since Sal was busy with dishes, Gran gave her a can of warm water to carry upstairs, and a towel.

She went lightly up the stairs, listening for their boarder, and was rewarded with the sound of coughing, followed by "Damn!"

The captain was sitting up in bed, his hand on his throat, a frown on his face. To her gratification, his expression lightened when he saw who it was. He spoke, and his voice was hoarse.

"What a predicament, Miss Massie. If I lie completely still and do not cough, I feel perfectly sound. Otherwise, I'm a medical calamity." He sighed. "At least Mr. Childers will be relieved I am staying in bed today."

She set down the water can and towel on the washstand. "Why would that be, Captain?"

"I think no shipwright bent on repairs wants a captain breathing down his neck, even if it is a requirement of the Admiralty."

"Too many cooks, eh?"

"Precisely."

He gestured for her to come closer and indicated the chair by the bed, to her way of thinking, much as he would make demands of a crew member. The thought diverted her; she sat down.

"My plan today is to remain in bed, but I daren't be idle." He glanced at her. "And none of those mutinous looks, Miss Massie! The war won't wait on a putrid throat."

I'm certainly going to have to watch my expressions around this fellow, she told herself, amused. "I know Pete still expects you to do your duty regarding his draught."

"Very well. I will concede that point. I am going to write a note which I hope he will take to dry docks." He looked at her, one eyebrow raised, and she felt her heart turn over. "No, Miss Massie, you are *not* to deliver the note. It is no place for ladies."

"I will concede that point," she teased, and he smiled.

"This note will be addressed to Matthew, one of my powder monkeys. He can't read, so it is up to Mr. Ramseur to do that. I am going to make Matthew my errand boy for today and possibly tomorrow. If Mr. Childers has any communication for me, Matthew will deliver it. I also will have notes for the harbormaster and my purser, which I am trusting to his attention. I will place a hackney at Matthew's command, which will please him no end."

"Most certainly," she said, "if he is like most boys. How old is he, sir?"

"I believe he is eleven. If not, then nearly so."

"So young."

The captain settled himself back against his pillows. "He came to the gunnery deck when he was eight."

"Heavens!" she exclaimed, unable to help herself.

"I was twelve when I become a young gentleman," Captain Worthy said. "I have been eighteen years in the navy, Miss Massie. The younger, the better. We aren't the army, praise the Almighty."

So you are thirty, she thought. *You were at sea when I was three years old.*

He shifted slightly so he was looking at her again. "I have a favor to ask you regarding Matthew."

Anything for you, she thought. She didn't know why he began that restless memorization of her face that was flattering and disconcerting at the same time. Perhaps he was feeling less sanguine than he let on.

"In five days' time, it will be Matthew's turn for shore leave. He came from the workhouse in Portsmouth, which is no place an alumnus ever wishes to revisit. Could he come here?"

"Certainly," she replied. "He won't mind staying in our family quarters, will he? I know we have plenty of rooms upstairs, but it would be lonely."

He nodded. "I was hoping you would say just that. You can put him to work, too." He chuckled. "He's a dab hand at running powder from the powder locker to the guns without blowing up any of us, if that's a skill you can use in your grandmother's kitchen."

She joined in his laughter, amazed at how easy it was to enjoy his somewhat morbid humor. "If he knows how to sew, he can do my mending."

"He has been learning to repair sail. I can't recommend him for delicate work."

It wasn't her business, but she wanted to ask, anyway. "Your other powder monkeys? What about them? They could come here, too."

"That's kind of you," he said. "One is on leave right now at his mother's house, about three blocks from the Barbican. The other two are twins, and their father is my gunnery mate. All sons of the gun, Nana."

He must not have realized he used her nickname. She couldn't think of any reason she wanted to correct a captain, especially since her name seemed to come off his tongue so easily. If he did it again, she knew she wouldn't mind.

"Is there a subscription library in Plymouth?" he asked.

"Yes, but…but…our subscription has lapsed," she replied, embarrassed.

He seemed not to notice. "Just take some coins from my purse in the top drawer. I want you to get me Gibbons's

Decline and Fall of the Roman Empire, the fifth volume. I have read one through four, and six, but number five ended up at the bottom of the Caribbean."

"Since you have already read volume six, Captain, you already know how those Romans declined," she said, unable to keep from quizzing him.

He laughed, then winced and put his hand to his throat. "Of course I know how it ends. Perhaps I have a tidier mind than yours."

She brought his purse to the bed. "I don't wish to pick your purse, sir. You do it."

He handed some coins to her, then gave her the purse, which she returned to the drawer.

"Now, are you ready for porridge?"

"I thought you would never ask." He handed her another coin and the note to the shipwright. "Have Pete deliver this himself in a hackney, and wait for Matthew to join him."

"Very well." She looked toward the washstand. "There's hot water, Captain."

"Which I intend to ignore today," he told her, relaxing further by putting his hands behind his head. "I will remain in all my dirt and whiskers today and, if possible, bathe tonight. The Mulberry has a bathroom?"

"Next to the scullery." She wasn't sure why such a prosaic conversation should make her blush, but it did. "Captain, we can bring a tub up here and haul water."

"I won't hear of it," he told her. "After a day of relative leisure, I intend to be well enough by nightfall to bathe and eat lamb chops." He gave her another glance. "And don't look so doubtful!"

She went to the door, but he called her back. "Miss Massie, perhaps you can find a copy of *Robinson Crusoe* at the library, too. And if you and Matthew and I have some spare time, you could read it out loud to us."

She nodded, pleased at his interest in what must be the lowliest member of his crew. "Is there anything else, Captain?"

It was his turn to look shy. "I don't even know how to ask this." Then he said, "I'd like to eat with you and Gran and Pete tonight, if it's allowed."

Nana thought of Miss Edgar, and her years of solitude. "It's allowed," was all she could say, and drat if her eyes didn't start to fill with tears, thinking of how pleased Gran would be.

"What did I say to make you melancholy?"

His voice was soft, and she called on all her resources not to fling her arms around him and give him a hug he wouldn't soon forget. "I'll tell you sometime," she replied, and left the room.

My God, what a lady, he thought, as the door closed behind Nana Massie. *I wonder if she had any idea how close she just came to getting a hug from a whiskery man with a bad throat.*

He would have asked Nana to eat breakfast with him, when she came back, but before he could ask, she assured him she had already eaten; he believed her. She didn't leave until she had appropriated all of his shirts and smallclothes. She had that same "I dare you to say no" look on her face from yesterday, so he did not argue.

"I couldn't help but notice the rash on your neck, Captain, when I applied the poultice," she told him, her cheeks red. "I am certain that comes from washing your clothes in sea water."

He had no plans to ever enlighten her about the merry hell smallclothes washed in brine played with his crotch and thighs. "Freshwater laundry is one of my chiefest delights on land, Miss Massie," he said. "I trust you are assigning this task to your scullery maid."

"I am," she said. "That way you can pay her a little something for her efforts."

"My pleasure."

She sucked all the air of the room when she left, which made it hard for him to concentrate on the leather box of ship's papers she had taken from his sea trunk under his direction and brought to the bed. Once he resigned himself to solitude, he spent the morning catching up on paperwork, stopping occasionally for short naps.

He was napping when his powder monkey knocked on the door. His eyes wide at seeing his commander in a nightshirt and in bed—something unheard of on the *Tireless*—Matthew nearly forgot to knuckle his forehead.

Oliver, keeping his expression serious, gave Matthew a moment to collect himself, before holding out his hand for the papers the boy carried. He gestured toward the chair and Matthew sat down on the edge of it, his cap tight in his fingers.

The news from Childers was bad. The damage to the stern was greater than he suspected, and several crossbeams in the hold would have to be replaced. Oliver stifled a groan and kept reading. *However,* he read silently, *I know the urgency. I will pull workers from the frigate going up in the ways and assign them to the crossbeams. I don't think we'll lose much time.*

"Bless you, Mr. Childers," Oliver said out loud. He beamed and looked at the powder monkey. "This is good news, Matthew."

The boy knew better than to address his captain first, especially when he hadn't been asked a question. His eyes brightened, though, as he looked at Oliver.

"Are you ready for some errands?"

"Aye, aye, sir."

Before Oliver could continue, Nana knocked at the door, then came in, carrying two books.

He could tell from the trees swaying outside the window that it was a blustery day. The red bloom on Nana's cheeks confirmed that it was also cold. He watched her, marveling again at how flawless her skin was, except for the disarming freckles across the bridge of her nose. He happened to glance at Matthew, and noticed the little boy was staring, too. *Yes, Matthew, that is what a lady looks like,* he thought. *We don't see many in the Channel Fleet, do we?*

To Oliver's delight, Matthew leaped to his feet and managed a rustic bow. Nana curtseyed back, her eyes full of fun.

"You must be Matthew, whom Captain Worthy is trusting with his messages," she said.

"Aye, sir," Matthew said, then stopped, confused.

It *has* been a long time, Oliver thought. "You should say, 'Aye, miss,'" he said gently.

She set the books by the bed, then turned to Matthew, who was watching her every move, to Oliver's amusement. "Before he sends you on errands, there is at least one meat pie in the kitchen. If the captain will permit it, I will take you down there."

"Only if you will bring one back for me," Oliver said, putting aside the papers.

"Perhaps, Captain," she replied, which caused Matthew's eyes to nearly pop from his skull. "I would rather you had clear soup and perhaps some applesauce."

Matthew couldn't help himself. "Gor, miss, for contradiction, he'll have you flogged!"

"He wouldn't dare," Nana replied.

Matthew stared back at him, the color draining from his face.

"You have to understand something about ladies, Matthew,"

he told the boy, as he observed the glee on Nana's face. "They think they know best. On land, perhaps they do. I would not for the world cross Miss Massie."

Matthew gulped. He inched closer to the bed and whispered, "Pardon me for speaking out of turn, sir, but doesn't she *know* who you are?"

"I don't think she precisely understands, Matthew," he whispered back. "I am humoring her."

The boy could think of nothing else to say. He bowed to Oliver and left the room. In another moment he was clattering down the stairs.

Nana watched the powder monkey go. She turned to Oliver. "Who terrified him most, you or me?" she said.

Oliver leaned back on the pillows. "Probably me. He's never even seen me sit down before, and here I am, sprawled in bed. And in a nightshirt yet."

"You don't sprawl," she said, and then blushed, realizing, perhaps, it wasn't an observation she should mention.

He looked at her, a question in his eyes.

"Maybe it's all your years swinging in a hammock," she explained. "You sleep very straight."

He hadn't ever thought of that before. "I suppose I do," he murmured. "You're an observant lady."

She only smiled again, knuckled her forehead in perfect imitation of Matthew's salute and left the room.

Don't observe me too closely, Oliver thought, as the door closed. *You might discover I can't take my eyes off you, either.* He pulled the leather case onto his lap again and took out a sheet of paper. He had nothing more than a pencil at hand, but it would do. It was time to compose a letter to Lord Ratliffe, to let him know how his daughter was doing.

My dear sir, he began, and got no further. His High

Exalted undersecretary at Admiralty House had asked for some word of Nana, to find out how she was faring, after she had bolted from his protection five years ago. It would be a simple matter to tell Lord Ratliffe, a concerned-if-absent parent, that times were harsh at the Mulberry, and Nana deserved better. *If she were my daughter, I would want to do more,* Oliver thought. *Surely Lord Ratliffe is of the same mind.*

Strangely, every instinct told him not to spill it all out. He could not dodge the uneasy feeling that there was more to the story than Lord Ratliffe was revealing. He had no evidence of anything, but Oliver knew his intuition was sound. It had saved his life and his ship on many occasions, and there was no reason to think things had changed, now that he was temporarily stoved up and cast ashore in a shabby inn.

If she were my daughter, he thought, and picked up the pencil. He set it down again, allowing himself the luxury of an errant idea. *If she were my wife, I could take care of her.* The idea was so absurd that he chuckled. Nana had more sense than to leg shackle herself to a captain in the Channel Fleet. And he had more sense than to ever suggest it. Still, the idea intrigued him enough to write "Captain and Mrs. Oliver Worthy" on a scrap of paper, then ball it up and pitch it into the fire.

> *My dear Lord Ratliffe,*
> *As you can imagine, in this season of blockade and war, times are a little tough in Plymouth. Let me assure you, however, that your daughter, Eleanor Massie, is doing very well. The Mulberry continues to enjoy the custom of the trade. It could use more, certainly, but I would assure you that Miss Massie is in good hands.*

He put down the pencil again, wondering if he was refer-
ring to himself. Hadn't he ordered victuals for the Mulberry?
He could do more. He picked up the pencil.

He heard Nana on the stairs—probably bringing him soup,
and another of Pete's draughts—and put the letter away. He
would finish it that afternoon and send it with Matthew, with
orders to give it to Mr. Ramseur, who would post it. He thought
about what he had written, knowing most of it was a lie. The
Mulberry was in desperate shape, and Nana was too thin.

Why was he lying to the one person who could do the most
good for his daughter? *I wish I knew,* he told himself as Nana
knocked on the door. All he knew was that his instincts had never
failed him before, and he couldn't see why they would now.

Another thought occurred to him, and he didn't even try
to brush it away. He had assured himself for years and years
that he knew better than to fall in love and inflict some poor
female with a husband who had no idea how long he would
survive the sea and a war that had outlived one century and
was wearing away on another.

That was the biggest lie of all.

Chapter Six

After another bout of misgivings, Oliver sent off the letter.

Sal outdid herself. There was a freshwater shirt, slightly damp under the arms, ready for him to wear to dinner that night. At Nana's command, Sal and Pete had heated and hauled water to the tub in the bathroom, where he enjoyed a lengthy soak.

Upstairs in his room again, he scraped away at his face, wishing there was something he could do to eliminate the myriad lines around his eyes, the product of years at sea, standing on a weather deck. *She would never believe I was thirty, even if I swore on a pile of Bibles,* he thought as he frowned into the tiny mirror. *And I declare I have only seen thinner lips on a Scotsman, Lord help us.*

At least he didn't have a paunch, like any number of high-fleshed landsmen he had noticed on his rapid journeys to and from Admiralty House. He couldn't think of any captains in the Channel Fleet who had a superabundance of flesh. He didn't think he could still fit into his midshipman's trousers, though. Parts of him had grown since those days, which was only to be expected. At any rate, none of the hired women he had serviced in various ports had ever complained.

And that is enough of that, he told himself, as he buttoned his breeches. Why would they complain? He paid them. He couldn't help but think of his father, and all his admonitions about cold baths and rigorous discipline of the mind. All baths at sea were cold, and no rigor of mind could ever compete with the combination of long months at sea, followed by a few weeks in port, where women were eager to please.

Think of something else, he ordered himself, as he tied his neckcloth and tried not to look himself in the eye. He stared at his throat as he finished with the neckcloth, grateful it wasn't giving him much trouble. The boulders and rocks were gone, and there were only the smallest of pebbles now. His head still felt stuffy because of the ache in his ears, but he was used to that chronic ailment of the deep-water sailor.

There wasn't any reason he couldn't return to dry docks tomorrow, and make Mr. Childers's life miserable. Oliver knew he should have felt more highly charged at the thought, but it was accompanied by the reality that he would only see Nana Massie in early morning and in the evening. He left his room, not even bothering to remind himself that he was impervious to females. That was a humbug.

Matthew waited for him at the foot of the stairs, springing up at once when he saw him.

"Matthew, are you wearing a new shirt?"

"Aye, sir." The boy paused, wondering if he should say more.

"And?" Oliver prompted.

"Mr. Ramseur got it from the slops chest for me," Matthew said, his eyes bright. "He thought I should look more presentable."

"He was right," Oliver agreed, touched to notice how many times Matthew had rolled up the sleeves to accommodate his small size. "I will tell him to charge it to me."

With Matthew walking behind him at a proper distance, Oliver went through the sitting room and the deserted dining room and into the corridor. He knocked on the door at the end of the hall, and Sal opened it, beaming up at him and curtseying.

He bowed in return, which set her giggling. "Sal, my compliments," he told her. "You took all the brine out of this shirt, which places me forever in your debt."

He had struck her dumb. Her hand to her mouth, her eyes wide, she could only bob another curtsey, then whirl about and run away. "Sal! You are supposed to usher us in," he called after her.

She didn't stop until she ran into Nana, who grabbed her, laughed, swatted the back of her dress gently and continued her on her retreat to the kitchen.

"Are you frightening *my* crew?" Nana teased.

"I paid her a compliment," he replied. "Honestly, I did."

"Did he really, Matthew?" she asked, looked around Oliver.

"Aye, si— Miss." The boy looked up at him, shock in his eyes.

"Matthew, if you ever doubted me, I would have had you flogged. But we cannot do that to Miss Massie," Oliver said. "She is a lady and a landlubber. She doesn't know our rules."

No she doesn't, he reminded himself, as he followed Nana down the narrow hallway, enjoying the sway of her skirts. She wore a lighter-colored dress, but he could tell she had cinched it tight across the back because it no longer fit her slim frame. *How can I get more meat on those bones?* he asked himself. *There must be a way. Perhaps Gran or Pete would let me help.*

Dinner was everything he had hoped it would be: broiled lamb chops, crusty but still pink inside; small potatoes cooked in a mushroom sauce; and the best navy bean soup he had ever eaten. Gran finished the dinner with a flourish, bringing in a dried plum duff, savory and moist.

True, a dinner at the Drake would have included more removes and the best smuggled sherry afterward, plus a tray of cheese. All the Mulberry could offer was hot cider and a block of cheddar, but the cider went down easily, and he was quite satisfied with the cheese, which was the same kind issued to ships at sea.

Oliver looked around the table. They were comfortably crowded together—Sal and Matthew on one side, Gran and Pete at opposite ends, and Nana next to him—and the small space reminded him of his own wardroom on the *Tireless*. He felt completely at home.

It was better than the *Tireless* because Nana sat beside him. At first, he wished that she had been seated across from him, so he could look at her without appearing obvious. He decided that having her beside him was even better. Now and then her sleeve brushed against his because she was left-handed.

She had apologized the first time she bumped his arm and offered to switch places, but he told her not to worry. She didn't press the matter or insist, which made him dare think she might enjoy the proximity, too.

Next to her nearness, Oliver found himself relishing the way Nana conversed with her grandmama. From Lord Ratliffe, he knew that Miss Pym's Female Academy must have trained and fit Eleanor Massie for the most elegant society. And here she was, so at ease and obviously loving the grandmother who probably had no education beyond what came her way from hard living in Plymouth. *Common* was written all over Gran's face, same as Pete's and Sal's, but there was nothing common in Nana's regard for these people dearest to her.

You walk such a fine line, he thought, as he dared a glance at Nana, *and you do it so gracefully.* He could understand why Mrs. Fillion bullied her into taking pasties, and the wigmaker had overpaid so outrageously for a hank of lovely hair. All Plymouth knew Nana was a diamond in a midden. So did he.

The only mystery to him throughout the meal was Gran herself, who seemed on the verge of tears. She didn't seem like a woman easily intimidated by a naval uniform, and he knew better than to use his shipboard voice in the confines of a building. He couldn't help but notice how she would glance his way and then bite her lip, as though keeping back tears. Maybe he could ask Nana about it later, when Gran wasn't around.

Dinner ended too soon to suit him, especially when the women of the Mulberry rose to clear the table. He didn't know what taboo he might be breaking, but Oliver couldn't bear the thought of Nana disappearing for a long time with dirty dishes. He cleared his throat, regretted it, then spoke up.

"Mrs. Massie, since you conn this frigate, may I ask your permission to come aboard in the kitchen, too? And Matthew? If we helped with the cleanup, then perhaps your granddaughter would consent to read to us from *Robinson Crusoe*."

He had startled her. He thought she would burst into full-blown tears then, but she mastered them, and nodded. "We welcome the help, Captain," she said. "We all enjoy hearing Nana read out loud."

Bliss. After Nana insisted he remove his uniform jacket, Gran gave him an apron and set him to work at the sink with Nana. He knew better than to even glance Matthew's way. The sight of his captain, lord and master in an apron would probably overset him and lead to either a fit of the giggles he would regret, or completely ruin him for the sea.

It did neither. Pete enlisted the powder monkey to carry the kitchen scraps to the backyard and burn them in a barrel. Then he set the boy to work chopping kindling for tomorrow's meals.

Sal scraped plates while Oliver dried and Nana washed. He put his credit at risk—if he even had any—and leaned close. "I think I am upsetting your grandmama, and I don't know why."

"I'll tell you later," Nana said as she handed him a plate. "She's not upset."

He raised his eyebrows. "Excuse my doubt, then."

Nana smiled into the suds, not even looking at him. "If you were around females more, you would understand the difference between tears of joy and the other kind."

Her revelation only left him more mystified than before. He directed his attention to the business at hand, when he wasn't sneaking peeks at Nana. *Why on earth doesn't this well-raised lady rail against the hand fate seems to have dealt her?* he asked himself. *I would.*

Since Nana had assured him Gran wasn't afraid of him or angry, he took his chance to speak to her in private when he asked Nana to go upstairs to his room and retrieve *Robinson Crusoe*.

"Mrs. Massie, I am probably overreaching all kinds of propriety, but I just don't have much time here," he started.

She stopped scrubbing the stove and held the cloth in front of her, waiting.

"I know times are hard here—this whole shore is being battered by the war in ways we don't often notice, when we are at sea. You are all bearing up admirably, but I'm worried that your granddaughter is too thin."

"It worries me, too," Mrs. Massie replied, her voice soft. "I hate it."

"If you will allow it, I will leave you with a sufficiency to buy whatever you need to eat here, after I am gone back to the Channel," he said. He tried to achieve some balance between outright command and feeble supplication. If he sounded reasonable enough, she might agree; if not, she would spurn his offer as condescending charity.

He must have hit it right. Gran's eyes filled with tears again, but he knew what Nana meant this time. She wasn't angry with him, or sad. Her relief was obvious, and as palpable as if she had thrown her arms around his neck and sobbed into his chest.

One burden lifted, he thought. "I'll set up an account for the Mulberry at Carter and Brustein tomorrow," he told her. "You have all been so kind to me, and I know this would relieve your mind."

She did something then that he had not expected. Before he could stop her, the woman took his hand and kissed it. With her apron to her eyes, she left the kitchen. He was relieved she did not question him, and embarrass them both by asking if he could afford such philanthropy. *I can afford it, Mrs. Massie,* he thought. *I could feed Plymouth, if it came to that.*

He had read *Robinson Crusoe* several times before; never did he enjoy it more. Nana sat close to the fire, book in her lap, and with the added fortification of a lamp close by. He sat on the opposite side of the room, free to observe her at his leisure. Sal and Matthew—after securing his permission—sat close to her on the floor, legs crossed. Gran, her face content, sat close, too, knitting. The rhythmic click of her needles reminded Oliver of his own mother, who never sat down without some work or other to occupy her hands. Pete fell asleep after the first chapter.

Oliver felt himself nodding off, too, soothed by the timbre of Nana's voice. Her accent was a delightful combination of the delicacy of her Bath upbringing with the little turn to the *R*s he often heard in the speech of the Devonshire coast. She had their same way of drawing out her *O*s he was familiar with from the same source, but which must have driven Miss Pym to chewing carpet tacks, if she was a stickler. *Miss Pym, you can't take all the Plymouth out of the lady,* he thought.

He couldn't help himself then—he was a man, after all. As she read of Robinson Crusoe's capture by pirates, he began to wonder what Nana would be like in bed. No question she would have to put on some weight before that romp. He wasn't a weighty man himself, but he'd be afraid of breaking her in half, at her present stone. She wasn't tall, but her height seemed to be in her legs. He had never seen them, of course, but he couldn't help imagining how nice they would be wrapped around his waist, and the soft sound of her breath, coming more ragged, in his ear.

Good God, stop this, he told himself, grateful that he sat in a distant corner and so no one probably heard the little groan he hoped he had stifled. He concentrated on her story, instead, and gradually fell under its spell, like the rest of her audience.

He was in perfect charity with himself when Nana closed the book, looked around, and then at him across the room. "I believe you and I are the only people awake in this room, Captain."

"I believe you're right."

"What do you suggest, sir?"

"Send them all to bed."

It was easy to do. A touch to the shoulder was enough to bring Matthew wide-awake and on his feet. Sal took longer. Gran yawned and agreed to settle down the children.

"I can sleep here on the floor," the powder monkey said. "It's softer than the gun deck."

Shocked, Nana stared at Oliver, who held up his hands to ward off her look. "He sleeps in a hammock! Honestly! Well, generally," he admitted. "We've all taken our turn on deck, I'm sure."

"He'll be in Sal's room tonight, and she will share with me," Nana said firmly. "Matthew, you are our guest."

The powder monkey knew better than to argue. With a smile in Oliver's direction, Gran led the way and Matthew and Sal followed. Nana still sat in the chair by the fireplace, the book in her lap.

Oliver couldn't believe his good fortune. Pete had gone to bed an hour ago, and Gran had deserted the field. He came closer and sat in the chair Gran had vacated, stretching out his legs and resting his shoes on the fireplace grate. Nana would have to go around his length to leave the room, so maybe she would stay a moment longer.

She seemed disinclined to move, or even to speak. He glanced at her face, and she looked away. He had no illusions she would stay for long, but he did have a question that she had promised to answer. But first, he had to thank her.

"Miss Massie, I'm grateful for your kindness to Matthew tonight."

She waved her hand at him, as though it was too unimportant to mention. "It was no trouble. He's a sweet boy and we have the room."

He could tell she wanted to say more, so he returned his gaze to the fire, and not to her expressive face.

"I don't think he's ever had lamb chops before."

Lamp chops. What a prosaic statement. They could have been husband and wife, discussing a child of theirs. The thought struck him like a gong that this must be what peace felt like: sitting before a fire, discussing lamb chops and talking about children, without a care or a worry beyond the limits of the room. It was almost unbelievable.

"I doubt lamb chops are a prominent entrée in a workhouse," Oliver agreed, when he recovered from the novelty of his thoughts. "I can tell you this—he's eaten shish kebab in a Moroccan bazaar before."

She thought about that. "You're telling me that although yours is an onerous life, it has its rewards." She leaned forward impulsively, as though she wanted to touch his arm. "I've never been to Morocco."

"No. You travel in quieter circles." He leaned back, liking the feel of the fire's warmth on his soles. Even more, he liked that this lovely woman could remain quietly in a safe place, thanks to the horrible work he, and men like him, did. "You were going to tell me earlier why Gran seemed so emotional about this evening."

"I was." Nana leaned back, too, and tucked her legs under her, so she was resting her cheek against the chair, and looked directly at him. "For ten years, we had a lodger named Miss Edgar, a former governess."

"That must have been a welcome, steady income for the Mulberry," he said, not sure his heart was up to her direct gaze.

"It would have been, except she ran out of money after year five." Nana spoke matter-of-factly, as though such a thing happened to every hotelier. "We kept her on and never spoke about it. We couldn't have turned her onto the mercy of the parish."

Others would, he thought. *No wonder the Mulberry never made any money.*

"Miss Edgar always ate alone in the dining room. Gran tried and tried to get her to do what you and Matthew did tonight, but she wouldn't hear of it. Even when she was living on our charity, she wouldn't join us here."

"Too good for the Massies, eh?" He said it softly, but the slight burned him. How could someone, especially some-one living on their charity, not see the goodness of the women who ran the Mulberry? How could someone be so stupidly blind?

Nana seemed to understand. "I think pride must be a terrible burden, Captain Worthy. Miss Edgar was poorer than Job's rooster, but quality, and therefore too proud to eat with us and have some company in her old age. She and Gran could have been friends. It broke my grandmama's heart."

She did touch his hand then. He held his breath, afraid that if he moved, she would realize what she was doing. She kept her fingers against the back of his hand, even pressing down on them. "When you asked if you and Matthew could eat with us tonight, she was so overwhelmed she could barely speak to tell me to lay two more places at the table. Thank you, Captain Worthy. I can't tell you what that meant to her, after Miss Edgar."

Before he thought, he turned his hand over and clasped hers. She smiled at him, then gently withdrew her fingers. "You made her very happy tonight," Nana said, showing no embarrassment at his brief attempt to hold her hand. "Me, too," she added.

If she had not said that, he would have stood up, extended his apologies and retired from the field. *I'm a fool,* he thought. *In for a penny, in for a pound.*

She continued to watch him from her comfortable pose, as though she often sat that way, curled in a chair's embrace. He longed to pluck her from her seat and hold her close in his lap, doing nothing more than keeping his arms tight around her.

Her hand still rested on the arm of her chair. He tapped the back of it once, lightly. "I want to ask you something that is absolutely none of my business," he began.

She didn't say anything, but watched him with an expression of interest and a little wariness.

"Blame Lord Nelson. He once said, 'A captain cannot go wrong who places his ship alongside an enemy's.' Not that you're an enemy," he hurried to add, then stopped, dumbfounded by his idiocy.

He could have planted a great, smacking kiss on her forehead then, because she seemed to understand his question before he asked it.

"You're not the first to wonder why on earth I left Bath when I was sixteen and came back here, when I had a father who was willing to educate me to become a lady."

She spoke almost as prosaically as when she had mentioned lamb chops. He could have kicked himself when she straightened up and looked into the fire again, instead of at him. "Many would like to know," she murmured, speaking more to herself than to him.

And you're not going to tell me, he thought. *It never was my business. Why should you?*

"Why do you want to know?" she asked suddenly.

He wasn't sure he even had a reason. Maybe he was more like Matthew, struck almost dumb by the pleasure of being part of a family, albeit an odd one. He had never had a home since he was twelve. Only a few days at a shabby inn on one of Plymouth's backstreets must have sucked him in deeper than he had realized, to ask such an audacious question.

He was not about to tell her of Lord Ratliffe's request that he spy on the Mulberry and provide a report. He was already feeling distinctly uneasy that he had written to Nana's father at all.

He could tell her that he cared about her and wanted to know if she had been hurt in some way. He knew he could not do that, either, because he was in no position to care about anyone other than his crew and his ship. Two hundred men and a 34-gun frigate had leeched all the love and devotion from him that he possessed. At least, he thought they had.

"I just want to know," he told her simply.

He held his breath when she rose, but it was only to close the door to the sitting room. He let it out as she returned to her chair and resumed her former, curled posture.

"I'll tell you, Captain. It's not that horrible, I suppose. Maybe only what I should have expected."

Chapter Seven

Nana braced herself to answer him, knowing how repellant he would find what she had to say, and what a reminder it was of her illegitimacy. *I can never escape it,* she thought. *I am a fool if I think I can.*

Pete and Gran knew. In her humiliation five years ago, she had thought to keep the reason from them, but her resolve had crumbled at first sight of their worried faces when she came home to them, carrying nothing except a reticule.

Telling Captain Worthy was different. Whatever warmth she had felt from him would be gone. She reasoned it was for the best; her explanation would serve as an antidote to what her heart had been telling her. She took a deep breath.

"My unmarried mother died in childbirth. My father, William Stokes, Viscount Ratliffe, was a lieutenant on the *Tonnant* then. I think he might have been in love with my mother, because he made no effort to deny his paternity."

"Big of him," the captain murmured.

"I suppose few do admit it, sir, so have some charity," she said, sounding sharper than she wanted to.

He said nothing; he obviously did not agree with her. She

could tell he would be a diverting man to argue with. Too bad that would never happen now.

"Gran extracted a promise in writing from Lord Ratliffe that he would see to my education and provide me with a future of some sort," she continued. "I stayed in Plymouth until my fifth year, so all my early memories are of here."

"What was your first memory of Plymouth?"

She could see he was interested in her as a child, which she found flattering.

"The seagulls, most certainly," she told him. She laughed, and put her hand on his chair arm. "I remember their sound. They were everywhere, especially when the fishing smacks came to port. Gran told me we were at the docks once, and a seagull landed on my head and stole a biscuit from my hand."

"I've seen that happen aboard ship," he said. "Pesky thieves, eh?"

She settled back again. "I cried when Gran took me to Miss Pym's. The only thing that kept me from dying of homesickness was that Bath has seagulls, too."

"You left home even younger than I did. Imagine."

So true, she thought, startled. "At least I was allowed home on holidays. Miss Pym couldn't understand why I wanted to go to Plymouth at every opportunity, but Gran loves me and I adore her."

She glanced at him. Even in the low light, the color that sprang into his sallow cheeks surprised her. *Captain Worthy, you must have loved someone, too,* she thought. *I wish it were me.* She was quiet a moment longer, wondering how any woman in her right mind would not want to be loved by Captain Worthy.

"I never met my father until I turned sixteen, but every year, he sent an artist to paint a miniature of me."

She stopped, not wanting to go on. He did not press her to continue, which made her heart sink. Obviously, the whole subject was disgusting to him. *Nana, what did you expect?* she reminded herself. *Better get it over with.*

"When I turned sixteen, Lord Ratliffe invited me to London. I went to his home."

"How did he receive you?"

"He was all kindness, and so polite," she said. "I could never fault him for his manners. They were easily as good as Gran's."

She needed him to laugh, and he did, lightening the tension in the room. She stared straight ahead then, too humiliated to look at Captain Worthy. "As calmly as if he were talking of the weather, he told me he had arranged for me to become a mistress for one of his cronies, in exchange for payment of his debts."

"Good God!" the captain exclaimed. He leaped up, and paced the room. He finally stopped by the mantelpiece and stared into the fire. "Did he explain himself?"

"I believe he considered that explanation enough. He assured me he had not educated me for nothing, and that any…" Her voice faltered. "Any bastard could surely not have hoped for something better."

Well, that was said. Perhaps she could continue, if only she did not look at the horror on his face. "That was why he had wanted a miniature every year. He told me he passed it around every year at his club until he found a taker. Someone who would pay his debts to have me."

Captain Worthy exclaimed something she had heard years ago on the docks that earned her a swat and no dinner, when she had repeated it to Gran. She dared herself a glance at his face, and it was stone-cold. As she watched, his expression turned to sorrow, as though the pain were his, too. It warmed her heart.

"I should be grateful, I suppose. He told me when I was eleven, there was a marquis who wanted me. Lord Ratliffe at least had the decency to turn him down, or so he told me." She made a face. "He said he wouldn't for the world have given me into the care of a beast who fancied children. It's funny, Captain. He seemed to think this meant he was a caring father."

Captain Worthy looked stunned. He sat down hard, as though his legs couldn't hold him. "I don't know what to say."

"I didn't, either. I just stared at him." She didn't try to stop her tears. "When I told him I would never consent to anything so sordid, he laughed at me. 'What did you expect, you bastard?' he said, and then ordered me to get out of his sight."

Nana wiped her eyes on her apron. As she leaned forward, she felt the captain's hand on the back of her neck. His fingers were warm and the gesture, though brief, was comforting.

"I left London immediately. A few days later, Miss Pym told me my father was no longer paying my expenses at her school, and I would have to quit Bath." She looked at him then. "Captain Worthy, I returned to Plymouth, where Gran loves me."

"Any regrets?"

She saw only kindness in his expression, which made her heart turn over. "Never. I've always known I was illegitimate. Gran never sugarcoats anything." She dabbed at her eyes again, but she was through crying. "One regret. I wish I had taken my Bath wardrobe to Plymouth, because I could have sold those lovely clothes for food and other things the Mulberry needed."

"That's the spirit," he said. "You left everything behind?"

"Nearly, sir. I doubt even the mail coach would have taken me in my shimmy."

He laughed. "You're a dab hand, Nana. I think you've inherited Gran's shrewdness, which is hardly a bad thing. Ever hear from that scoundrel again?"

"No, thank God." She knew she could trust him, no matter how he really felt about her disclosure, but she had to ask, "I trust this story I have told you will go nowhere."

"No fears on that account. You told Gran and Pete, didn't you?"

She nodded. "I wasn't going to say anything, but it just spilled out."

"So the old boy's in debt, is he?" Captain Worthy asked.

"I certainly didn't help his pocketbook," she said dryly. "I wonder how he plans to resolve his dilemma now?"

"Good question," the captain replied. He put his hand to his heart. "Nana, that's all the excitement I can manage for one night. You'll have to excuse me."

"Certainly." She got up and opened the door, knowing that he would probably leave the Mulberry tomorrow and take up residence at Drake's Inn. What else would any man do?

He stood in the doorway a moment, as though reluctant to leave her, which surprised her. "I'll be at the dry docks tomorrow. Three weeks of choler and frustration there will make the blockade seem like a visit home at Christmas."

She knew she wasn't imagining things when she noted the wistfulness in his voice. He had no home. She had asked him that first night if there was someone she could send for to help nurse him. *Of the two of us, I believe I am the luckier,* she thought. *Lord, smite me when I whine.*

He did something then that startled her. The captain gently cupped her face in his hands and then touched his forehead to hers, holding it there until they were breathing in unison.

"Remember this, Nana—not a bit of what happened was your fault."

She nodded, treasuring the feel of her head against his, breathing deep of him and the reassurance she felt. "You would still be my friend, then?" she asked.

"I would be your friend."

He went upstairs to his chamber slowly, his feet feeling as though they carried lead weights. As if in weird opposition to his feet, his mind raced backward and forward, as he thought through every word he had written only that afternoon to Lord Ratliffe. He knew he had glossed over the state of affairs at the Mulberry, painting a far rosier portrait of the situation because of his own intuitive uneasiness. He only hoped it was enough.

He finally decided there wasn't anything he had written to cause Lord Ratliffe to turn his attention again to his daughter in Plymouth. The biggest problem he could foresee, in his future intercourse with the man, was how to avoid calling him out and shooting him dead.

In bed, he stewed about that for another hour, wondering if he could appeal to the First Lord and request that someone other than Lord Ratliffe hear his reports from the blockade. He had plenty of time to think up a plausible reason why, considering that he should not have to see the man for another month or two.

Still, he worried. Maybe he should have painted an even rosier picture of the situation in Plymouth. Lord Ratliffe was surely still on a financial lee shore. Suppose he decided to prey upon his daughter again?

If he did, what could you do, anyway? Oliver wondered. It was not a thought to send a man comfortably into the arms of Morpheus. He had barely dropped off to exhausted slumber before morning came, and with it, Matthew knocking on his door, bringing breakfast.

Gran must have decided he was fit enough for bacon, eggs

and black pudding, as well as a much smaller bowl of porridge. If only Nana had come along with the food, too, to sit with him while he ate. She was nowhere in sight.

He had to ask Matthew, and it reassured him to know that Nana had gone early with Pete to the fish market. He took his time dressing, hoping that Nana would return before he had to leave for dry docks. All he wanted was a glimpse.

When he had given up hope he would see her, he opened the front door to leave, and found Nana sweeping the steps. She looked the same as yesterday; prettier, if anything. The sun was shining this morning, which lent a dull red glow to the auburn in her hair.

He gestured for Matthew to go ahead, carrying his leather paper case, and looking serious at the importance of his duty. With a half smile on her face, Nana leaned on her broom and watched the boy go. She moved off the narrow walkway so he wouldn't miss a step.

"Matthew, you'll be back here in a few days, if you think Captain Worthy can spare you," she told him.

The powder monkey bobbed his head. "Aye, miss."

"I'll come back tonight, if I think the *Tireless* can spare me." Oliver wondered at the surprise in her eyes at this simple declaration. Surely she didn't think last night's revelation had in any way lessened his regard for her?

She took a moment to recover. "There you go, quizzing me again," she chided. "Of course you will be back. Sal has all your shirts in the washroom and I will tell her to hold them hostage, should you decide you prefer another lodging to ours."

Not in a million years, he thought. To his gratification, she leaned the broom against the door and walked with him to the waiting hackney. Again he had the same, indescribable feeling of peace, as though this lovely creature were his wife, walking him to the conveyance that would take him back to sea. It was prosaic beyond belief, but he knew the memory would keep him warm this winter on the blockade.

He looked at the pansies in their pot by the front gate. They appeared none the worse for wear, after his poor, if involuntary, treatment of them.

"I hope you didn't have to…to… Who cleaned them up?"

"I did," she replied, looking up at him with something close to glee in her brown eyes. "Everything deserves a second chance."

She still stood there until he was inside the hackney and the driver was gathering up the reins. "Dinner is at six," she said as she stepped back and waved.

Yes, dear, he thought; *I'll be home.* He noticed Matthew was watching her, too. "What do you think of her?" he asked.

Matthew sighed. "Oh, sir," he said, and nothing more.

I agree, Oliver thought. Two chowderheads here. *Perhaps we're both safer on the blockade. All we have to worry about there is keeping the French in port, and staying alive as we do it. The fewer distractions from England, the better.*

That was the rub. Less than a week ago, he would have believed it. Now, torn by the simple fact that he had to spend nearly ten hours or so away from Nana Massie, he knew he was lying to himself, which might even be worse than lying to others.

Nana's resolve to not think about Captain Oliver Worthy— at least until he returned that evening—lasted less than ten minutes. It might have lasted another fifteen, if only she had sent Sal upstairs to retrieve the rest of his laundry. But Sal was busy washing dishes, so she went instead.

The captain had left the rest of his whites outside his door.

He had wrapped some coins into a piece of paper, wound it shut at each end and scrawled "Sal" on it. Nana hefted the paper and smiled. "Captain, you're too generous," she said out loud. "Bless you."

She picked up the laundry, tucking it over her hip. Her mistake was looking down at his nightshirt, then raising it to her face to breathe in its odd fragrance of brine, mixed with wheat from the poultice, and the pleasant odor of someone else's body. She thought she detected a hint of bay rum, but mostly it was the smell of ocean salt, which seemed to combine within it the sharp tang of tar and something milder, which she decided was just the captain himself.

Nana rubbed it against her cheek. She knew she had done the right thing last night by telling him so plainly what her father had done. If it did not serve to remind Captain Worthy of her own illegitimacy and utter unfitness for genteel society, then it had reminded her. She wiped her eyes with his nightshirt, grateful, at least, that he had said, "I would be your friend."

She knew she would be busy in the morning, and she was. The afternoon surprised her, though, because it brought two lodgers to the Mulberry. One was an artificer, who had come to fix one of the few complicated mechanisms in the ropeworks at the dry docks. "Two days at most, mum," he had told Gran when he came inside the entrance hallway. "I hear you keep a good, simple table."

The other was the wife of Daniel Brittle, sailing master on the *Tireless*. "I daren't take my man home for five days, even to Torquay, because he would only pine for the ship the whole, livelong time," Nora Brittle confided as Nana showed her upstairs to a room at the back of the inn. "This way I can see him." She winked elaborately, and Nana blushed.

I can't let this pass, Nana thought, as she added more linen to the room's washstand. "Mrs. Brittle, may I ask how you heard about the Mulberry? We're off the main streets."

Mrs. Brittle had no objection to a chat. "Dan's been staying aboard the *Tireless,* but Captain Worthy suggested we take up residence in your inn. He told my man, 'It's quiet, clean and the food takes no liberties.'"

"That sounds like Captain Worthy," Nana replied, laughing.

"You know him, dearie?"

"A little," she replied, feeling the blush rise to her cheeks. "He's staying here, too."

Mrs. Brittle opened the wardrobe and hung up her cloak. "Dan says he's the best man in the Channel Fleet, and he wouldn't sail with none other." She looked at Nana, observing her high color. "I was going to say he's kind, too, but it looks to me like you already know."

Nana could only nod, as she felt the heat increase in her face. "He's been good to us," she managed to say.

Mrs. Brittle wasn't through. "Dan told me only this afternoon, 'I don't know what miracles they work at the Mulberry, but they've raised Captain Worthy from the dead, like Lazarus!'"

"The captain did look bow down when he came here," Nana agreed, remembering a little Plymouth cant that would have sent Miss Pym to her smelling salts.

"Keep up the good work, dearie!" Mrs. Brittle said as Nana left her to her unpacking.

Oh, Lord, Nana thought as she hurried down two flights of stairs. *He is getting us lodgers. Bless the man. We can open the dining room.* When she reached the kitchen, she grabbed Sal around the waist and swung her around. Gran beamed at her from the Rumford, where she was stirring a kettle of soup.

Nana looked again. They hadn't had to use that size kettle in more than two years.

She hugged Gran next, giving her a kiss on the cheek, but let go when the doorbell clanged again.

"Better get that, Nana. If it's another lodger, we serve dinner from six to seven!"

It was two lodgers, representatives from the royal armourer, delivering cannon for the new ship under construction in dry docks. "Just tonight, miss," the older man told her, as he put down enough coins for them both. "But we'll be back with another lot next week, if you've room."

"We'll have room," she assured him. *Oh my, yes, we'll make room, if we don't have it,* she thought.

Captain Worthy came back to the Mulberry at half past six, looking used up and weary. She had been watching for him since six, and opened the door as he came up the walk, moving slowly.

She stood on tiptoe to take his cloak from him, which he relinquished with a sigh. "Long day," he told her. "That damage to the stern was so great I'm fair gobsmacked that we even limped into port." He just looked at her a moment, and then he started to smile. "It appears to me that you're about ready to dance up and down, Nana. Either you're really glad to see me, or something good has been going on here."

It's both, she thought. *It's both.* "The dining room is open now and there are five lodgers!" she exclaimed. "But you know that already, don't you?"

He shrugged, already looking better. "All I did was drop a few hints."

Before she even knew what he was doing, he kissed her on the cheek. It was too brief for her to take issue with him; she wasn't sure she would have, anyway.

"You deserve some good fortune at the Mulberry," he told her simply, then turned and started up the stairs. "I'll be down soon."

She watched him go. Before he reached the first landing, he was whistling.

Chapter Eight

Nana discovered one problem with more lodgers. Because the dining room was open again, Captain Worthy couldn't invite himself into their living quarters for dinner. By the time dishes were washed and the kitchen prepared for breakfast, it was too late for more than a smile or a few words on the stairs.

She told herself it didn't matter. The captain had a little more than three weeks to see his ship worthy for sea, his men properly housed during the lull and all made ready for a return to the Channel Fleet. She had no place in the scheme of things. Anything else, particularly after her candid conversation about her origins, was just her wishful thinking.

Or not. She knew he was resourceful, but Captain Worthy exceeded her expectations by solving her dilemma by the next evening's meal. The solution came in the form of a note delivered to the Mulberry in the afternoon by Matthew and taken directly to Gran, who handed it to her to read.

"'Mrs. Massie,'" she read out loud, "'I regret I am unable to complete my duties at the dry docks in time to arrive at the Mulberry before dinner hours have expired. Would it be too much trouble for you to keep something warm on the hob and let me eat in the kitchen for the next few weeks? Yours, Worthy.'"

Mine, Worthy, she told herself, when she put down the note and looked at Gran, who was looking back, a serious expression on her face. *I know that look,* Nana thought. *Perhaps I should allay her fears and remind myself that Captain Worthy is busy at dry docks and nothing else.*

"Gran, he already knows about my background. I told him, that night we started *Robinson Crusoe.*" It hurt, but she added. "You needn't worry about the captain. He has more sense."

"I suppose I needn't worry," Gran echoed. She turned back to the veal cutlets she was dredging.

Nana hugged her. "Gran, I'm not my mother."

Gran continued her dredging of the meat more vigorously, until there was a great puff of flour around the pan. "No, you are not," she said, her voice weary.

How could I be so unkind? Nana asked herself. "I'm sorry, Gran," she said simply. "I never knew her, but I shouldn't be so heartless as to forget that you did. Besides, he simply needs more time at the dock. There can be no other reason."

Oliver felt few qualms that night as he arrived at the Mulberry long after seven o'clock. He only hoped he had not been observed in his arrival, because he came not from the direction of the dry dock, but from the Barbican, where Brustein and Carter had their office. He had been too long at sea, where he was used to quick obedience, to understand why two solicitors would take so long to draw up a simple transfer of a minuscule amount of his funds to an account for the Mulberry.

The figure wasn't large, just a modest sum to keep the Mulberry in food, no matter how much prices rose as the war deepened. And the better the bill of fare, the more likely the Mulberry would see a steady influx of lodgers. He was no fool. The inn would never have the trade of the large inns closer to the waterfront, but that was no reason to give it the heave-ho.

David Brustein and Elias Carter had done their best to dissuade him. "Sometimes little businesses are better off gone, Captain, if you'll pardon me," Brustein argued. "All you are doing is prolonging the inevitable. The Mulberry Inn should have closed years ago."

They were beginning to irritate him, because he wasn't used to argument. He was hungry, too, and even more eager for the sight of Nana. He looked at his watch.

"Gentlemen, is there some part of this reckoning you do not understand? I've stated what I want you to do with my own money, and you are giving me grief." He set his watch on the table between them. "If the second hand sweeps around one more time on this discussion, I will conclude that you are tired of my business. I can remedy that tomorrow morning with a visit two doors down to Wallace and Sons."

That's better, he thought, as Mr. Brustein leaped to his feet, stammering apologies. Oliver pocketed his watch, told them he would explain the matter of funds to Mrs. Massie and left their office.

Gran would know what to do. Instinct told him she was a careful woman of business, in spite of Brustein and Carter's opinions. He dared *them* to keep a struggling inn open as long as the redoubtable Mrs. Massie had.

And then he was home again, and there was Nana at the front door. He couldn't believe she was watching for him, mainly because he didn't think it was healthy for his opinion of himself to dream someone cared that much. He decided she was checking the progress of the wind, which was blowing a gale from the northwest: perfect wind to make for Spain. Thank God the *Tireless* was in no shape to sail. Not even the king himself could have dragged him aboard right then.

That is a first, he told himself. Better not let it get around the fleet that Captain Worthy actually preferred a storm in a port.

He let her take his soggy boat cloak, bending down a little to make it easier. He could have done that himself, and quicker, but he enjoyed the feel of her arms against his back as she took the cloak from him.

"I'm sorry, but we ran out of veal cutlets," she told him. "Will soup do?"

He nodded, scarcely hearing, because all he really wanted to do was look at her, storing up her beauty like a sea sponge took on water.

She made a little noise of disgust. "How can I quiz you if you won't rise to the bait? There's plenty of veal. More of Pete's draught, too, if you're difficult."

"Miss Massie, you are wicked," he told her, following her down the narrow hall to the kitchen. He glanced in the dining room, where several patrons were smoking clay pipes and playing cards. He crossed his fingers that she wouldn't suggest he could eat in there, but she never even looked in the dining room.

It was veal all right, delicate and warm and accompanied by mushrooms and gravy with a distinct flavor of ale. Bread both fluffy and yeasty helped sop the gravy, and rice pudding with currants finished him off. Nana shook her head at veal and gravy, but served herself a bowl of rice pudding to accompany his.

They ate in companionable silence. He felt himself relaxing, forgetting himself so much that he even leaned back in his chair. *I'm tired,* he thought. *I should go to bed. But that would mean too many hours without Nana in my sight.*

"You're tired. You should go to bed," Nana told him.

He looked at her, startled. *Hopefully you didn't read the rest of my mind,* he thought, as he stood up.

She stood before him, looking like a schoolgirl with her hands clasped in front of her. He would have given ten years off his probably too-short life to have had the courage to grab her by the shoulders, pull her close and kiss her with all the fervency of his heart. Luckily, the moment passed.

"Thank you again for sending business our way," she said.

He shrugged. "It's not hard. A few words here and there, and then if your place is good enough—and it is—word of mouth takes over. I won't tease you or Gran—times are hard and no one's getting much custom. Mr. Childers did tell me there will be two more frigates under construction soon, but the crews are housed at the dry docks."

"I know," she replied, but the look she gave him was hopeful. "Maybe they'll have wives and sweethearts who want to visit them."

"Nana, you're a raving lunatic optimist," he declared.

"How else would anyone survive at the Mulberry?" she said as she bobbed a schoolgirl's curtsey and went into the scullery, coming out in a minute with hot water in a can and towels. "Chamber Three reminded me ten minutes ago that we are still an inn. Good night, Captain Worthy."

He nodded to her and returned to the last of the rice pudding. He looked up to see Gran standing silently by the door, her eyes on him. He made to stand up, and she shook her head. She came to the kitchen table and sat down.

I'm too obvious, he thought with dismay. *I should allay her fears once and forever.* Then he remembered his visit to Brustein and Carter. *At least I can coat her misgivings with good news.*

"Mrs. Massie, I have established a fund for the Mulberry

with Brustein and Carter," he told her, after setting down his spoon. "They will circulate a paper to the local victuallers and all you need do is sign your name to all bills."

"I am having second and third thoughts about this, Captain," she told him.

"You needn't," he said, knowing that none of his air of command would in any way sway her, if she was determined to change her mind. "I have no ulterior motives beyond a desire to see you all in better health and earning a living."

A woman of experience—what kind, he didn't know—she saw right through him, as he knew she would.

"Captain, let me say this. I will say it only once, because you are a gentleman," she said, never taking her eyes from his face. "I lost my only child to the Royal Navy, and I will not sacrifice a granddaughter, too. You cannot ruin her. We will starve first."

That was plain, he thought. *I shall be as plain.* "Mrs. Massie, when I was a midshipman, we put into Portsmouth after two years in the Orient. All over town, I kept noticing women in black. I asked one of the mates if every woman wore black in Portsmouth. He told me, 'Aye, lad, it seems so.'"

Gran stirred in her seat. She opened her mouth to speak, but closed it when he kept talking. He knew that if he stopped now, he would never have the heart to continue, because his was breaking.

"Even now, when we return from a voyage, or land in a foreign port, I can't help myself, but it's the first thing I look for. Are the women in black? Aye, Gran, they are. I told myself I would never deliberately do that to some kind lady. I am also the son of a vicar and too much a gentleman to ruin her. Please believe me."

There. He got through it. He even believed it, because he

knew he had to. She might doubt his word, but she would not call him a liar. He was counting on her common upbringing to weigh in his favor. As staunch as she was in defending her granddaughter, he hoped his superior presence might give him some weight.

It did, but barely. "Very well, Captain," she said at last, after he had started to sweat inside his wool uniform. "I have to trust you, don't I?"

"No, you don't," he was honest enough to reply. "You can, though, and I hope you will." He stood up. "I have to tell you, I see myself as a walking dead man. There are matters afoot right now in Spain that will tax the *Tireless* to the limit. Let me do this one good thing for you and your granddaughter."

"Very well," she said again, and this time there was finality in her voice.

He allowed himself the tiniest sigh of relief. He went to his room, where he lay awake until nearly dawn.

Two or three times before the sun rose, he had convinced himself to move to the Drake. There wasn't anything else he could do at the Mulberry except be reminded every time he saw Nana Massie that it was possible to fall in love without intending to.

He tried to disgust himself by considering her questionable lineage. His was an ordinary family. No Worthys had any connections, beyond his mother's uncle, who commanded a frigate and had secured him a position on the *Temeraire*. All else he had achieved by his own efforts, but still, his was a respectable family with a good name.

He knew such men as he would never consider a permanent alliance with a bastard, no matter how charming. It just wasn't done. He knew his brother officers would call it bad form. At least he reckoned they would, if he hadn't been who he was: a highly successful commander of men and ships. He also knew that once those skeptics got to know Nana Massie, they would be as charmed as he was. Once people had their chatter and gossip, she would be accepted in any circle because her manners were impeccable, she was delightful and he was distinguished enough to cover any sins that fathers visited on their innocent children.

He finally gave up sleep as a bad idea and padded in his bare feet to the window, looking out on a grey morning. *I simply must quit thinking along these unprofitable lines,* he told himself. *I am heading back to the Spanish coast. There is no place for a wife in my life. There never has been, and there never will be.*

Oliver told himself he didn't want to set eyes on Nana at breakfast; it was time to stifle whatever pleasant camaraderie they had developed. He also knew if she wasn't there, he would eat slowly enough to hang around until she appeared.

She was there, pouring tea for two vendors who were trying to chat her up. *I wonder how long it will be, before she starts to look better fed?* he asked himself as he took a seat. *I will probably never know.*

"Tea, sir?" she asked him, ready to pour.

He put his hand over his cup. "Actually, coffee would be better, if you have it."

"We do."

She returned with coffee, followed by Sal and Pete, who laid the food on the sideboard. He looked at it appreciatively: bacon, sausages, porridge with cream, eggs and toast with jam. No one could fault the Mulberry's breakfasts now.

Nana was sitting at his table with her own bowl of porridge when he returned with a full plate to his seat. She ate silently, until finally he put down his fork.

"You can talk to me, you know," he suggested.

"Gran says never to bother men who are eating."

"I don't mind," he said, certain she had no idea how he yearned for just those trivialities of table chat that Gran frowned upon. By custom at sea, he often took his meals alone, his only company a chart or Admiralty dispatch. Before he went to sea, he remembered how his own parents had discussed the day ahead, or perhaps difficult parishioners, or the virtues of lamb over pheasant for dinner.

"What will you do today?" he asked.

"Gran wants me to inventory the linen," she told him.

She was looking at his toast. He tore it in half and gave her the bigger part. She shook her head and indicated the other one, which she took and covered with plum jam.

"I will probably be mending sheets this afternoon." She made a face. "There now. I dare you to come up with a more exciting day."

"I couldn't possibly," he told her, wondering what the two vendors at the other table would do if he suddenly leaned across the table and kissed Nana. He had the oddest feeling that Nana wouldn't mind in the least, which did nothing to firm his resolve to put her completely out of his mind.

"Oh, you could," she said.

What? Kiss you? he thought. *Good God, Oliver, pay attention.* "You mean, my day?"

She looked at him patiently, as though he were a not-too-bright child.

"Uh, I will go aboard the *Tireless* and walk around my wounded frigate and dare any of the workers—which includes my crew—to spend an idle moment. They're stepping a new mainmast today."

"Take me along," she asked. "I have never seen that."

"Dry docks is no place for a lady."

He glanced at the vendors, who were looking at Nana and then laughing softly. *She is a lady, you dimwits,* he wanted to declare. *Just down on her luck a bit.* Nana, her face flushed, had turned her attention to her porridge bowl. He narrowed his eyes and gave the men his quarterdeck glare, famous in the Channel Fleet. It had the desired effect. The vendors quickly turned their attention to their food.

She was embarrassed now. Before he could say anything, Nana got up and left the room.

There wasn't any reason to stay in the dining room any longer. The eggs had turned to slate and the coffee tasted worse than gall. Even the sky outdoors, seen through lace curtains, looked as though the clock had turned back and it was oily dawn again. *How does she manage to take all the life from a room when she quits it?* he wondered.

He walked the three miles to dry docks. Rain threatened, but it suited his mood. At a high point in the road, he looked toward the sound, squinting to see several ships, looking no larger than sloops of war or hoys. The sloop probably bore dispatches meant for the Admiralty. He knew Marshal Soult was somewhere around Burgos in the north, which meant Sir John Moore and his army would probably head in that direction, now that Napoleon had crossed the frontier again with his own *Grand Armée.* Ferrol was his duty station in the Channel Fleet. *I should be there,* he thought. *And soon.*

By the time five days passed, Matthew had returned to the Mulberry for his shore leave, and Nana had convinced herself to think of something besides Captain Worthy. The men from the royal armourers had come and gone a second time, and recommended the Mulberry to an accountant and his clerk, in Plymouth for an audit that would take several weeks. Mrs. Brittle had returned to Torquay but her husband stayed on, which meant the sailing master generally rode to and from the inn each morning with the captain. Mrs. Fillion had even sent the captain of a sloop of war their way, saying the Drake was full.

Nana wasn't entirely sure of that, mainly because the two captains and the sailing master spent several evenings together in the dining room, long after everyone else was asleep, poring over charts and talking quietly, as though they had planned this visit. When the captain of the sloop returned to his ship, Captain Worthy walked him down to the docks, still deep in conversation. When Captain Worthy returned, he was silent and grim-faced.

So grim, in fact, that when she took his boat cloak, she just held it and said, "I wish there was some way I could help you."

He looked at her, surprised, then startled her by enveloping her in a firm embrace.

Pete had hugged her once, and the brother of the schoolmate at Bath had tried to, but this felt nothing like her previous experiences. She couldn't have moved if she wanted to, but she didn't want to. She was sure she shouldn't be so brazen, but she found her arms tight around him in the next second, as though she wanted to absorb him within herself, or at least, his war-weariness.

He said nothing, merely held her so tight she could feel his uniform buttons against her breasts. She decided the sensation was not even remotely unpleasant. In height she was level with his heart, which beat against her ear. She closed her eyes, hoping he would forget what he was doing, and just stand that way with her until the *Tireless* was ready for sea in two weeks.

"For goodness' sake," he said finally, and released her. He

held her off at arm's length, but seemed to have no qualms about looking into her eyes. "That was the best help I could have had, Nana." He crouched down a little to peer closer at her on her own level. "This would be a good time for a massive change of subject, but I can't think of what it would be, can you?"

She shook her head, speechless.

He rubbed the top of her head and started for the stairs. He paused with one foot on the first step. "I needed that."

I do not understand men at all, she told herself as she watched him go. *They are so self-centered. I needed that, too. Perhaps he didn't notice.*

The next morning, after Captain Worthy left the inn, a new lodger came to stay. Nana answered the jangle of the doorbell because Gran and Sal were upstairs changing sheets, and Pete and Matthew had left earlier, baskets on their arms, to visit the greengrocers. She put down the pillowcase she was mending and opened the door in midjangle.

A man with eyes as brown as her own stood there, looking rumpled as only someone can who has come off the mail coach. He carried a valise, and had slung a satchel over his shoulder.

She couldn't help but smile at him, because his own expression was so engaging—not at all like Captain Worthy, who lately wore a perpetual frown. He came as close to looking carefree as anyone she had ever seen before.

"Mademoiselle," he said with a slight bow. "It isn't near Christmas yet, but I hope that you have room at this inn."

Amused, she nodded, and opened the door wide. "Please come in. I am certain we can accommodate you, even if you are not a magi."

"Touché," he exclaimed, and kissed his fingers.

His name was Henri Lefebvre, and he was a painter of portraits. "Large, small, groups and individuals," he told her as he signed the register and took the key she handed him. His accent was obviously French, with a curious admixture of northern England, maybe even Scotland in the lilt of his English. She looked down at the register, trying to read upside down what he had written.

Obligingly, he turned it around. "I am from Carlisle," he informed her. "But you do not believe that, do you?"

"Not precisely," she said, captivated by his quick speech.

He bowed again. "I am from Paris, of course. Do not frown at me, mademoiselle! Your own Sir Arthur Wellesley once said, 'Just because a man is born in a stable, this does not make him a horse.'"

Nana laughed, in spite of herself.

"I have not been in France in years," he assured her, "but I am as I said I was—a painter of portraits. Thank the Lord Almighty Himself there are many rich squires and their fubsy wives in Carlisle who like their portraits painted." He winked broadly. "But only if I can make them look slightly less old, gouty, fat, bald or without teeth. Name your defect." He laughed. "Name them all! I can make them disappear! Poof!"

She put up her hand, as if to ward off the flow of words that seemed to spill out of him. "I did not mean to question you, Mr....Mr...."

"Lefebvre," he said. He put his thumb and forefinger to his lips and seemed to draw out the syllables. "Le...feb...vre... Ah, yes. You purse your lips as though you were going to kiss some lucky gentleman. Lefebvre."

Nana blushed, which made him sigh and slap his forehead.

"Ah, to be young enough to blush!"

* * *

"He speaks in exclamation points," Nana told Captain Worthy that night—late that night—over steak and ale pie, the crust only slightly soggy from the long wait for him to show up.

"I suppose he is the stereotypical Frenchman, then," the captain said. "The only ones I see are those willing—no, eager—to administer a broadside to my ship." He leaned toward her. "I am not in favor of the French. You may add an exclamation point to that."

Nana wasn't sure how it happened, but they seemed to have come to some declaration of nondiscussion about what happened yesterday evening. Perhaps if nations can declare embargos, and decrees and orders in council, people could, too, Nana decided.

She was happy enough to watch him eat, his eyes on her occasionally, but more often on the dinner in front of him. He shook his head at seconds, and leaned back in his chair, that breach of naval etiquette he seemed willing to commit in her presence.

"Did he say why he is here in Plymouth?" he asked.

"He supplied all kinds of information," she replied. "He said he is on holiday."

"Here? Excuse my skepticism," he said dryly.

"I suppose it makes sense. Monsieur Lefebvre likes to paint landscapes, even though he says none of his clients want to buy them."

"I have to wonder how good he is, then."

"Good enough, I think," she told him, getting up and going to the cupboard by the scullery. She handed him a picture. "He sketched this portrait of Sal. I don't think it took him more than five minutes. She was so excited she burst into tears and threw her apron over her face."

The captain examined it. "Yes, I would agree he's good

enough." He stood up and stretched. "Well, let us hope he finds plenty of land here to paint. Does he plan an expedition to the moors?"

"He didn't say."

She got up, too, following him out of the family quarters and past the lodgers' dining room. She paused at the door to the sitting room, hoping he might be inclined to spend a few minutes there with her. To her disappointment, he continued to the stairs.

He seemed reluctant to go upstairs. "Are you still reading to Matthew and the others?" he asked.

"Oh, yes. Robinson Crusoe has made himself a canoe now."

"Is Matthew being helpful?"

"He is. Gran is making him a shirt that fits him, and he went into transports when she tried the sleeves on him. Imagine what he will do when she finishes it!"

He went up a few steps. "Could I ask you a favor? It's a brazen one, but maybe you could humor an old seadog."

"Anything."

"Call me Oliver. I never hear my name spoken, and it's a nice one. Good night now."

Oliver. Nana said it under her breath so no one could hear, as she finished her duties that evening and went to bed. Because Matthew had taken Sal's alcove next to the scullery, Sal was sleeping in her bed. Nana eased herself next to Sal, careful to make sure she was asleep, and whispered "Oliver" again.

By the time her eyes grew heavy enough for sleep, reality had crowded into the bed with them. She couldn't call a post captain by his first name, not in a million years. She would just be encouraging something destined to go nowhere, even if he did like the sound of his name and he said he was her friend. She tried to imagine a world where first names were never spoken, and couldn't. She noticed the captain did not even call his mates by their first names, but only Mr. this or that. These were people with whom he must have been on the closest terms, and the dignity of his office didn't allow the intimacy of first names.

Still, she liked the way he called her Nana, even though she wasn't entirely certain he realized he was doing it. Before he came to stay at the Mulberry, she had thought it was high time to abandon her baby name. She changed her mind; the sound of it on Captain Worthy's lips warmed her heart. Maybe he did know what he was doing, she decided. She did not think he called her Nana when there was anyone else present.

Such contemplation was fruitless. With a sigh, Nana closed her eyes.

She woke early and hurried to help Gran in the kitchen, stopping only for porridge, because her grandmama insisted. With Matthew's help, she and Sal had breakfast ready on the sideboard before the early-rising auditors had time to fret and start examining their cutlery. She knew Henri Lefebvre would be among the last in the room. He seemed unconcerned about time, probably because he was on holiday. Besides, he had told her yesterday that the best light for painting came when the sun was up, but not too high. But the captain would be there.

"Good morning, Captain," she said, as he came into the room.

He frowned, sat where she indicated and took a sip of the coffee she had already poured for him. "So it's to be 'Captain,' eh?"

"I don't think I can call you anything else, sir."

He said nothing more about the matter, but she could see the disappointment in his eyes.

Chapter Nine

The wind blew raw from the northwest, setting the water dancing in Plymouth Sound. The only ship venturing out was another sloop of war, with shortened sails.

The sailing master sat beside him in the hackney, his eyes also on the sloop. "I wouldn't chance it. Must have important dispatches."

Oliver nodded, his mind on the sloop, but his heart on Nana. She hadn't walked him to the hackney this morning, but then, the weather was foul. He shifted uneasily, because he knew that didn't matter. She had walked with him yesterday, even though she had to hold down her skirts in the high wind. She hadn't even minded when he took her arm, declaring she needed more ballast. The difference was the sailing master, who had gone earlier yesterday. Nana knew better than to intrude when others were present.

He knew he was thinking it, so he forced himself to let the thought swirl around in his brain like brandy in a snifter: Nana knew her place. He doubted it was anything Gran had ever said—not Gran, who loved Nana so well. Perhaps Miss Pym had let Nana know—probably since she was a little girl of five and new at school—that the world was going to treat her differently.

Suddenly he hated Lord Ratliffe with a fervor he usually reserved for the French. Damn the man! Why couldn't he have left Nana alone to spend another two years at Miss Pym's, and then provided his daughter with a respectable dowry that would have made her pretty face appealing enough for an accountant, or possibly a naval surgeon? Maybe even a master shipwright or an Admiralty secretary? How difficult would it have been to have done the right thing?

At least Mr. Brittle knew better than to talk to him when he obviously didn't have much to say. By the time they arrived at Union Street and began the descent to the docks, Oliver forced himself to think about the *Tireless*. With any luck, he still had not quite a week and a half when only a hurricane would be excuse enough to keep him from weighing anchor and pointing the bow toward Spain again. Another ten days to try to convince himself that what he had always believed was still true: that single men were the lucky ones.

The wind didn't keep Mr. Childers from stepping the new mast, as he had promised. Encouraged by the bosun and crew, Oliver had even lent a hand with the lines to raise the mast. It was a small enough thing, but he knew his men liked it when he shared their work. Everyone was quiet as the mast swung upward and then settled into its well in the hold with a pleasant thump. It looked bare as a bodkin now. By afternoon, the yardarms would be hanging again, and the rigging would follow.

His mood turned filthy then, when Mr. Childers came up to him, rubbing his hands and smiling. "Captain Worthy, I have the best news."

"The war is over?"

"One could wish. This is almost as good. My shipwrights

tell me the *Tireless* will be seaworthy in less than a week. Four days, I think."

"Good God."

"We've thrown all the extra help we could into your little beauty here and trimmed a whole week off my estimate."

Damn Childers. Oliver looked at the man, smiling and pleased with himself. He had done exactly what Oliver had wished for, when he limped into Plymouth with his frigate two weeks ago.

Call me the greatest actor in the world, Oliver thought, as he smiled and clapped the shipwright on the back. "That is the best news I have heard in weeks," he lied. "Mr. Childers, you are to be commended."

"Two and a half weeks! I didn't think we could do it, Captain."

"Is she sound?"

"As a roast, sir. She'll be tight as a drum. Throw any simile at her."

"Then I am pleased as punch," Oliver said. It was a feeble joke, and never had he meant something less, but Childers laughed until he had to sit down on a pile of rope to recover himself.

Oliver had to grasp at straws. "I wonder…will the victuallers have completed their work in four days? What about water?"

Mr. Ramseur, standing nearby, spoke up. "I have made all those arrangements, Captain. All we'll need is a favorable wind."

"That's….uh…that's excellent, Mr. Ramseur," Oliver said. He plowed past his own misery then and concentrated on his crew. "This will leave one quarter of the crew still unable to make any shore leave." He turned to the shipwright. "Mr. Childers, if I release that last group right now for four days' shore leave, will you still be able to bring the *Tireless* in on time?" Please say no, he begged in his mind.

"I can, Captain, I can, especially since you had the wisdom to release the foretopmen first, and save the gunners for last. The topmen are back, and they're the ones I need to help with the rigging. Good of you to plan ahead, sir."

Ah, yes, good of me, Oliver thought sourly. *I'm a naval prodigy.* He turned to his second mate and spoke with more force than necessary, all things considered. "Don't just stand there! Release the rest of the crew. Then send a dispatch for Mr. Proudy to return at once. Then you'd better give yourself three days, starting the moment you've done the above."

Mr. Ramseur tried to protest, but Oliver overrode him. "Nonsense! Isn't there someone named Dorie in Kingsbridge you're desperate to see?"

His mate colored promptly, but nodded.

I wish I had your courage, Oliver thought. *Or at least your optimism that you won't be fish food in a fortnight.* He took out his watch, and affected a kindlier tone. Mr. Ramseur didn't deserve to be barked at because he was in love and human. "Release those men now, sir. I'll write to Mr. Proudy myself. You can be in Kingsbridge in no time if you move your ass."

Without another word, Ramseur saluted and ran onto the *Tireless.* Mr. Childers chuckled. "Were we ever that young?"

I never was, Oliver thought. *I've had all the answers since I was a midshipman: never fall in love, because it would be a cruelty. I was dead wrong and I am a twit.*

He didn't feel like eating luncheon with Mr. Childers or anyone else. He spent the afternoon with the purser, reconciling the stores with the lists, and then on deck, watching the yardarms swung into place. His attention was diverted once in the afternoon by Mr. Brittle, who handed him a spyglass and directed him to look at the hill above the dry dock.

"It's that Frenchman," his sailing master said, amusement

in his voice. "He's been there all week. And if he's not there, he's by the Cattewater, and then at the Hamoaze."

"People have odd avocations," Oliver said. He found Lefebvre in the glass and watched him, sitting on a rock and sketching. "It's funny, Mr. Brittle. I am so used to these water-ways that I forget the beauty. Still, I suppose it's a release from painting red-faced squires and children disinclined to sit still."

He collapsed the glass and returned it to his sailing master, but looked toward Lefebvre again, a speck now on the slope above the harbor. *I wonder if he would do me a portrait before I sail,* he thought. He remembered the sketch Nana had showed him of the scullery maid. Maybe Lefebvre would dash off a drawing of Nana. He could do it discreetly, so she wouldn't know and be embarrassed by a post captain's fool-ishness. He could tack it next to his compass and look at her lovely face every time he opened his eyes. It would be some consolation.

Weary and out of sorts, he returned to the Mulberry long after eight o'clock. He knew that Nana usually watched for him, so he straightened up when he left the hackney and squared his shoulders. No sense in looking like a forlorn hope.

Could Lefebvre capture that smile, and the way her eyes seemed to light up? He thought maybe he liked her best that morning he had watched her sleep on the cot outside his door, her eyelashes so long and her absurd freckles. *I could pretend that I was sleeping by her. Lord Almighty, I am an idiot.*

She was waiting for him. He managed a smile that didn't get near his eyes, and let her take his boat cloak, as usual. He didn't fool her for a moment.

"What's wrong, Captain?" she asked, her own eyes troubled. "Didn't they step the mast?"

"Nothing's wrong," he said too quickly. Everything was

wrong. Maybe he wouldn't say anything. It was just too hard to speak the words that would remind him of his duty and ruin his stay at the Mulberry. It might even make her sad for a while. He didn't know for sure. All he knew was how sad he felt.

"There is good news, actually." He took off his hat and set it carefully on the newel post. "Mr. Childers is a remarkable shipwright. The *Tireless* will be ready for sea in four days— ten days ahead of schedule."

He didn't know what to expect, but she astounded him by gasping and then giving a deep sob that he felt right down to the pit of his stomach. She dropped his cloak, put her hands to her face and took several deep breaths, until she gained some control over herself. She picked up his coat—he had been too dumbfounded to move—and draped it carefully over the banister, next to his hat.

"We'll miss you, Captain," she said, not looking him in the eye, which wasn't like her at all. "Let me go hurry along dinner. It might need more warming up."

She didn't invite him to walk with her to the kitchen, but turned almost blindly and went down the hall, touching the wall as though to guide herself. As he watched, scarcely breathing, her shoulders began to shake and her head went down. She paused for a moment, bending forward to place her hands on her knees. It lasted just a second. She went into the kitchen.

He sat down on the steps, horrified at what he had seen. He felt more gawky and foolish than Mr. Ramseur; younger than Matthew, his powder monkey; older than the oldest one-eyed, one-legged tar begging in the Barbican. He sat there a long moment, until he reminded himself that post captains didn't sit on stairs and act like fools in love. He had made up his mind years ago, and he knew beyond any reckoning that to be married and present such news would be infinitely worse.

He wouldn't say anything to her. It was war and ships went to sea. The two of them would overlook what just happened the same way they had both overlooked that ill-advised embrace in the hall a few days ago. If he didn't say anything, she wouldn't. Hadn't he decided that Nana knew her place? So did he.

He took his cloak and hat upstairs and lay down on the bed with his hand over his eyes. A few minutes later, there was a knock. He didn't speak; it wasn't Nana's knock.

"Captain Worthy?"

Sal stood outside his door. With a sigh, he got up and opened it.

"Gran says dinner is ready." She looked at him, a question in her eyes.

He had snapped at Mr. Ramseur earlier, but he'd be damned if he'd frighten a scullery maid. "I'll be right down," he told her, willing himself to be calm. "Is everything all right in the kitchen?"

He expected an honest answer from a little girl, and he got one. "No. Nana won't come out of her room and Matthew is moping," she said, her voice troubled. "You're going to sea?"

"It's what I do," he said patiently.

"You'll take care?"

"Aye, I'll do that, too," he told her. "I like a whole skin, same as you, Sal."

She smiled at that. It seemed to reassure her, but then, she wasn't more than ten and had no idea what ships at sea, and the men who sailed them, really did.

Gran's excellent chicken and noodles, thick and full of peas the way he liked it, was gall and wormwood. He ate because he had to, all the time wishing Nana would come out of her room and sit with him. He had so few days left to see her. In three days he would have his sea trunk and private stores transferred back to the *Tireless.* By all rights, he should be aboard now.

Over pudding, he informed Matthew that tomorrow he would be required back on the frigate. He could tell the powder boy was disappointed, but knew better than to express it.

Oliver lingered as long as he dared over the pudding, even asking for a second helping he didn't want, in the hope that Nana would come out. To his relief, she did. He wasn't brave enough to look too closely, but her face was pale, though composed. Her eyes were stark and red, and he knew she had been crying, but she sat with him, saying next to nothing, while he burbled on about the work ahead, in the frantic days before a ship put to sea.

He was silent then. He wanted to tell her how much he would miss her, but he held back. There was no point in offering encouragement. She seemed to understand, and gradually relaxed enough to smile at a feeble witticism he forgot as soon as it left his lips. *I'll get through this,* he thought. *It's far better that she never have an inkling of the depths of my love.*

She spoke finally, seeming to choose her words carefully. "Gran told me what you have done for us with your solicitors," she said. "I've never heard of such kindness, but believe me, we are grateful."

I would do more, if I dared, he thought. "It's a small thing, Nana."

"Gran says she'll continue your arrangement only until that time when we're on our feet again," Nana said. "Mr. Lefebvre tells me he sees more ships going in and out, and I think the war is going to give us more custom here."

"Monsieur Lefebvre is right." He pushed back his chair and stood up. The room was suddenly too small and Nana too close. "I've arranged for the hackney to pick me up at five o'clock tomorrow morning, so I won't be here for breakfast."

"I'll have some food for you to take along," she said.

"You needn't."

"I know," she said. "It's really all I can do, though, isn't it?"

He wasn't entirely sure what she meant, but it seemed to tax her to the limit. With a brief look into his eyes, she got up quickly and went back into her room.

He felt like an old man as he climbed the stairs to his room, stood at the door a moment and then went up another flight to knock on Henri Lefebvre's door. He could see a light under the door, but it was a long moment before the door opened.

The artist stood there, his shirtsleeves rolled up. If he was surprised to see Oliver, he did not show it.

"Come in, come in," he said. "Excuse the mess. It's a condition of the work I do."

Oliver nodded. He looked at the table, covered with sketches of the view of the Hamoaze, a sight he was familiar with. He went to the table, as Lefebvre hovered at his elbow, as if to protect his drawings.

"You'd enjoy the view from my quarterdeck, as we come into the sound," Oliver told him. He looked closer. "Is that the *Tireless?*"

"*Oui,* Captain."

"She looks so small." He picked up the sketch. "My world. Some days, you'd be welcome to it." He set it down and turned to face the artist. "You should come to Plymouth in spring, when the hills are green and the sheep multiplying."

"Perhaps I shall. Capitan, may I help you?"

No one seems to want me around, Oliver thought. *Not Matthew, not Nana, and not this Frenchman.* "Yes, you can, if you would. Could you make a sketch of Miss Massie for me? She's so charming, and I'd like something to remember her by."

Lefebvre smiled. "That I can do."

"Don't let her know. That would just embarrass her." *And me,* Oliver thought.

Lefebvre turned back to his table, and sorted through his sketches of the harbor and the dry docks. "Here we are."

He handed Oliver a small portrait of Nana, looking directly at him and smiling. "I couldn't resist, either, Captain. After I sketched that little kitchen maid, I asked Mademoiselle Massie, and she agreed. I can sketch another, so you may have this one."

Oliver took it. The artist had almost caught the animation of Nana's brown eyes, and the energy. He looked closer. "No freckles."

"You want freckles?" the painter asked, surprised. "I am so used to my clients not wishing to exhibit defects, that I left them out."

"They're not defects," Oliver said, handing back the sketch. "Put 'em in, if you will. What do I owe you?"

Lefebvre shrugged. "A shilling?" He laughed. "Two, with freckles."

Oliver felt his own mood lightening and he smiled in return. "Three, if you can find a color pencil in your arsenal to match that hair color."

"Done, monsieur! I will have it under your door by morning."

Lefebvre was as good as his word. By the time Oliver woke up at 4:30 a.m., the sketch was under his door. The Frenchman had trimmed the paper and put the little drawing in a paper frame. Oliver looked at it for a long moment, then tucked it in the pocket of his waistcoat. He would tack it above his compass, at true north.

He went down the stairs quietly, shoes in hand, and put them on in the hall. Nana stood in the shadows, a robe over her nightdress, a small bundle in her hand.

"Black pudding, boiled eggs and ham," she told him. "Common fare, but that's our specialty at the Mulberry."

And uncommon inmates, he thought, as he took knotted cloth from her. "I sent Mr. Ramseur off to Kingsbridge yesterday afternoon. He's desperate to see his Dorie."

She smiled, which relieved him. "Maybe he'll work up the nerve to propose."

"And then I will have two mooncalves sharing the quarter-deck with me!"

It came out louder than he intended. Nana put her finger to her lips. "Remember, kind sir, that one of the Mulberry's chiefest virtues is the quiet," she whispered.

The hackney pulled up in front of the inn. Oliver glared at it, but made no move to leave the hallway, not with Nana there, looking so lovely and smelling faintly of roses, and calling him "kind sir."

"Captain, were you never in love?"

He thought he hadn't heard her right, so he leaned closer. She put her hand lightly on his shoulder and stood on tiptoe. "Were you never in love?"

Her breath was warm on his cheek. He thought of all the cold winds from the Channel to the Bering Sea that had scoured his cheek, and the hot winds of North Africa and the dog latitudes that burned him. He prided himself in knowing, from the wind, how to keep his ship aright and sail close to the wind. How could he explain Nana's breath on his cheek giving him more heart than any breeze from any point of the compass?

Just keep your hand there for another week or two, he

thought. *That's all I ask, and by God, it isn't much.* "Yes, as a matter of fact, I was in love once," he whispered back. Best to couch it in the past tense. He sailed in four days and it would be past tense.

"What about you, Nana? Lost your heart yet?"

"Yes," she answered, her voice so soft. "It's a dreadful business, isn't it?"

He could have declared himself then. No one was around. The inn was dark. The hackney would wait. "There will be another one along someday, Nana," he said instead, and hated himself.

"I doubt it," she replied. She looked at him, and he could not help seeing the tears in her eyes. "How…how did you get over her?"

I can't, he thought. *I won't.*

The hackney driver saved him, getting down and stomping up the front walk to knock on the door. Oliver opened the door, turning around at the last moment to touch her under her chin. "I recommend a sea voyage, courtesy of King George."

She laughed softly. "You're a coward, Captain Worthy."

I am indeed, he thought, as he followed the jehu back to his conveyance. *There isn't a bigger coward in the entire Channel Fleet.*

Chapter Ten

Mercifully, Oliver was too busy to think of Nana more than fifteen minutes out of every half hour in the next few days. He could set aside his personal misery to appreciate the trim of the new mast, and the rigging all replaced and taut again.

With Mr. Childers's approval, Oliver and a skeleton crew took the *Tireless* from the Hamoaze and into the sound, to shake down the new stern. He conned the helm himself, enjoying the feel of the wheel and the frigate's response. "No shimmy now," he told his best helmsman, who he knew was itching to take the wheel. "She's a lady again. You take her," he said, relinquishing the wheel, and allowing each of his helmsmen a turn. With Oliver as scribe, they discussed any idiosyncrasies to report to Mr. Childers.

"You care what they think, don't you, sir?" Proudy asked him, when the *Tireless* was moored in the wet dock now.

"Aye. Let this be a lesson for you, Mr. Proudy. It's their ship, too."

When Proudy left him, he went to his quarters and tacked Nana's picture above his berth. Monsieur Lefebvre had still been sparing with the freckles on the bridge of her nose.

He stood on his quarterdeck as the sun started to go down, thinking of Nana, now that the press of business was done and Mr. Childers had left the dock. He glanced at the low hills on the west back of the Tamar, then opened his glass to spy out Lefebvre. Oliver waved, and chuckled when the Frenchman waved back.

He rode back to the Drake with his first mate, watched the perpetual whist game and resisted with surprising ease any desire to join in. Captain Virgil Dennison from the sloop of war, *Goldfinch,* caught them up on the latest news from Corunna— none of it good. He walked back to the Mulberry, knowing his own walking would soon be confined to a quarterdeck.

He passed the guildhall, pausing a moment to listen to the chorus within, practicing selections from *Messiah,* which Mrs. Fillion had told him was an annual event. Christmas again, he thought. Even after all his years at sea, it still mystified him that life on land continued in its usual round, season by season, even in time of war and great national emergency.

Dennison said Napoleon himself had crossed the border again into Spain with his *Grand Armée,* to remind the citizens that his brother Joseph Bonaparte was supposed to sit on their throne and not flee from it. Soon Oliver and the *Tireless* would be playing their own little game of darting into ports—some under rebel control now—to learn what they could and take the news to Admiralty and Horse Guards.

It was inevitable, with each of the precious days that passed, that he was thinking more and more of what lay ahead. He discovered something curious: rather than think less and less of Nana, he found each moment in her presence more concentrated and sweet. Maybe this was how married captains felt.

Perhaps he imagined it, but she seemed to have put on weight. Her face looked a little fuller, and her dress not

cinched so tight across the back. Well, good. His deal with
Gran was working. Sal was not so pinched-looking, either.
Even Pete lingered over second helpings in the kitchen. Gran
was Gran; he doubted she had ever put on an extra pound.

Nana still kept him company in the kitchen. Even when he
came home in time to eat in the dining room, there was no
pretense he should stay there. He went straight through to the
kitchen, enjoying the bustle around him as dishes came and
went from the dining room.

"Isn't it too noisy for you, sir?" Nana asked, after she returned
from the dining room and sat down across from him again.

"Not at all. Nana, I eat alone on the *Tireless*. It's a custom
of the sea I do so, unless I invite others," he told her. He could
tell by her expression that she didn't think much of the idea.

"Are you ever lonely?"

How to answer that one? He decided upon honesty. "All
the time, Nana."

Her eyes filled with tears, reminding him forcefully of his
situation. He leaned across the table until his face was close
to hers. "Nana, don't cry for me."

"Who said I was crying for you?"

She got up to leave the room, but she wasn't fast enough.
He took her by the hand, and surprised them both by kissing
it. He released her fingers and leaned back in his chair as she
stood there. "Now that's one more thing for us to carefully
overlook," he told her.

Oliver made a point to talk to Gran that evening, settling
his account with her, and telling her that a carter would come
for his sea trunk tomorrow, leaving just his duffel bag. "I'll
sleep here tonight, but I'll leave by three or four in the morning.
The tide turns midmorning, and there's a fair wind to Spain."

She nodded. "We owe you a great deal, Captain Worthy."

"You owe me nothing. I've never enjoyed time onshore more than this."

He went upstairs to pack. Nana was nowhere in sight, but Pete waited for him in the hall.

"Sor, could I have a moment?"

"Certainly, Pete. I've wanted to thank you for all you've done during my stay."

"It's nothing, sor, compared to what ye've done for us."

"I wanted to, Pete, and I have the resources."

Pete wasn't through. "Could you do me one last favor, Captain?"

"If it's in my power."

The old sailor grinned. "It is, sor. It's for Nana."

"Then yes, of course."

"Every year since she's been back from Bath, I escort her to the guildhall for *Messiah*."

"I heard them practicing this afternoon."

"She likes to listen and I don't mind, but my arthritis…" His voice trailed off. "Could ye escort her tonight?"

"It will be my pleasure." He never meant anything more in his life. "You're sure Gran won't mind?"

"Oh, she'll mind, but I can manage her," Pete replied.

He was obviously uncomfortable. Oliver opened the door to his room and ushered him inside, to sit down at the table. Oliver sat across from him.

"I know Gran thinks I have designs on her granddaughter," he said bluntly. "I don't. I told myself years ago that I wouldn't marry, and won't encourage any female to think I will." He couldn't sit still, but got up to pace the room. He stopped in front of Pete, who watched him with an inscrutable expression. "Did you know Gran's daughter?"

Pete shook his head. "I started workin' for Gran in ninety-one, when Nana was three and the bonniest little girl I ever saw."

"I'll wager she was."

Pete smiled at the memory. "She had her hair short then, too, and it was even curlier. She went everywhere Gran went, and she had the sunniest disposition. You'd always see the two of them shopping for the Mulberry, Gran with her big basket and Nana with a little one, skipping along and stopping in every shop to say g'day. She had everyone's hearts even then."

She has mine now, Oliver thought.

"She cried buckets, but Gran was glad enough to send her to Bath. The last thing Gran wants is for her to give herself to the navy, like Rachel did with that bastard Lord Rat."

"Ratliffe," Oliver corrected, amused.

"You know him?"

"Briefly. I see him at Admiralty House." No need for Pete to know that it was Ratliffe he reported to these days. *I need to change that,* Oliver thought. *I can't stomach the man now.*

"Nana's moping," Pete said, looking at Oliver. "And you're moping, too, sor."

That's blunt, Oliver thought, surprised. *I could deny it, but he's seeing right through me, man to man.* "Aye," he replied simply.

"I think you should marry her," Pete forged on, "unless you're squeamish about hedge babies."

Blunt again, you old tar. "That's not it, Pete. I just can't bear the thought of marrying that lovely lady and turning her into a widow. I've seen too many widows and written too many letters to them, telling them their husbands are dead, but thank God it was quick and their men didn't suffer. Give your children my sympathies."

The words spilled out of Oliver. "That's a crock, of course—you know what death at sea is often like. Could I do that to someone I love? Never."

Pete watched him a moment. "You'd rather Nana just drooped and perished for love of you?"

"She can't seriously be in love with me," Oliver said, amazed. "What could she possibly see in me? I feel older than Methuselah and would never be here when she needed me."

"I've been watching you, sor…"

"Thanks," Oliver interrupted sourly.

"…and when you and Nana are talking, or when you're watching her—you do it all the time—you don't look like Methuselah."

"Damn your eyes, Pete!"

Pete only shrugged. "I'm not in your navy now and I can speak my mind. There's one thing else you need to know about women. They're awfully good at waiting. And as for what she sees in ye…" He shrugged again. "What man ever understands that?"

They sat staring at each other until Pete finally slapped his hands on the table. "It's your life, sor. Take her to *Messiah* tonight, at least. And dress warm."

Oliver did, wondering at first why a guildhall overheated with concertgoers could possibly be cold. Nana offered no objection when he announced he was taking her tonight instead of Pete. The color he noticed that had been absent from her face for a few days bloomed again, and he marveled how brown eyes—his own were brown and ordinary—could be so lively.

He met her in the kitchen, where she was putting baked potatoes into a small bag. She wasn't dressed any fancier than usual, but then he remembered she had left her good clothing behind in Bath when Ratliffe ended her stay there. Above the fragrance of potatoes, he could still catch a whiff of roses about her. He wondered if it was her soap.

He offered his arm and she took it shyly. Out of habit as they walked, he stopped and turned his face to the light wind several times, just to make sure it still blew from the right quarter. She laughed out loud the second time he did that, and it warmed him.

When they came to the small gathering in front of the guildhall, he tried to move her forward. "Wait inside while I stand in line," he said.

She didn't move. "Oh, no, you don't understand. Didn't Pete tell you?"

"Tell me what?"

"We don't actually go inside, so we never need tickets. Why do you think I brought the potatoes?"

It was his turn to laugh. "Because you get peckish between 'Comfort Ye, My People,' and 'The Hallelujah Chorus'?"

She led him past the line and around the corner of the hall. His grin widened as he noticed a set of steps leading up to what was probably the closest exit to where the choir would be standing. He followed her. She sat down a few steps below the landing and patted the stone beside her.

"They always prop the door open a little, unless it's raining. You can hear very well, and there is an excellent view of the Cattewater, too. The potatoes are for your hands."

He sat down beside her, overwhelmed by her nearness and delighted he wasn't inside a stuffy hall, packed cheek-to-jowl with people he didn't know. Sitting hip-to-hip with Nana Massie on the stairs reordered all his thoughts about paradise and heaven, as explained at length by his father the vicar.

I could waste this opportunity, he thought, *or I could make two miserable people happy. Three people. Pete seems to think I am worthy of his dear Nana.*

"Stand up a minute, Nana," he ordered. "I'm only newly recovered from a bad throat and potatoes won't be enough."

They stood up and he enveloped them both in his boat cloak. "That's better," he told her as they sat down even closer together, his arm tight around her.

She could have objected, but to his delight, she didn't. She nestled under his arm with a sigh and rested her head against his chest.

There was no defense against that. He kissed the top of her head and rested his chin there, as the door opened slightly and the overture began. With his arm around her waist and his eyes on the harbor below, he never heard Handel to better effect.

By "For unto Us a Child Is Born," he had to ask, "Nana, do you wash your hair with roses?"

He felt her nod. "Sort of. Gran saves the rose petals from the front yard." She paused. "I'm especially grateful you didn't throw up on those."

He laughed so loud that the bass closest to the open door said, "Shhh," which gave Nana the giggles. "That's the wig-maker," she whispered, when she could speak again. "I hope I do not lose all credit with him. What will I do next year when I want to listen here?"

"We can go inside next year," he whispered back, and knew he was committed.

She was silent then, but her arm came across his chest to hold his side, as though she wanted to gather him into her, as she had done when they embraced in the hallway.

There was no resisting her, but he did hold out for a few more choruses. To the accompaniment of "Glory to God in the Highest," he kissed her gently and long, savoring the softness of her lips and the energy of her response. Her hand went to his face and then into his hair, where her fingers were warm against his scalp.

He touched her face in turn, relishing the feel of her tender skin against his rough hands, all the while kissing her until they were both breathless. He held her off then slightly, to watch her face now when she was so ready to kiss and be kissed. The little-girl look to her was gone, at least for now, replaced by a woman equally beautiful, but different in a subtle way he could not have explained.

She put her hand to her own face. "I hope you don't think I do that on a daily basis," she said, her voice shaky.

"First time?" he asked.

She nodded, then shook her head. "I did let a boy kiss me once in Miss Pym's garden," she whispered. "It…it wasn't quite like that."

Her artless confession only served to increase his humility even more than his ardor. She was handing him something precious, and he knew it right down to the soles of his feet, which were getting cold against the guildhall stones.

He knew he could never again listen to Handel's oratorio and think of Christmas or Easter. With peace in his heart and Nana in the circle of his arms, he listened as she softly sang "He Was Despised," along with the contralto in the hall. He could literally hear a clock ticking inside his brain as he counted down the hours and minutes until the *Tireless* would put to sea in the morning. He had never felt so sad to be going back to the Channel Fleet and his work, which was difficult and dangerous and he knew would occupy him fully.

But here was Nana and the night music, and the pungency of a tide rolling in that would roll out and help the *Tireless* on her way. Even the tug of the moon was working against him. He had never felt so puny before. He could almost hear his father thundering from the pulpit, "'What is man that thou art mindful of him?'" They were simply two little people in a world at war. *And still we kiss and cling,* he thought, *as though we could stop time in its tracks.* What folly, but how right it felt.

He wasn't rightly sure how much more kissing he could manage before a sharp-eyed constable would declare him a public nuisance, but there she was and all he could do was kiss her. They were both getting better at it with every attempt, right up to "The Hallelujah Chorus."

"We're supposed to stand up," Nana said against his lips.

They both started to laugh. A hand to her face, Nana put her other hand over his lips to quiet him. He kissed her fingers as he hauled her to her feet, still wrapped tight in his boat cloak. He never should have pressed against her, considering the advanced state of his ardor, but he already knew that affecting missish airs was not her suit. A speculative "Hmm" was all she could manage, which only increased the high humor of the moment.

"Hmm?" he echoed. "That's it?"

"See here, Captain," she whispered, even as she stepped back. "I am improvising."

Smiling to himself, even as he felt the blood rush now to his face, he unwrapped Nana from his cloak. "Time to go home," he told her, even as the cold fact came surging back that he had no home, and it was all wishful thinking.

He steered Nana around the crowds coming from the guild-hall because he didn't want his dear one to chat with anyone but him. *You people of Plymouth can have her sweet face and good nature when I am gone to sea,* he thought.

A misty rain began as they slowly walked toward the

Mulberry. He had taken her under his cloak again, and she had voluntarily put her arm behind his waist to hug him tight. He was already recognizing that as a gesture peculiarly hers, like the way she watched for him each night, and sat with him while he ate, looking so interested in what he had to say about the *Tireless.* She would be a captain's ideal wife.

Some things aren't to be, though, he told himself. *I will go no further with this.*

To his surprise—and if he were honest, to his chagrin—she solved the matter in her own forthright way, the moment they entered the Mulberry, the entrance hall lit only by one lantern.

Gracefully retreating from his cloak, Nana stood with him at the foot of the stairs, and tugged at his shoulder. Accustomed to this now, he leaned down and she kissed his cheek.

"Good night, Captain," she told him. "I want above everything to come upstairs with you, but I'd rather break your heart than Gran's."

He had to smile at her frankness. He kissed her forehead. "I wasn't going to suggest it, my dear, even though I want to. I wouldn't do that to Gran, either, or more especially, you. What a pair we are."

"A good pair," she assured him, and his heart warmed.

He pulled her into his embrace one more time, and she offered no objections, folding into him in an almost boneless way that made loving her the simplest thing he had ever done, in all his complicated life.

"There *is* one thing," he whispered into her hair. "In light of the fact that for the past two hours we have thoroughly thrashed the Advent Season and, I might add, George Frideric Handel, I think you are almost—well, nearly—required to call me Oliver."

He felt her laughter against his chest. "I agree, Oliver," she said.

"Much better." He held her off and looked at her. "I do require one more thing. Promise me before I ask it."

"No lady should do that," she protested.

"You must."

"Yes, then."

"Don't see me off this morning. It's too hard."

She started to cry, and he held her tight again. "Promise."

She nodded. "I'll try."

"Go on to bed now, and don't look back," he ordered.

She did as he said, squaring her shoulders and walking away from him without a backward glance.

Oliver knew he wouldn't sleep, so he lay in bed with his hands behind his head, counting all the ways and reasons he loved Eleanor Massie. *I must survive this war,* he told himself. *I want her for my wife and children of her body.*

At three o'clock, he dressed again and repacked his duffel. He looked around the room, with its shabby, comfortable furniture, and view of the ocean, dark now, but out there, always out there: a friend sometimes, an enemy other times.

He put on his cloak and slung his duffel over his shoulder. Mr. Proudy shook his head whenever he hoisted his own duffel, but Oliver knew he never stood on much ceremony. Besides, he had seen the great Lord Cochrane himself carry his own duffel.

He went down the stairs, and stopped.

Nana had almost kept her word. Wrapped in her robe, a pillow under her head, she had curled up on the settee in the front hallway. He looked closely at her in the light of the lantern, which still gave off its soft glow. She must have worn herself out with crying, from the tear streaks on her face.

"Bless and keep you, my love," he whispered. "God knows if we shall see each other again."

Quietly, he took his cloak from his shoulders and laid it on her. She stirred, but did not waken. He had another cloak aboard the *Tireless*.

He had not ordered a hackney on purpose. He had a long walk, but Mr. Proudy would have the *Tireless* trimmed and anchored in the Cattewater. The jolly boat would be waiting quayside. His men would row him out to their frigate; the bosun would pipe him aboard, and life would go on.

Everything had changed except the duty ahead.

Chapter Eleven

When Nana woke up that morning, enveloped in the familiar cloak, she managed to take several deep breaths before bursting into tears. She pulled the cloak as tightly around her as she could.

How could that man have been so quiet, coming down the stairs? she thought, when she had exhausted herself with tears. Then, *Why did I have to fall in love with someone destined only to go away?* And then the cold bath: *He never said he loved me. How could he? I am illegitimate.*

Knowing that Gran would be upset, Nana willed herself into calmness as she lay there in the dark. She reminded herself of all the times she had cried when she had to return to Bath and Miss Pym, leaving her dear Gran and Pete, and even Plymouth, not the kind of town any of Miss Pym's other students lived in.

She wondered how navy wives survived such painful separation. *I have none of that,* she reminded herself with sorrow. *There is nothing binding me to that beloved man who will never be out of my thoughts—no declaration, no promise, no pledge, no ring, no shared words of love, no experience beyond a few weeks at the Mulberry Inn, and an unforgettable performance of* Messiah. For all she knew, Oliver Worthy behaved like that in every port.

As she lay there dry-eyed in the dark, Nana wondered if her own mother had suffered torments when Lord Ratliffe went to sea. *At least I will not know the panic and horror of ruin,* she reminded herself. History did not repeat itself.

She didn't know what time it was, but soon Sal would be rising to start the kitchen fire, heat water for guests and prepare breakfast. Gran mustn't find her here, collapsed in a soggy heap on the settee.

Nana took off the cloak when she entered her room. There wasn't any point in hiding it. She would just spread it across the end of her bed and wrap it around her at night.

If breakfast felt a little like sleepwalking, so be it, she decided a few hours later. It was easy enough to smile at the guests because she did appreciate their presence. She relied on her naturally cheery disposition to get her through the meal, and it did. And once she knew she could manage, cleaning the rooms was easy enough. Mercifully, Sal took the floor Captain Worthy had vacated, so she didn't have to go into his room and see him irretrievably gone.

The floor above was simple: Henri Lefebvre preferred that she not disturb his room. The other rooms were easily cleaned and prepared for the next lodgers. *I can manage this,* she told herself over and over, as she scrubbed and tidied.

At midmorning, she realized he only made her promise not to see him off from the Mulberry. Dropping her broom and dustpan, Nana ran down three flights of stairs, pausing only to throw her cloak around her shoulders.

She knew that for centuries, wives and sweethearts gathered at the Hoe to watch the ships leave Plymouth's harbors and enter the sound. She turned her face to the wind, wishing it would blow hard from the south and keep the *Tireless* bottled in the sound. The wind blew from the north and west, where it had been blowing since the third day of the Creation, when God decreed it.

She slowed to a more ladylike pace when she came to the Hoe, that headland where Sir Francis Drake had bowled and watched for the Spanish Armada. Other women were there: several of the hard-looking women Gran always told her to ignore, and well-dressed ladies, the wives of officers. She saw Mrs. Brittle, wife of the sailing master and probably a veteran of many such moments.

Mrs. Brittle motioned her closer. "Come for a last look, dearie?"

Nana didn't think there was anything in her own expression to cause such sympathy on Mrs. Brittle's face, but when the sailing master's wife held out her hand, Nana grasped it like a rope thrown to a drowning man. In another moment, Mrs. Brittle clasped Nana as though she were her own child.

"There now, there now," she soothed. "I wish I could tell you that it gets easier, but I'd be lying." She pointed. "There they are, love. My Daniel's probably shouting his orders, keeping the sails trim." She shaded her eyes with her hand. "It's a tricky harbor."

Nana was almost too shy to ask. "What…what would Captain Worthy be doing?"

"Some captains turn the leaving of a harbor to their first mate, who gives the orders. Captain Worthy sometimes takes the helm himself, to leave Plymouth Sound. He's probably at the wheel, love."

"He doesn't trust his crew?" Nana couldn't help asking.

Mrs. Brittle hugged her closer. "He trusts them more than

most! Daniel thinks Captain Worthy is a true deepwater sailor, never happier than when he is conning the ship."

I hope he has another boat cloak, Nana thought. *I wish I had taken the time to show him how to make a wheat poultice for his neck and ears. I wish a lot of things.*

They stood close together, watching the ship leave the sound and enter the swell of the Channel, where the rollers and troughs waited. "How long have you been coming here?" Nana asked.

"Some thirty years. They *do* come back to port." Mrs. Brittle indicated a well-dressed lady standing by herself, and lowered her voice. "It's only Mrs. Proudy's second time, poor thing."

"Should we say something to her?" Nana whispered back.

Mrs. Brittle shook her head. "I've tried. She's not like us, Nana. Her father's a baronet. We have too much of the common touch about us, dearie."

I'm the bastard of a viscount, Nana thought, *and it's a wider chasm than you can begin to fathom.* They watched until the *Tireless* disappeared from view, then walked down the hill together. She glanced at Mrs. Brittle then, grateful for her hearty kindness

"You live in Torquay?" Nana asked, shy again.

"I do, love. Don't you know, our house overlooks Tor Bay. Sometimes the *Tireless* puts in there. As testimony that they return from sea now and then, Dan and I have four children."

Nana laughed, even as her face turned red. "May I come and visit you sometime?"

"Anytime you're lonely, come for a chin-wag."

I'm lonely now, Nana told herself, as she said goodbye.

Lodgers came and went in the next few days, and it was easy enough to keep too busy to think about anything but the work of the Mulberry. The start of each day began with her mind on the end of it, when she could retreat to her room, wrap herself in Oliver's cloak and cry herself to sleep.

She couldn't fool Gran. One afternoon, after spending far too long shining the brass doorknob and dreaming that Oliver would come through the door any minute, she looked up to see Gran watching her.

"If you polish that any more, you will wear a hole in the knob," Gran said, her voice gruff, but kind.

Nana managed a laugh. "Silly of me."

Gran stayed where she was in the hall. "I've been going over the accounts and Christmas looks more promising," she said. "Would you like a length of muslin for a spring dress, or a new muff? What would you like, my dear?"

"Captain Worthy," Nana blurted out. The words hung between them like channel fog. When she realized what she had said, she put her hand to her mouth. "Oh, Gran, I…"

She didn't know what she was going to say, but it hardly mattered. In the next moment, she found herself sobbing into Gran's apron as the woman held her close on the settee. She cried until she felt as drained as a water keg after a two-year voyage.

She found a dry spot on Gran's apron and dabbed at her eyes, hoping no one had heard her outburst. She finally dared to look at her grandmother, knowing she had to reassure her.

"Gran, please know this. I didn't— We didn't—do anything to shame ourselves, or you."

There was no mistaking Gran's sigh of relief.

"I wanted to, Gran, even though I knew better," Nana said honestly, picking her way through a narrow lane of emotions. "I hope you're not ashamed of me for even thinking it."

Gran had her own struggle then. "Never," she said. "You're

my darling and I trust you." She managed a ghost of a smile. "Isn't that onerous?"

Nana blew her nose. "The worst." She took Gran's hand. "What I would like to do, if there is an extra shilling, is ask Mr. Lefebvre if he would make a sketch of me that I could send to Captain Worthy."

Gran considered her request. "You haven't promised the captain anything?"

"Nothing. I don't even know what he really thinks of me," she said simply. "I just want to do it."

"It's not proper."

"I know. Miss Pym would give me such a scold," she replied. "I would deserve it, but I would still want to send Captain Worthy a picture." She leaned her head against Gran's shoulder. "Maybe the apple didn't really fall so far from the tree."

"Yes, it did," Gran said firmly. "But send him a picture, anyway. I think… No, I know….he's a lonely man."

Shy but determined, she approached Henri Lefebvre later that day. "Just a small picture. Maybe that one you did of me after you sketched Sal?"

"That one?" Lefebvre asked. "I could do another one. Perhaps a better one for someone serving so valiantly in the fleet."

"I only have a few pence," Nana said, embarrassed again. "I have an idea."

"Ask way, mademoiselle." He made an elaborate bow. "How could any man refuse you?"

Easily enough, she thought. "Here's what I would like."

Lefebvre walked with her to the back of the guildhall, where she sat on the steps in Oliver's cloak and asked him to paint her there. He worked quickly, and finished before the sky clouded over and the rains came.

She spent an evening composing a letter, heading it Dear

Captain, because she hadn't the courage to write Oliver. She told him she had gone to the Hoe and, in Mrs. Brittle's company, watched the *Tireless* leave the harbor. She wished him Godspeed and signed it, Your Friend, Nana.

It was too bloodless, but she knew she did not dare write what she really felt, considering that he had not stated any official position of his own. She stared at the antiseptic words, willing him, somehow, to read, instead, her heartfelt love and constant devotion, no matter where the winds took him, or whatever befell him. *You have my whole heart,* she thought, as she fashioned an envelope and put in the sketch from Mr. Lefebvre. *I had no idea of my own heart's depth, until I met you, Oliver Worthy. I just wish I were worthy.*

Considering that she hadn't a clue what to do next, she enlisted Pete as an accomplice.

"Address it to him, then put the ship on the next line, and Channel Fleet below," he told her. "Do you know his station?"

"Ferrol. I don't have any money to frank it," she said.

"No need. There's a sloop of war in the harbor right now. I'll take it to the captain and he will do the rest."

"Suppose the sloop is not going toward Ferrol Station?" she asked, thinking of all the ways her foolish correspondence could go astray.

Pete clapped his arm around her shoulders. "It's the *Goldfinch,* Nana. Captain Worthy and Captain Dennison were in conversation at the Drake no more than ten days ago. He'll know where to find your captain."

"How do you know all this?" she asked.

"I watch things, too, Nana," he replied. "Trust me to do this for you."

She watched him go down to the docks, tempted half a dozen times before he was even out of her sight to call him back. She knew so little about men—their habits, their constancy. "I just want you to have a picture of me," she whispered, as Pete disappeared from view. "Just a picture."

Despite her state of mind, Christmas was the best in years. There were no guests currently staying at the Mulberry. Even Mr. Lefebvre had gone to visit friends in Cheltenham. Gran had thrown caution to the winds and purchased a duck, which Pete dispatched, Sal and Nana scalded and plucked and Gran cooked to a brown, crackling goodness.

And five days later, Mr. Ramseur knocked on the door.

Occupied in the dining room with a governess changing post and two hemp vendors, Nana had sent Sal to the door.

The first glimpse of the high fore-and-aft hat and a boat cloak made her knees weak. Feeling her face draining of color, she sat down at the nearest table. A closer glance told her the officer wasn't much older than she was. Surely the navy wouldn't send children with bad news.

"Yes?"

He took off his hat, tucking it under his arm. "Are you Miss Massie?"

She nodded, not sure of speech.

He smiled at her. "Don't look so alarmed! I'm Lieutenant Caleb Ramseur, of the *Tireless*. I have a letter for you, and something else."

Wordlessly, she held out her hand for the letter he was offering, wishing her fingers wouldn't shake. She took the letter, and a small package wrapped in canvas.

She couldn't help but look behind him. Did Oliver not even want to see her? Tears prickled the back of her eyelids.

He seemed to understand. "Oh! Why am I here and not the Old Man?"

She had to smile then, particularly since he suddenly realized what he had said, and his face went as red as hers was white.

"It's nautical cant, Miss Massie, only no one ever says it where…er…the Old Man can hear. May I sit down?"

"Excuse my manners, Lieutenant. Of course you may."

He grinned at her. "Still don't have my land legs yet." He couldn't have overlooked the question in her eyes. "Miss Massie, we had just got to Ferrol Station when wouldn't you know it, a French freighter bound for Martinique tried to leave the harbor. You never saw a slicker capture."

"I still don't understand," she said honestly. "Mr. Ramseur, why are *you* here?"

"The Old Man told me to take the freighter to Plymouth, a prize of war." He couldn't hide his pride. "It was my first command, from Ferrol to Plymouth."

"Congratulations, sir," she said. She held up the letter and package. "And this?"

"There wasn't much time, but the Ol'…Captain Worthy wanted to send you a Christmas present." He sighed. "We ran into contrary winds and I'm late. Merry Christmas anyway."

Nana laughed. "Same to you, Lieutenant." She looked around for Sal, who was standing in the door to the kitchen, wide-eyed. "Sal, please bring Lieutenant Ramseur some cake. A large piece, I think."

"Oh, I shouldn't.…" He started to rise.

"Chocolate," she interrupted. He sat down again.

Sal brought a slice of cake. The second mate didn't waste a moment demolishing it. He did pause long enough to gesture with his fork toward the package in her lap. "Captain said I was to watch you open it and tell him your reaction." He took a huge bite. "He said he's sorry he couldn't be here himself to see it."

He stopped eating long enough to hand her a folding knife from his uniform jacket. She picked out the stitches in the canvas and unfolded over a foot of cotton wadding.

One last turn of the wadding revealed a pearl, slightly pink and the size of a wren's egg. "My goodness," Nana said, scarcely able to speak, her voice an octave higher than usual. She set the pearl on the table, afraid to touch it. She looked at the lieutenant, who was watching her face, his eyes appreciative. "Does the Admiralty know there is a mad man on the blockade giving away pearls?"

Mr. Ramseur burst into laughter. "Mr. Proudy wanted to wager that you would faint!"

"What about the…uh…Old Man?" Nana asked, hugely amused.

Mr. Ramseur sobered up immediately. "If he knew we were even *thinking* about placing a wager on a lady, he'd have tied us to the grate and flogged us himself." He took another bite of cake. "Must remember that—'mad man giving away pearls.'"

"'On the blockade,'" she added. "Get it all. Mr. Ramseur, I couldn't possibly accept this. It's worth a fortune. He'll end up in the parish workhouse, right next to the Massies."

It was the lieutenant's turn to stare. "Surely you aren't serious."

"Of course I am!" she retorted. "He has been so kind to us, to be sure, but generosity has its limits!"

"You don't know, do you?" Ramseur said finally, after weighing his words.

"Know what?" Nana demanded, bewildered. She started to rewrap the pearl.

"The Old Man is one of the richest post captains in the Royal Navy."

Nana stopped what she was doing and stared at him, her mouth open. "Surely you aren't serious," she said in her turn. "But…his father was a vicar. I know that much. Unless church service has changed vastly, that's not an avenue to inherited wealth."

"True, true." The second mate ran his finger around the rim of the plate to get the last of the icing. "You do know about prize ships, don't you? Under Admiralty Orders, prize ships are the property of the captain alone, and not the whole fleet. The Old Man doesn't have to share with anyone except his crew, and by God, he is generous with us, too."

Pete spoke up from the doorway. "No wonder he never worries about desertion, when in port. I can't think of one captain in one hundred who would have given his crew so much shore leave as Captain Worthy did, when the *Tireless* was in dry docks."

Ramseur grinned. "It's more than that. We like him, too. He's fair." He rose then, and tucked his hat under his arm again. "I'll give him a report about your expression, Miss Massie."

Shaken, she rose and curtseyed to his bow. "I had no idea. Simply no idea." There were a thousand things she wanted to say, none of which Mr. Ramseur needed to hear. "Tell him we will discuss this when I see him next."

"He thought you would say that."

"The Old Man is going to get a piece of my mind," she said. She turned to see Sal at her elbow, with the rest of the cake. "Here you are, Mr. Ramseur. Share it as far as it will go with the hoy's crew."

Nana walked him to the front door. "Lieutenant Ramseur, has the *Tireless* received any mail yet from Plymouth?"

"Not yet. Maybe there will be some letters by the time I get back."

When she returned to the dining room, Gran was there, looking at the pearl, amazement on her face, and listening to Pete talk about Admiralty Orders and prize ships. Nana handed her the pearl and the wadding. "Please put it in a safe place."

"The Tower of London?" Pete teased.

"Heavens, Pete, don't quiz me!" Nana said. "This is all too much." She picked up the unopened letter. "I think I need to read this."

She retreated to her room, closing the door quietly behind her. With a sigh, she wrapped herself in Oliver's boat cloak and opened the letter. It made her smile.

It was short, beginning with no salutation, written in a hurry, which confirmed what Mr. Ramseur had said, and made her laugh.

> *I know, I know: Miss Pym would never approve. Hang Miss Pym. It's Christmas and there are no stores in the fleet, unless I were to send you a checked shirt from slops, or steal the rather ostentatious crucifix the captain of the French freighter we captured is wearing. Oh, the Frogs! Why are they so much trouble? We have to go with what we have, and I have a pearl for you. Feliz Navidad from Ferrol, O. Worthy.*
>
> *P.S. O. Worthy should probably not be counted worthy in matters of proper social intercourse. O. Worthy is cold, his feet ache from standing on them for hours and hours, and he does not particularly give a rat's ass about Miss Pym. Neither should you.*
>
> *Merely O.*

Who could not laugh at that? *I wonder if he knew how badly I needed a laugh,* she asked herself. *Maybe he needs one, too*. Nana folded the letter, tucked it under her cheek and closed her eyes. She slept all through the night for the first time in weeks.

Chapter Twelve

She didn't even want to know where Gran had hidden the pearl. All Nana wanted to do was read Oliver's amusing note over and over again until the paper went limp from folding and unfolding. *I am becoming useless to humanity,* she decided, as January blew in colder than usual and sleet made walking difficult.

She wondered how Mr. Lefebvre managed to continue sketching, but he did, going out in all weathers and returning white-faced and shivering. Maybe it was his French background, but he wasn't the sort of man she felt would welcome commentary on his habits. Still, one particularly raw afternoon, just after the year turned, she couldn't help herself.

"Mr. Lefebvre, I can't but wonder why you are so devoted to landscapes in the dead of winter," she asked, after bringing him a pot of tea and biscuits in the dining room.

He did smile at that. "Miss Massie, this is still such a welcome break from painting portraits of landowners! *Sacre bleu!* The demands they make when my paintings look like them!" He sipped his tea. "I'll be here a few more months, and then I am even contemplating a return to La Belle France."

"You are probably in no danger of losing your head now," Nana said, "but with the war, isn't it impossible to travel to France?"

"There are always ways."

I suppose there are, she thought. *I wonder if I am the most naive female in Plymouth.*

That evening, she was the most surprised.

Everyone else had gone to bed. She was pacing the floor in the sitting room, trying to wear herself out enough so she could sleep, when someone knocked on the front door. Startled, she glanced at the mantelpiece clock. Midnight. "Who would trudge up the hill to the Mulberry on a night like this, when the Drake beckons?" she murmured out loud.

Then she knew who would do precisely that, and ran down the hall. She jerked open the front door and walked right into an embrace.

"You had better be Captain Worthy," she said, with her face close against his chest.

Oliver put a hand on each side of her face and kissed her. His face was wet and cold, but his lips were warm.

They just stood there, the rain pelting down, until Nana pulled him inside. Before she closed the door, she glanced beyond him to see a carriage and horses. "Did you forget to pay the jehu?" she asked.

"No. I have to go to London."

Disbelieving, she tried to undo the clasp holding his boat cloak together. He put his hands gently over her fingers and pulled them away. "I mean it, Nana. Even stopping here puts me behind schedule and liable for a court martial. But I had to." He kissed her again more gently this time, as though to atone for bad news. He pulled her down beside him on the bench in the hall.

"You can stay awhile when you return?" she asked, already bracing herself for his answer.

He shook his head. "Things are going from bad to worse in Spain, and I must deliver a message to Horse Guards from one of our connections on the coast near Ferrol." He put his finger to her lips, smiling when she kissed it. "You make my job so hard! Not a word of what I just said to anyone. Not even Gran or Pete."

If he could make light of this, so could she. "I haven't divulged a state secret in at least a fortnight," she said. "You're safe with me."

"I know," he replied. "I'm certain no man ever felt safer." He pulled her as close as he could.

"See here, I'm supposed to be irritated with you for that Christmas gift," she said, after they finished kissing again.

"You'd be even more in the boughs if I'd given you the ruby or the emerald. It was Christmas, Nana. I didn't have anything else."

"I wished I had something for you."

"How about that sketch on the guildhall steps?" he said, his eyes merry.

"I mean something of value."

He stood up then, pulling her with him. "Nana, you gave me that every day I was here at the Mulberry. Even now." He wrapped his cloak around her, as he had on the guildhall steps, and she walked with him out to the post chaise.

"I'm dreaming all this, aren't I?" she asked, as he unwrapped her and held her face in his hands again, as though memorizing her.

"No. I'll be back as soon as I can." He grabbed her close in a tight embrace that left her almost breathless and released her just as quickly. He opened the chaise door and stepped up, then looked at the coachman. "London now, and spring'um."

Oliver slept between Blandford and Salisbury, wrapped tight in his cloak, which he fancied carried some of Nana's rose scent: surely his imagination, but a comfort, nonetheless. When he wasn't sleeping, he wished she were beside him. How had he managed so many years at sea without Nana Massie waiting for him? He thought of the times he had put into Plymouth, oblivious to her existence. *I owe you that, at least, Lord Ratliffe,* he thought.

Through the sleet, he glanced out the window at a motionless telegraph, one of many large signaling devices stretching from Plymouth to London, and wished—not for the first time—they were capable of sending detailed messages in spite of storm or darkness. That much modernity would obviously have to wait for another age, he told himself, as he hunkered down and tried to return to sleep.

He reached London on a grey day thirty-eight hours later, only to be stalled by late-afternoon traffic. Oliver didn't mind the delay, because he was trying to force his sleep-deprived brain into a decision. The lords of the Admiralty had specified he deliver all communications directly to them. He had never failed them. He looked down at the note he had taken from his waistcoat pocket, knowing that when it got to Horse Guards from Admiralty, there would be an instant summons for a meeting at the highest levels. By the end of a typical day, bureaucrats scattered. This was no typical day: he had to be there first.

He knew the note by heart. Don Rogelio Rodriguez, his contact from beyond Ferrol in the land controlled again by France, had urged him to memorize them whenever he could.

Oliver closed his eyes. *We are retreating with all dispatch to Corunna, in the hopes of finding transports to return us to England. Soult is right behind. If there are no transports, we will be cut off. Your obedient servant, Col. Sir John Moore.* He opened his eyes. There was more, and it all needed instant attention.

That's it, Oliver thought. He rapped on the side of the post chaise, opened the door and leaned out. "Horse Guards," he ordered. "Then take me to Admiralty."

Horse Guards it was. Note in hand, and trusting that his sea legs wouldn't give him grief, Captain Worthy shoved all dignity aside and ran up the front steps. When he left without the note, a lieutenant was running with it inside the building.

Oliver sank back inside the post chaise with relief, until he reminded himself that his next stop—so close—was Admiralty House. Hopefully the lords would be in a forgiving mood, if they knew how important the note was. Maybe Lord Ratliffe had left early, so he could have access to one of the lords, instead.

His luck was on a lee shore. Lord Ratliffe was even standing in the corridor when the porter ushered Oliver toward his office.

Bow and smile, Oliver told himself as he approached the viscount. *Even though you'd like to have his guts for garters. Bow, at least. It's required.*

He did his duty, then followed Ratliffe into his office. The viscount held out his hand for the note. Oliver shook his head. "My lord, since it was of the utmost urgency and the hour for close of business was approaching, I took it directly to Horse Guards."

"You did *what?*" Ratliffe shouted.

Startled at the vehemence, Oliver repeated his message. "I

know the situation on the ground near Corunna, my lord," he added. "I used my judgment."

"Your judgment," Ratliffe mocked. "Your judgment! Since when do you know more than the lords of the Admiralty?"

Since forever, Oliver thought, as his mind reeled. "I was there, my lord, with my Spanish contact. Sir John's aide-de-camp rode up from the general's current position and handed me the note."

"Who is your Spanish contact?"

That's the second time he's asked me, Oliver thought. "My lord, I shall not say."

Lord Ratliffe's face turned a peculiar mottled purple color. More irritated than alarmed, Oliver observed the viscount, looking for any resemblance to Nana. Thank God there was none. *Hopefully, Nana will learn—if she doesn't already know—that I am best handled calmly,* he thought. *Never this.*

"My lord? Would you like me to get you a glass of water?" he asked, all politeness. "Perhaps I should leave."

Ratliffe gasped for breath. He stabbed the air with his finger a few times, then jabbed it at a chair. "Don't go anywhere!" He stalked from the room, slamming the door behind him.

Oliver experienced his first moment of uncertainty concerning his action. One side of his brain assured him he had done what the lords would have wanted. The other side warned him to say little to anyone. Maybe both were right.

He stood where he was in the center of the room, his eyes going by habit to the outside window, where the bend of the trees told him all he needed to know about the wind gauge. Time was wasting and here he stood.

As he glanced toward the door, his eyes grazed Lord Ratliffe's cluttered desk. *It's a wonder anything gets done* here, he told himself. He took another look, and another, and felt his breath coming faster.

He was at the desk in three strides, standing over it to stare down, his face draining of color, at a familiar sketch partly covered by a document. With fingers that shook, he lifted off the document from a drawing of Nana Massie, done by Henri Lefebvre, who had sketched both drawings tacked to the deck beam over his sleeping cot. He let the document fall back into place because his fingers couldn't hold it.

He took Lord Ratliffe's advice and sat down. In fact, he hung his head between his knees for a brief moment, because little points of light had begun to obscure his vision. He forced himself to breathe deep for a few seconds, then he slowly raised his head.

Maybe the sketch would be gone now. Maybe he had imagined the whole thing. He had had so little sleep in the last five years, and lately, he was seeing Nana everywhere.

The portion of the sketch that had caught his eye was still there when he raised his head. He sat back, his mind working fast. Lefebvre. Lefebvre. England was full of émigrés from the revolution. Lefebvre.

"Oliver, you are an idiot," he exclaimed, then looked around, because to his own ears, his outburst filled the room.

No one came running. He heard no footsteps. He willed himself to stay in the chair and think through the impossible. The partly rosy picture he had painted for Ratliffe of the situation at the Mulberry obviously hadn't been enough. *What have I done?* he asked himself. The viscount was obviously still counting on tough times in Plymouth to force Nana's hand.

"I will take care of that immediately, your lordship," he said, softly this time, but biting off each word.

Lefebvre. Then he remembered, and it was as if someone

had slammed a fist into his stomach. The name had no direct bearing on his duty, but, sitting in Admiralty House, he remembered there was a leader of cavalry with the name of Lefebvre-Desnouettes, a favorite of Napoleon, captured only months ago in Spain, and now paroled in Cheltenham.

"My God," Oliver said faintly. Maybe it was a common French name. *Not likely,* he thought. *With all the hundreds of details that cross your path daily at sea, you still should have remembered that name.* "Colonel Desnouettes, have you a brother or cousin who is a spy?" he asked softly. "Seen him lately?"

The fist in his stomach plunged in deeper. "Lord Ratliffe, how are *you* connected with a French spy? Since Nana wouldn't, does Bonaparte pay your bills now?"

He closed his eyes and leaned back, forcing his tired brain to reflect. A spendthrift at the mercy of his creditors, Ratliffe's money problems had obviously not been solved when Nana Massie proved so uncooperative and refused to be sold for her father's debts. This bankrupt man remained bankrupt still, Oliver reasoned. *And now he has turned to spying against his country for money.*

You have scarcely any evidence, he told himself. *If you make such a shocking accusation, the lords will lock you up in Bedlam and throw away the key. The very least they would do is remove you from command of anything larger than a rowboat.*

He got to his feet, desperate to return to Plymouth and find out for himself. *Slow down,* he told himself. *First, you must secure Nana's safety.* He had already planned to do it one way during this visit to London. There was a better, even more certain way: one he had vowed never to do. *Times change,* he thought, willing himself calm as the door opened. *I have changed, too.*

Looking no more rational than when he had run from his office, Lord Ratliffe stormed in first, followed by a much more benign-looking Henry Phipps, Earl of Mulgrave, First Lord of the Admiralty. Relieved, Oliver let out his breath slowly. Ratliffe could not have found a better man.

His words stumbling over each other, all the while he pointed at Oliver, Lord Ratliffe railed at length about his gross stupidity in sending the message first to Horse Guards. The earl listened patiently, glancing over once to catch Oliver's eye and transmit what looked like the briefest of winks.

Not even Lord Ratliffe could go on forever. He concluded his observations by pointing dramatically at Oliver and declaring, "My lord, I demand you ask for this man's commission."

Lord Mulgrave cleared his throat. He removed his spectacles, breathed on them, wiped them clean, then repeated the entire process. By concentrating hard on the medallion behind Lord Ratliffe's desk, Oliver managed to retain his composure.

"My lord?" Ratliffe prompted, impatient.

"William, I can't do that," the earl replied. "We'd be losing one of the navy's finest sailors, one who thinks on his feet and had the brains to take that message directly to Horse Guards." He turned to Oliver. "Good work, lad. I'd have done the same." He looked at Ratliffe, whose face was assuming its mottled hue again. "William, do sit down and fan yourself with something. Better yet, take a few days off in the country, why don't you?"

The viscount sat down in his chair suddenly, and the earl turned his attention to Oliver. "D'ye have a moment, my boy? Let's chat about that missive from Sir John. No, no, Ratliffe. Leave this to me. Come, Oliver."

Oliver left the room without a backward glance. *I hope I never see that wretch again,* he thought. *At least it's nice to know that Nana will never invite him to our home for the holidays.*

But he was getting ahead of himself, something he had been doing for two months now, since he first met Nana. Standing in the hall, he debated whether to tell Lord Mulgrave his suspicions and realized he had no evidence. Instead, he recited the message from Sir John Moore and the situation of his retreat toward Corunna.

"It's an ugly business, my boy. I won't keep you here a minute longer," Lord Mulgrave said.

"There is one thing. Two things, actually."

"Say on."

Oliver told the First Lord what he needed and asked how to go about doing it. Lord Mulgrave listened, grinning broadly, and nodded.

"I will do precisely as you wish, Captain Worthy," he said. "My own solicitor will speed things along for you tomorrow. Go to Grey's Inn first thing and ask for Robinson. As for the other matter, I will contact the Court of Faculties and bend my will on them a little, what say you?"

"I am in your debt, my lord," Oliver said simply.

"Tut, my boy, tut. I must admit to some surprise. Aren't you the man in the fleet who for years has assured us that he would never be so stupid as to ask some poor female for her hand?"

"That very idiot, my lord. Hard to imagine England controls the waves with such nincompoops sailing her ships, isn't it?"

"My thoughts precisely. Tell me, boy, does this female of your choice have any idea that you are richer than God?"

"No."

"How will she take such news?"

Oliver smiled for the first time since he left Plymouth. "She'll be irritated."

Lord Mulgrave rubbed his hands together. "Even better!

Nice to know you have a heart and other working parts. Just don't scare her to death on your wedding night."

"No, sir." Oliver bowed. "My Lord, do excuse me. If I don't get a little sleep I will fall down the steps, crack my head and be of no further use to the Admiralty." He couldn't help it then; he was so tired his shoulders sagged. "My Lord, I don't know how to thank you."

Lord Mulgrave rested his hand on Oliver's shoulder in a rare show of affection. "It is we who owe *you.* You have kept your oath to the Crown a thousand times over. Good luck."

I need more than luck, Oliver thought grimly as he gave the coachman instructions to find him lodgings close to Grey's Inn. *Not only do I have my puny plans, but I must also find out Lefebvre's game and stop him. And do this in time to sail with a good tide. Father would consider prayer a right good step now.*

He closed his eyes to begin one.

Lord Mulgrave greased the skids beyond belief, on his behalf. By ten o'clock, Oliver had willed his entire property and all goods to Nana Worthy, effective upon his death. With the solicitor trying not to gape, Oliver set up liberal allowances every quarter, starting that day. By noon, and after a payment of forty shillings, he had a special license issued to him from the Court of Faculties and Dispensations, good for a wedding at any time and in any parish in the realm.

He was no closer to a solution about Henri Lefebvre, though. As the post chaise raced toward Plymouth, he knew his first task was to verify his suspicions. It was certainly no crime to sketch a pretty woman surreptitiously and send a sketch to her father. If that was his job, then why did Lefebvre continue to hang around Plymouth? What was he really sketching? And what about his strange connection to Ratliffe?

He knew the answer, even as he berated himself for his lack of suspicion, especially in time of national emergency. Lefebvre must be keeping an eye on all naval shipping. For all Oliver knew, the Frenchman had a counterpart at Portsmouth, and maybe even Exeter, doing the same thing: watching for transports, looking to see if England planned to shore up Sir John Moore in Spain with more troops, or let him wither.

By the time the post chaise passed Exeter, Oliver had a plan so feeble it made him wince to think about it. He would not involve Nana, but he needed Pete's help. He needed the old sailor to instantly do as he said and not hesitate for anything. The whole scheme depended on speed.

He arrived at the Mulberry the following afternoon, dismissed the post chaise and went inside the inn, not bothering to knock. To his infinite relief, Nana and Gran were nowhere in sight; he needed Pete. The old sailor sat in the kitchen, slicing vegetables. He looked up in surprise to see Oliver, and started to rise.

Oliver motioned him to sit down. He sat beside him, telling him to listen and not talk. He told him first of his will, and then of his wish to marry Nana immediately. To the question in Pete's eyes, he told him next about the sketch on Lord Ratliffe's desk, his fear that the viscount might still seek to ruin his daughter to pay his debts. And there was the not-so-trifling matter of treason.

Pete was no fool. "Lefebvre and Lord Rat? Damn them both" was all he said, as Oliver continued talking, stating his fears that the Frenchman was spying on naval shipping.

"I can't prove anything right now and there isn't time before I must sail again," he said. "Pete, can you arrange for a diversion this evening around the dinner hour to get everyone out of the Mulberry? And let me have a key?"

"I can do that, sir," Pete said. "Let's put you in the room across the hall from Lefebvre right now, and not say a word to Nana. Better if no one knows you're here but me."

"That's a hard thing," Oliver admitted. "I really need to talk to her."

Pete nodded. "Aye, sir, you do, if you're planning to spring marriage on her. But let's trap the Frenchman, and then Nana."

Oliver took his arm, suddenly unsure of himself. "Do you think Nana will even consider what I'm...er...proposing?"

Pete laughed, but sobered instantly. "She'll consider it, but she may decide to do what's best for you."

"I don't like the sound of that."

"You shouldn't," Pete said frankly.

God, what does that mean? Oliver thought. *Surely she knows how much I love her?*

Pete took an extra key for both rooms and Oliver followed him upstairs. "No lights now, sir," he told him. "Lefebvre knows no one is in this room."

"Very well. I'll lie down and wait." Oliver sat on the bed and removed his shoes.

Pete set the extra key to Lefebvre's room on the table by the bed.

"What do you have in mind, Pete?" he asked.

"D'ye still have those drills on board ship where someone yells 'Fire in the paint locker'?"

"Aye. Are you planning to burn down the Mulberry?"

"I would never!" Pete declared, an indignant expression on his face. "I was thinking more in terms of those ugly curtains in the kitchen. Nana said only yesterday she wanted some new ones. She'll be able to afford them if she marries you, won't she?"

"She can replace them with cloth of gold or ermine, if she

likes," he said. "I trust you not to burn down the Mulberry, Pete. I've grown rather fond of this old place."

"Don't you even worry, sor."

Chapter Thirteen

Oliver may have been dozing, but years of experience with fires at sea woke up him up the moment he smelled smoke. A heartbeat later, he heard Pete shout, "Fire! Everyone out!"

He grabbed the key to Lefebvre's room. "Get out," he muttered as he heard the Frenchman slamming drawers. In another second, he heard him throw open his door, pause long enough to lock it, then pound down the stairs.

Oliver was across the hall in a step, key in the lock and turning. To his relief, Lefebvre had left the lamp glowing. He ran first to the table, covered with sketches of trees and shorelines and gulls coasting on currents of air. "You have some talent," he admitted, as he dug through the pile. Nothing.

He forced himself to stop and think. He had heard a drawer slam in the seconds before Lefebvre left, so he went through each drawer in the bureau. Under stockings and smallclothes he found a sketchbook. Oliver pulled it out and ran to the lamp. Page after page of more Plymouth scenes: the Barbican, the Drake, the Hoe, the Citadel. More Nana. *At least he has good taste,* Oliver thought.

He came to the end of the sketchbook. Nothing. Had the

man already forwarded his sketches? He started to close it, then noticed that the back cover was more padded than the front. "What have we here, Monsieur Le Spy?" he asked out loud.

He ran his fingers carefully along the inside edge of the back cover, close to the spine, then pried it up with his fingernail. "Well, well," he said, scarcely breathing, as he lifted out a sketch of ships riding at anchor in the Cattewater, then another of the dry docks. In another of the mouth of the Tamar River, he could make out the *Goldfinch,* Dennison's sloop of war.

His skin crawling, Oliver replaced the sketches and returned the book to the drawer. Lefebvre was watching the harbors, seeing what came and went. It was only a matter of time before troop transports might sail, if Horse Guards so ordered. That news could send a fast ship to France to deliver the news and an appropriate response. Napoleon was no fool. And if no transport sailed, then Boney had no fears of further British aid to France.

He looked for correspondence. The room was small and he located nothing of a letter to Lord Ratliffe, or anyone else. Still, the open ink bottle on the table, with fresh ink on the quill tip, hinted a letter.

He stood in the center of the room. *Where would I think no one would look for a letter?* he asked himself. He raised the mattress. Nothing. Too simple. *No one does that,* he thought.

Then he dropped to his knees and felt under the bed for the night jar. He pulled it out quietly, and there was a letter resting on top, ink still damp. *Cousin,* read the salutation in French. He could make out the first paragraph, which told of Christmas.

He heard footsteps on the first flight of stairs. The next paragraph began with more trivial commentary, then this sentence: *No transports yet. I wish I knew what Horse Guards intends...* That was all. He replaced the letter and slid the chamber pot under the bed. He was back in the room across the hall, door just closed, his heart thundering in his chest, when Henri Lefebvre turned the key in the lock across the hall.

Good God, did I remember to lock it again? Oliver asked himself. He sighed when he heard Lefebvre click open the door. *I guess I did. I think I have a totally grey head now,* Oliver thought. *Give me a frigate any day. I'm no good at spying.*

He had no choice but to remain where he was, which chafed him no end, thinking of General Lefebvre-Desnouettes, detained at Cheltenham, and obviously to be the recipient of that letter. Perhaps letters and drawings went to Lord Ratliffe, who funneled them to the general. *Cousin,* he thought. *I have no proof of anything else.*

When he was about to explode from impatience, the dinner bell rang at the foot of the stairs. *You'd better be hungry, Henri,* he thought.

Lefebvre was. Within five minutes, he had locked his door and gone downstairs. Oliver forced himself to wait a few more minutes, then, shoes in hand, left his room and padded quietly downstairs, where Pete was waiting for him.

He put on his shoes and pulled Pete outside the front door for a hurried conversation. "I found some evidence, but he's naming no Admiralty names," he told the old sailor. "I've got to get rid of him before I sail, but I'm not up to murder. I'd welcome any suggestions."

"I have one, sor," Pete said. "Have ye noticed what's riding at anchor in the Cattewater?"

"I haven't looked yet."

"Two East India merchants, the *Norfolk Revels* and the *Tidewater.*"

"The *Revels?* I know her captain. Durfee and I were midshipmen together. Well, Pete? I'm slow here."

"Nah. You're tired and have other matters on your mind. They're both short of crew and the *Revels* sails to India in two days."

Maybe he wasn't so slow. "Pete, might you know where Captain Durfee is staying?"

"Where else but the Drake?" Pete coughed. "Does he owe you a favor?"

"More than one."

He found Captain Durfee at the perpetual whist game. A whispered conversation in the hall, smothered laughter from Durfee and detailed instructions on where to find Lefebvre sufficed. Oliver was back at the Mulberry within the hour.

He knocked on the door this time. To his heart's delight, Nana opened it and walked straight into his arms. He could have held her there for hours, except that he didn't have hours.

There was time to kiss her, though; he hoped he'd never be in so much hurry that he couldn't take a moment to savor her sweet lips, and relish the way she held him so close, as though he would disappear if she didn't.

"Oliver, we had a fire in the kitchen," she said.

"Everyone's all right?"

"The only casualties were the kitchen curtains. I have no idea how it happened." She hauled him in close again. "Oliver, I'm already missing you and you haven't left yet."

They laughed together. He pulled her into the sitting room and closed the door. *Now what?* he asked himself. *I've never done this before. Let's see if she'll let me take her onto my lap. That was easy.*

"Nana, I did two things in London that you'll have to know about," he began, then could have slapped himself, because it sounded so stupid. *Dolt,* he thought, *she can hardly overlook a fortune and a special license.*

"Whatever it was, I'm certain it's a good idea," she told him, nestling into him in that lovely, boneless way he so enjoyed. "Maybe," she amended. "I'm still not certain about the pearl."

Oh, Lord, that dratted pearl. And she thought *that* was extravagant? Better just spit it out. "Nana, I went to Grey's Inn and registered a will leaving everything I own to you."

"You did *what?*"

At least she didn't screech like her father. He looked down at her face. No mottled color, just suddenly pale.

"You heard me, Nana. Everything." He thought it prudent not to mention just how much "everything" really was. A thousand pounds a year would sound grand enough to any inmate of the Mulberry. He could break the news to her later, maybe thirty years from now when they had grandchildren.

"I'm almost afraid to ask what the second thing was you did," she commented. "Purchase Bedlam as a domicile? You know you'll never live that far from the ocean."

"Uh, not quite." He pulled her away from him so he could look her directly in the face. "Nana, I bought a special license. Will you marry me?"

If he thought she was pale before, she went even whiter. "You can't be serious," she said finally. "What will people think?"

This wasn't going well. "I've told the First Lord of the Admiralty I'm getting…well, I want to get married… He reminded me of the many times I've said I would never do such a poppycock thing."

"But you didn't tell him who I was?"

"Well, no, I hadn't asked you."

The good thing was, she hadn't leaped up from his lap, even though she was sitting upright now. She put her hands on his chest, but at least she wasn't pushing. He could see all kinds of emotions crossing her expressive face, the face that would never fare well in card games, or hide any honest feeling. The look she ended up with was a measuring one, as if trying to figure out how to tell him what he needed to hear. He almost didn't want her to speak.

"Captain, men like you don't marry bastards."

She said it quietly, gently, as though trying to remind him of the facts of life. *You lovely lady,* he thought. *I had better be as honest.*

"Maybe they don't, Nana, but you're the only lady who has ever held my total, undivided attention."

"Most would not call me a lady."

He could hear uncertainty in her voice now. "They would be wrong, Nana."

Then it was wrenched out of her, like fingernails ripped from a hand. "I would die if you were ever ashamed of me, Oliver!"

This wasn't going as he had planned. Gracefully, and with total composure, she got off his lap, smoothed down her dress and folded her hands in front of her.

"Nana, I…"

She stopped him with her hand placed gently on his head. "This isn't a good idea, Oliver, as much as I love you."

He could have groaned out loud then, but he could see she was poised to leave the room, so he remained silent and still. He felt her fingers trembling on his scalp. He could see how she struggled for words, not finding any. She took her hand off his head.

"Captain."

He felt his heart sink into his shoes at the word.

"Captain, everyone has a place in this world. I think now that part of my Bath education was to remind me of that. My father seemed to understand it."

"He was wrong," Oliver interrupted. He tried to rise, but she put her hand on his shoulder this time, forcing him down.

She took a deep breath, pulling up strength from somewhere, and looked him in the eye. "I won't have you a laughingstock of the fleet, unable to command the respect of your superiors, peers and crew, and trapped in thankless assignments, because you followed your heart instead of your brains and married an illegitimate woman with nothing to recommend her."

He didn't know what tack to take then, what plea would dissolve the determined look on her face, making her appear both absurdly young, with her short hair, and aged because of the sorrow in her eyes.

"Nana, I've been following my brains for nearly twenty years, and they have gotten me nowhere," he said, biting off each word. "I had all the answers. I was even smug about it."

He watched her face, thinking—was it wishful thinking?—that there was some wavering in her resolve. He spoke more gently then. "Will you at least consider the matter?"

He knew, as he spoke, that he had lost. He had to sail with the tide, and she knew it. Time was his worst enemy and her greatest ally. Like the oyster's answer to irritation in its shell, time would smooth over her disappointment and strengthen her resolve. The resulting pearl, so beautiful, would only prove she was right.

"Think about it," he repeated. "Nana, I love you."

She closed her eyes against the pain his words seemed to cause her, and she swallowed. "I'll think about it," she said, and fled the room.

Gran had kept dinner waiting for him in the kitchen, but after Oliver stared at the food until the gravy hardened, she removed the plate. He knew he should go to his ship, but he stayed where he was, wishing Nana would come out of her room.

He wanted to blame someone. There was Gran, who had every reason to hate the navy. He knew how she felt about him, and officers like him who lived deep when in port and abandoned women all around the world. Her own daughter had been such a victim.

He glanced at her, sitting silent by the stove, staring into space. He could destroy her with a word, and crumble the Mulberry into ruin.

It was easier to blame the times, Napoleon and certainly himself. He knew nothing about courtship and marriage because he had steeled himself against it, refusing to consider something as preposterous as love in time of war.

How proud can a man be? he asked himself in misery. How arrogant to think that he was not like other mortals, who fell in love. Now that it had happened to him, he couldn't convince the love of his life to take his hand and walk with him, even if the journey would be uncertain, at best. He was the least worthy of all.

It was a galling thought and it propelled him to his feet. "I have to talk to her," he told Gran, and left the kitchen.

"She isn't in her room," Gran called after him.

He stopped in the doorway. "Where…where is she?"

"I don't know."

He went back into the kitchen and stood before Gran. "What do you mean?"

He hadn't meant to snap it out, but that was all he knew. Gran, bless her, seemed to understand.

"She grabbed your boat cloak and ran out of here," the woman said.

He could have sunk to the ground with relief. There was

only one place she could be. "I know where she is," he said. "Gran, come with me and talk to her. Please."

Gran shook her head. "She won't listen to me." She stood up then and took him by the arm, clinging to him in tears until he felt obliged to put his arm around her. This was not the flinty innkeeper but a woman still groping her way around her own enormous loss, twenty-one years earlier.

"She won't listen because you've spent her whole life warning her against mariners?"

She nodded and sobbed harder against his chest. He felt only pity then, and held her close.

"Never mind, then. Never mind," he crooned.

They just stood there, companions in misery, until the woman in the doorway cleared her throat.

"Mrs. Massie, will you let go of that post captain and secure me a room? And by the way, what is going on?"

Startled, Oliver looked around to see Mrs. Brittle, the wife of his sailing master, standing in the doorway leading to the outside hall. He let go of Gran, who continued to sob.

"Mrs. Brittle, she won't have me," he said, sounding like a schoolboy, and for once, not caring.

"You're a little young for her, sir!" she retorted. When he did not laugh, she sobered up immediately. "Please don't tell me something's happened to that pretty little Nana."

The words tumbled out of him. "I proposed to her, and all she could think about was how bad that would be for me, to marry someone illegitimate and poor. And now she's bolted. Capered off."

Mrs. Brittle came into the room. "My goodness, Captain, we have to remedy that right away."

"We?" he asked, feeling suddenly hopeful.

"Me. I went through this some thirty years ago."

He could have cried. "You'd help me?"

"Of course!" she declared. "You're a wonderful catch for any female, even if you are a bit gruff and get mighty thin about the mouth when things don't go your way."

"That would be anytime this last ten years," he admitted. He looked at her, a question in his eyes. "Why are you here, if I may ask?"

"Simple. I was hoping you would release your officers and petty officers for a day or two. Since the *Tireless* is in port, I'd like to see Daniel."

"I can, although we're sailing with the tide tomorrow."

Mrs. Brittle put her gloves back on. "Tell me where she is, then, and you go out to the *Tireless*."

He hesitated, and she fixed him with a look not unlike one of his own. "I've a hankering for Daniel, Captain Worthy! And you want Nana."

"Oh, I do."

"Then where is she?"

He smiled. "On the guildhall back steps."

Mrs. Brittle nodded, then spoke to Gran. "Dry your eyes, dearie." She held out her arm to him. "You can escort me to the guildhall, then find a waterman to get you to the *Tireless*."

"Aye, aye, sir," he told her.

The steps weren't the same without Oliver beside her to keep her warm. And by now, the boat cloak was starting to smell of roses, and no longer his briny self. From the guildhall steps, Nana couldn't see the *Tireless,* and that was just as well. Tomorrow afternoon, when Oliver sailed with the tide, she'd stay away from the Hoe, too.

In time, she knew he would come to realize the narrowness of his escape from marriage to her. She didn't know what she was going to do about his willing all his income to her, but he was a good captain. He would probably stay alive and outlive her anyway, so a will concocted on impulse wouldn't be an issue. She planned to die of heartbreak by Sunday noon.

Nana rested her chin in her hands. *You silly nod, people only die of heartbreak in very bad novels,* she reminded herself.

It was dark now, and getting colder. The street was silent. She almost thought she could hear water lapping on the distant docks. With a pang that made her sob out loud, she knew it was a sound she never wanted to hear again, as long as she lived. Maybe she would take a little of the captain's money and run away to the interior of Canada, where there was only ice and snow, and no seagulls.

She heard people on the street then, a woman laughing and then a man joining in. She sat up. She knew that laugh; in fact, she adored it. *I suppose I must face him,* she thought. *Only a coward would do what I am doing.*

She heard someone coming around the guildhall walk, and braced herself. She looked closer. It wasn't Oliver. She heard his footsteps continuing down to the harbor, to her utter dismay.

It wasn't Gran, either, come to take her home, and congratulate her on her resolve in not marrying a sailor.

"Dearie, do you mean I have to drag my bones up all those steps just to sit with you?"

"Mrs. *Brittle?*" Nana asked, astounded.

"The very same. Hang it all, you're worth the climb."

Puffing and fanning herself, in spite of the cool air, Mrs. Brittle plumped herself down beside Nana.

"What…what…"

"What am I here for?" the woman asked when she could speak. "Your wedding tomorrow, before the tide turns."

Nana burst into tears, burrowing herself into Mrs. Brittle's cushiony bosom. She cried until her face was slick, then accepted the handkerchief the sailing master's wife held out to her, no questions asked.

"You know I can't marry Captain Worthy," Nana said finally.

Mrs. Brittle chuckled and pulled her closer. "Why not? Are you already married to someone else?"

"Of course not," Nana said, feeling out to sea. "You know why, and my reasons are indisputable."

"They certainly are, dearie. I'm glad you were able to sort out the captain. He needed to be told he was foolish to expect any happiness."

Nana had expected a scold from Nora Brittle, but there was none. She just held her close. When she spoke, the woman's voice was tender.

"I really came all the way over bad roads from Torquay because I wanted to be with my Daniel before he sailed." She chuckled. "He's not much to look at. He weighs too much, and he has indigestion when he eats anything with onions. His grammar's better than mine by a long chalk, but his Geordie accent is still so thick you could slice it. The dratted man can't remember our children's birthdays to save his wretched hide. No wonder, really, because he was never there when any of them were born."

Nana felt a huge weight leaving her shoulders. "You love him anyway, don't you?"

"Heavens, yes."

Nana took a deep breath. "Aren't you afraid he'll sail away and you'll never see him again?"

"All the time. It's my worst nightmare."

"But you'd marry him all over again?"

"Yes."

Mrs. Brittle pulled her close again, and Nana felt brave enough to admit her worst fear. "It's more than just being an innkeeper's granddaughter," she whispered. "I'm illegitimate."

The woman chuckled. "So am I. Haven't the slightest idea who my parents are. I grew up in a workhouse and was a scullery maid in Torquay, like your Sal." She hugged Nana. "You had Gran and a Bath education, though."

It was all said so calmly, but the implication was as obvious as if Mrs. Brittle had thundered it from the pulpit in St. Paul's Cathedral.

"So why am I being so foolish?" Nana asked out loud.

"I'm not saying there won't be a barrier or two for both of you," Mrs. Brittle told her. "You'll always run into people who don't know what love is."

Nana nodded, drawing comfort from Mrs. Brittle's generous embrace. "I hope he's coming back. I think I broke his heart."

She could feel Mrs. Brittle's chuckle more than hear it. "He'd better be back, and with Daniel! I didn't come all this way over bad roads to sleep by myself tonight. Just wait here a minute more, dearie. The captain's tough. They'll be along."

They were. In a few minutes, Nana heard the men talking as they walked together to the guildhall. In another moment Mrs. Brittle stood up and waved to her husband, who came halfway up the steps to retrieve her.

"Is there room at the inn, Nana?" he called to her.

"For you, always," she said, her heart full.

Mrs. Brittle waved to her from the bottom of the steps. "See you tomorrow, dearie. Good evening, Captain. I left you a warm spot."

And then it was the two of them. Without a word, Oliver seated himself on the step Mrs. Brittle had vacated. He didn't say anything, but his arm went around her gently as she leaned against his shoulder. In another minute she had found that comfortable place under his arm where she fit so well.

She didn't know how to begin, but she knew she had to speak first. "My hair is awfully short, and I only have three dresses. Well, two. The third one has a scorch mark up the front."

"Does it?"

"Oliver, I..."

He let out a long breath. "Thank God that captain went away!"

She kissed his cheek. "Does he bother you?"

"All the time."

"Well, I love him, too. And if you don't mind all my shortcomings..."

He didn't speak for the longest time, and when he did, she could hear the catch in his voice.

"Your hair will grow," he said patiently. "As for three—or two—dresses, I probably wouldn't know one from the other." He paused then, and she waited. "My life has no guarantees, Nana. I could die tomorrow."

"I could, too, my love," she reminded him. "It's the great leveler. Why do you think you're so special?"

He chuckled and didn't say anything else, content to hold her. After a few more minutes, she straightened up.

"My rump is cold and these stones are hard. I think you'd better propose again."

"I'd rather not get down on one knee on these steps." He turned a little to look at her and put his hands on each side of her face, drawing her close. "Eleanor Massie, I love you more than I can adequately express. Will you marry me tomorrow morning early, so I can take the *Tireless* out of Plymouth Sound with the tide?"

"That was so loverlike," she told him, and kissed his lips. "Yes, a million times over."

"I don't have a ring."

"You have a license."

They laughed.

Chapter Fourteen

Oliver returned Nana to the Mulberry Inn, holding her hand all the way, kissed her good-night and spent a few minutes next with the vicar of St. Andrews, who looked over the special license, then finally nodded. "The navy. The navy" was all the man said, after a shake of his head.

He had another waterman row him back to the *Tireless* that night, where he told Mr. Proudy and Mr. Ramseur the good news, and packed up his best uniform and sword.

"You're all welcome to the wedding tomorrow morning at St. Andrews at nine o'clock," he told his highly appreciative audience of lieutenants. "Any of the men who wish to come may do so. We'll sail at one o'clock, with the tide."

"I'll pray for a sudden squall, falling barometer and a foul east wind," Proudy said. "A man ought to have one night with his bride. Even you, sir."

The lieutenants were both laughing when the bosun piped him over the side again.

Oliver stopped at the Drake long enough to invite Mrs. Fillion to St. Andrews, and asked her to spread the news to any of her cohorts in the Barbican.

"I shouldn't wonder but the church will be filled," the innkeep said. "Stop by here afterward for a wedding breakfast, Captain."

"You can manage something on such short notice?" Oliver asked, touched.

"We'll do nearly anything for Nana," she told him. "Remember that."

Gran met him in the hall when he returned. She put up her hand as he opened his mouth for another apology.

"Nana's twenty-one and of legal age, Captain Worthy."

He felt like a schoolboy before the headmaster, and not the veteran captain he was. "I'm sorry to dredge up so many comparisons, Mrs. Massie."

"This is different. I'd rather she didn't marry a seafaring man, but you're the best of the lot, and even Nana is entitled to a lapse in judgment."

He smiled because she did. His grin broadened when she kissed him on the cheek, and informed him that Nana already knew what to expect on her wedding night.

"We sail with the tide, Mrs. Massie," he said, his face bright red. "That'll have to wait."

"Oh, really? Everyone at St. Andrews tomorrow will be praying for terrible weather. I hope you've tossed out a weather anchor on the *Tireless*."

He had. He wasn't the son of a vicar for nothing.

She sniffed the air. "Take a bath. You tars always smell so salty."

Oliver had blown out the candle, but wasn't asleep yet when Nana knocked on his door. He hadn't expected that. "Yes?" he asked, hesitant.

"May I come in?"

"Briefly. Briefly. A man can only stand so much."

She came in, closed the door behind her and pulled up a chair to his bed. Even in the gloom, he felt her excitement.

"Mrs. Fillion just sent me a dress. Gran is taking it in right now. It's blue."

The words tumbled out of her, and he smiled. He put his hands behind his head, the better not to touch her. She smelled dewy and fresh, as if she had just come from the bathroom. He could probably cajole Pete into heating some water for him in there in the morning, especially after Mrs. Massie's admonition.

She didn't speak for a long moment, and he began to wonder why she had come.

"I have a confession, Oliver."

The words came out so quietly he wondered if he had heard her right. She looked so serious, he thought he should lighten the mood.

"That boy who kissed you in Miss Pym's garden kissed you twice instead of once?"

"Just once. It's not that," she said simply. "I don't want to deceive you, mainly because I am certain you would never deceive me."

He felt a pang, considering that he hadn't told her about any of his encounters with her father, and certainly not his suspicions. Some things Nana probably didn't need to know.

"You'd better confess then, before I decide to tickle it out of you." He made as if to rise.

"Oh, no!" she said. "If you did that, Gran would be really disappointed in us."

"Well, then?" he prompted. "I doubt it's something we can't clear up right now, considering the heavy weather we've just been through."

She took a deep breath. "When he was here a few weeks ago, Mr. Ramseur told me how wealthy you are. I already know."

"That's it?" he asked, bewildered.

"Yes!" She looked at him earnestly. "I don't want you to ever think for one second that I love you because you are wealthy."

He couldn't help himself. He laughed out loud. She leaned closer and put her hand over his mouth. "Hush! What will Gran and Pete think?"

He caught her hand as she tried to remove it, and kissed her fingers. "Nana, there's only one way to reassure me— when did you first decide you loved me?"

She managed to extricate her hand from his grasp, but she took it only as far as his chest, where she rested it over his heart.

"Well?"

"I'm thinking," she scolded him. "Don't rush me. Oh, I know. It was that first night when I leaned you forward to put that wheat poultice around your neck."

He stared at her, mystified.

"You needed me," she said simply. "And you're so handsome. That made me pay attention, and then I couldn't look away from you. After a while, I didn't want to look away ever again." She shrugged. "Don't laugh at that. I suppose marriages have started on stranger footings."

"No one ever accused me of being handsome."

"Then I don't know what is wrong with the females in naval ports around the world. They must be blind. Good night, my love."

She left as quietly as she had come. He knew he wouldn't sleep all night now, but after shaping his pillow into a soft ball, he rested his head on it and closed his eyes. He opened them only once in the middle of the night, when he heard a storm shriek in from the Irish Sea. He smiled. His wedding day was going to be sleety, windy and thoroughly nasty, thank the Lord. He wouldn't dare take the *Tireless* out of Plymouth Sound.

In his bath the next morning, Oliver listened to the wind howl and try to bully its way inside the Mulberry like an unwanted lodger. The pounding rain was music to his ears. After a thorough scrub, he decided there wasn't much he could do about his briny smell. He doubted he could ever rid his body of it. *At least I haven't seawater in my veins,* he thought, *despite what my crew thinks.*

He sat in the bath until the water began to cool, still a little surprised at himself over the coming event. Mr. Brittle had agreed to stand up with him. His sailing master, a man at sea thirty years without mishap, could by his mere presence, reassure Nana that men did survive service with the Royal Navy.

He and Nana had decided last night not to be foolish about seeing each other before the wedding, considering that the Mulberry was no London hotel, and concealment impossible. Even then, he was not prepared for his first glimpse of her that morning, with little seed pearls tucked here and there in her curly hair, and wearing a powder-blue short-sleeved dress with rather more exposure of her bosom than he was accustomed to observing.

She charmed him by spinning around in her new dress, with its little flounce and puffed sleeves. "The wigmaker sent over this netting of seed pearls this morning," she said, after another pirouette. "Gran says I must wear a shawl or I'll catch cold. My, you look handsome."

"Same old me, Nana. I did get my best uniform from the *Tireless* last night." He kissed her cheek and whispered, "Gran says I smell too much like salt water."

She sniffed. "I like it." She took his arm then, suddenly serious. "Oliver, I'm just about scared to death."

"Me, too, Nana. What a pair we are."

They rode to St. Andrews together in a hackney, Nana bundled in her old cloak, her cheeks rosy, her wonderful eyes so bright. "I hope you have no cause to regret this," he told her, swept out to sea by her beauty.

"I won't," she said, her words spoken softly into his sleeve. "Not now."

When the hackney pulled up in front of the old church, he was amazed at the crowd of people going into St. Andrews. There was Matthew, grinning and looking well-scrubbed within an inch of his life.

And there was Captain Dennison from the *Goldfinch*, which must have slid into port just ahead of last night's storm. *I must find a minute to talk to him, and see what the score is,* he thought, his mind returning to war.

Nana stopped as they came inside the church. "Do you know, the day after you arrived at the Mulberry, I came here with a cod in a basket and lit a candle for you? It was your pence, too."

He laughed out loud, which caused heads to turn, especially those of his crew, who probably had no idea that he possessed body parts and passions, much less a laugh. Even Mr. Ramseur looked startled.

Taking a deep breath, he turned Nana over to Pete, who was dressed in his best, tucked his hat under his arm and walked toward the front of the church, to stand beside Mr. Brittle. On the way up the aisle, he stopped for a word with Dennison, who looked exhausted. "Come to the reception," Oliver whispered. "You can tell me the news."

"It's not good, but could be worse," Dennison whispered back. "Go aft, Worthy, before I flog you!"

"Cold feet, sir?" Mr. Brittle asked, when he reached the front.

"Freezing. Why do men do this?"

"Because we're men, sir. It's the only legal way to get the women we crave."

He couldn't help but smile at that, even as he watched Eleanor Maria Massie, white-faced and serious, standing beside Pete Carter, hanging on to him for dear life. Her face had not been out of his thoughts for longer than a five-minute stretch since he met her. If he died tomorrow or fifty years from now, her name would be on his lips as a last sacrament.

As the processional began and everyone rose, he thought of the brother officers he had stood up with, men with more courage than he, obviously. The most recent had been two years ago in Portsmouth, when Captain Nathaniel Barker married his lovely lady. Six weeks later, Nate and all hands went down with their ship in the Baltic.

I can't do this, he thought. He must have stirred, because Mr. Brittle spoke to him out of the corner of his mouth. "Stand right there, laddie," he whispered.

He stood. He was glad he did, even though he seemed to hear the vicar's questions from a long way off, and even Nana, so close, looked as though observed through the wrong end of a telescope. He gave his responses firmly, and so did Nana. And then she was his wife. He could have wept from the sheer joy of it, but that would have tried his crew beyond their capacity, so he refrained.

And then it was down the aisle to sign the registry, then leave the church between a corridor of cheering sailors. Out in the sleet and wind, Dennison led the way to a waiting post chaise.

"I'm *not* going to Admiralty with you," Oliver said.

"Didn't ask you," Dennison joked, with a wink at Nana, who blushed. "She's a beauty. I can't imagine where you found her." His face became deadly serious. "You need to

know what's going on. Let me drive you the tiny distance to
the Drake."

Oliver helped Nana into the post chaise, happy enough to
be authorized now to give her a gentle boost with his hand on
her rump. Nice, that.

"Business always first, Mrs. Worthy," Dennison said, after
he directed the coachman to the Drake, three blocks away. He
leaned forward across the narrow space. "Oliver, there's
trouble in Austria. Boney has gone back over the border and
left the pursuit of Sir John to Marshal Soult."

"Slowing down, then?"

"Only slightly. It's a bad retreat through snow and mountains to Corunna. I'm to report to Admiralty and direct transports be sent immediately. It could be a last stand there, if we
don't supply them for Sir John's army."

"We knew it was coming," Oliver said. *There's no way that
Henri Lefebvre needs to see transports languishing in Plymouth
suddenly rigged out and made ready to sail. No way in the
world,* he thought.

The post chaise stopped. Dennison opened the door. "Now
I'm off to Exeter, Honiton, Axminster, Bridport…"

"…Dorchester, Milbourne, Blandford and Woodyates Inn,"
Oliver continued. "It's the route to London, Nana. We've
memorized it." He gripped Dennison's hand. "A word of
advice, Virgil—take your news either to Lord Mulgrave or
directly to Horse Guards."

Dennison questioned him with his eyes, but nodded. He
glanced at Nana, then back to Oliver, his eyes merry. "And
what about a kiss for the bride?"

"Nana makes up her own mind," Oliver replied. "He is a
good friend, Nana love."

She obligingly turned a cheek in Dennison's direction. He

pulled her to him and smacked her on the lips, anyway. "Didn't your mum warn you about sailors, Mrs. Worthy? Fair sailing, Oliver."

Oliver helped her out, and Dennison closed the door. "See you back at Ferrol Station!" he called. "Be gentle with him, Nana!"

Nana pressed her hands to her cheeks. "My blushes," she murmured. "Is he a *friend?*"

"One of the best, Nana love."

There wasn't time to talk with Nana, once they went inside. Mrs. Fillion whisked her away into a circle of women, which made him cringe inside, thinking of all the good advice they were offering his darling. *It's a good thing receptions aren't held before the wedding,* he decided, as his own crew gathered with other officers in Plymouth and immediately began to talk shop. He looked wistfully at Nana several times, wishing to get her away from everyone.

And then he saw Lefebvre, laughing and chatting with other celebrants, and remembered his duty. He looked around. Captain Durfee was easy enough to spot, with his booming laugh. When an interval offered itself, he took the captain of the East India merchantman aside, but still in view of Lefebvre.

"That's the man," he said, indicating with a nod of his head. "Dennison's on his way to Admiralty with more news of the war, and the last thing we need is that Frenchman sketching what goes in and out of the Sound in the next few days."

Durfee looked Lefebvre up and down. "Appears the laddie is about to embark on a voyage to Bombay. Where might I find him tomorrow?"

Oliver gave him several suggestions and Durfee nodded. "We'll nab him before he has time to sharpen a pencil. Who knows? Maybe he'll even make a good sailor."

"If he doesn't, leave him in India," Oliver said. "I'd prefer it."

"That I can do." Durfee held out his hand. "Now, why don't you lay aside your duty—and your uniform—and enjoy some portside comforts?"

Oliver shook his friend's hand, too embarrassed to say anything. Durfee went back into the public room, after a sidelong look at the Frenchman.

Nana gave him no grief. He located her in the crowd and led her to the stairs to sit down for a brief conversation.

"I'll be back at the Mulberry as soon as I can, but it will probably be after dark," he said.

"And what if the wind changes?" she teased, her hand on his chest.

"It won't dare." He nudged her shoulder, enjoying the liberty of such a casual gesture. "I suspect Mrs. Fillion and her friends have been giving you all manner of good advice."

She turned to look at him, her face so close to his that her eyes looked crossed. "I intend to ignore at least ninety-eight percent of it. Mrs. Fillion did mention one thing."

"And?"

"Perhaps I will tell you afterward."

At least she didn't seem frightened of him, Oliver thought, as he rounded up his officers for the trip to the *Tireless*. Pete assured him he would see Nana back to the Mulberry. None of the guests seemed surprised by his departure, but why would they? This was a navy town that moved with the rhythm of tides and winds. Puny human affairs counted little.

He noticed then that Gran wasn't there and asked Pete.

"She blubbered all through the wedding and went back to the Mulberry," he said.

"Was she happy?" Oliver asked, uncertain.

Pete nodded. "Over the moon. Women are strange creatures, sor, if you haven't noticed."

* * *

Oliver didn't return to the Mulberry until midnight, and wasn't surprised to see the inn dark, with only a lamp glowing in the small foyer. On the front table was a note in Nana's handwriting. He held it close to the lamp and smiled, amazed at how quickly she could take the chill off even a January night with a storm raging outside.

> *To whom it may concern: Nana Worthy is upstairs in Captain Worthy's old room. She is not a light sleeper, but she always wakes up in a good mood.*

The room was dark, but there was still a glow from the fireplace. He just stood in the doorway for a precious moment, savoring the sight of her in his bed. She was on her side, facing away from the door, so he could admire the curve of her hips. *I'm married now,* he thought. *I did what I said I would never do.* The enormity of his responsibility to his wife settled on him less like masonry and more like a blanket, which relieved him, since his whole life was wrapped up in duty.

This was different from duty. He was used to dealing with forces he could not change, only bend to. He hadn't wanted a woman who would challenge him at every turn; he didn't need that. He had married a woman who would love him, and let him go, because she was a child of the Channel, who understood external forces.

He was out of his clothes in a minute and into his nightshirt. Nana had left him plenty of room in the bed. After locking the door, he climbed in beside her, molding himself to her shape and putting his arm over her and around her waist. Her eyes still closed, she turned her face toward his and he kissed her.

To his amusement, she muttered something and backed herself in closer to him. He kissed her neck then, happy for her short hair, which meant he did not have to fight his way through tangles and tresses to get to it. She obliged him by unbuttoning her nightgown and sliding it off her shoulders so he could kiss her there, too.

"Thought you weren't coming," she murmured, her eyes still closed. "Tried to stay awake. Failed miserably."

He laughed into her neck, then unbuttoned more of her nightgown so he could touch her breasts. She put her hand up involuntarily, as though to stop him, then sighed and put it on his cheek instead, as he continued his exploration.

It had been a long time since he had enjoyed the comfort of a woman. Even then, he didn't remember any other woman's skin to be as soft as his wife's. Her breasts had a pleasant weight to them now, thanks to improved menus at the Mulberry. Thank God she was no longer wand-thin. He ran an experimental hand across her ribs, pleased with the result.

"I'm nervous," she whispered, "but I think it's time to make my nightgown disappear, don't you?"

He couldn't have agreed more. She sat up then, and they bumped heads. She laughed softly as she pulled her nightgown off, rolled it into a ball and pitched it toward the chair by the window. "That's so if I get cold later, I'll be able to find it."

"You won't get cold," he assured her, pitching his night-shirt next to hers.

He wanted to see her better, but the way she still put her hand over her breasts made him think she wasn't ready for a lamp near the bed. That could wait. He could see her well enough in the light from the fireplace and he knew what to do.

He settled beside her again, running his hands over her body until she accepted the idea and relaxed, giving herself over to what he hoped was the gentleness of his fingers. She did have beautiful breasts, and no objection to his kissing them. Her breath began to come faster, especially after he took a nipple in his mouth. She murmured something that sounded like his name.

He knew she was shy, so he took her hand and wrapped it around his growing member. She hesitated only a moment, then began to caress it gently.

By now, he had put one hand behind her head, and the other on her pubic mound, where he massaged her rhythmically. Her hand went involuntarily again to her privates when he coaxed her legs open, then dropped to her side. Gradually her clenched fist relaxed, as her breathing accelerated and his fingers went inside her.

She was more than ready, but still, this was her first time. He had never deflowered a woman before, and this was his wife, who would be the only female he ever shared his bed with again. No sense in rushing things, no matter how long that lifetime turned out to be. Instead of mounting her then, he ran his hand down the inside of her thighs, relishing their warmth and smoothness. How did women stay so soft? he asked himself. It may have been his last coherent thought, because she took her hand from his organ and nudged his hip, trying to slide herself under him.

"You're certain?" he whispered into her ear, and then kissed it as she murmured something that didn't even sound like words.

He rose up then, and other than reminding her a time or two to relax, if she could, he moved inside her, amazed at the simplicity of her response as she did as he asked, putting her legs around him, anchoring him to her.

"You're finally close enough," she managed to say, as she

moved in rhythm with him, chuckling the time or two she got off rhythm, and then applying herself wholeheartedly to learning the mating dance that had been going on since Adam and Eve left the Garden in some disgrace, and struck out on their own.

He did not expect her to climax this first time, and she didn't, but splayed her hands across his back as he came, as though trying to keep him safe at such a vulnerable time. He had never felt so protected before in his entire life, by this simple act. His brain was mush, but some imp told him she could probably be ferocious in his defense. The idea was absurd, but he tucked it away to consider, probably during a late night when he was standing watch and wishing he was back in his wife's bed. *That will probably be any night until this war ends,* he thought.

When he finished, he didn't feel like moving, so he didn't. She offered no objection to his weight beyond rearranging her legs on his legs, the better to support him, and beginning a slow massage of his back that roused him more than he thought possible, considering his exertions.

He finally rose up on his elbows. "Do let me know if I'm cutting off all circulation," he whispered. "Nana, I love you. There just aren't words."

She nodded, raising up her head to kiss him. Her hair was sweaty now, which brought the rose fragrance of her into a fullness of odor that made him breathe deep. He sat up finally, not leaving her, but relishing the sight of her body beneath his, her arms extended across the bed now, nothing of shyness over her bare breasts anymore. She just looked at him, her eyes lingering on the place where they were still joined together, then traveling up his chest and to his eyes. Her gaze was so direct and honest and still virginal, in a way that would always touch him, and probably arouse him, too. She was a woman in a thousand, and he was far luckier than any man he knew.

He left her with some reluctance, lying down next to her. Her hand was under his head this time, and he enjoyed the comfort of it when she drew him close so he could rest his head on her breast.

"I trust I met some expectations," she said, which made him laugh.

"Exceeded them, Nana love," he assured her. "I hope I didn't hurt you."

She shook her head. "I feel sore in places I've never felt sore before, but I expect that will pass."

"Most assuredly." He couldn't help himself then. "You don't see too many bowlegged females traipsing about, do you?"

She jerked the pillow out from under her head and hit him with it, which made him whoop and tickle her until she stopped hitting him because she was laughing so hard. She threw the pillow after him when he got up, but lay back a moment later and allowed him to wipe her privates with warm water from the brass can someone had thoughtfully provided hours ago. In another moment he was back in bed, and she was curled up against his chest this time.

When he was quiet, she put her hands over his ears.

"You're listening for the wind, aren't you?" she asked.

"I have to."

"Not tonight you don't," she told him. "Go to sleep, my love. The sea is always out there."

Chapter Fifteen

Nana woke up to silence. The wind had stopped. She looked at her husband who slept so peacefully beside her, his back to her, his shoulders bare. He still lay carefully composed, as though in a sleeping cot swinging from a deck beam. She watched him sleep, admiring his well-developed shoulders, appreciating the way they tapered down to a fine waist. If anything, he was on the thin side, too. *Too bad I cannot bully him the way he bullies me about eating,* she thought, then reminded herself that bullying wasn't precisely her nature.

She moved closer to him and put her arm across his chest. He grasped her hand immediately, which surprised her.

"I didn't know you were awake," she said, resting her cheek against his back.

"I was just lying here thinking how badly I don't want to move," he told her, as he turned over to face her. He sighed. "But there's a frigate down there and it needs a captain."

She ran her hand across his face, feeling the stubble of his whiskers. "I know it's selfish, but will you have time to think about me, once you're back on the blockade?"

He kissed her palm as her fingers caressed his face. "I

already do, Nana. It can get pretty quiet on an early-morning watch—just you, me and an ocean." He looked toward the window, where the dawn was making an effort.

Nana kissed his chest. "Right now it's just you and me."

He didn't need a gilt-framed invitation. Their first coupling last night had been followed by another one in the wee hours, and now this: more intense because she knew they were both feeling the imminent separation. She gave herself to him gladly, more accustomed now to the feel of him inside her, and the rhythm of his love, which this time carried her to another level.

She tried not to cry out. This was an inn, after all, with paying lodgers entitled to their own rest. She buried her face in his shoulder, gasping as she clutched him across his back, attempting the impossible of absorbing him and trying to turn herself inside out, at the same time. He climaxed after her.

"How does anyone survive this?" she whispered as he kissed her sweaty hair.

"It's a dangerous business," he agreed, slowly continuing his motion until her eyes rolled back in her head again. "Really dangerous," he added, when she lay still finally. He kissed her shoulder, then took a playful bite of it.

He did not leave her, but when he turned his head, she knew he was thinking about the ocean again, and the *Tireless,* and the men waiting for him on board. Almost instinctively, she tightened her legs around him, then relaxed them when he looked down at her and shook his head.

"I have to go," he reminded her. He didn't move, though, and she was content to bear his weight until that moment when he did rise.

He just stood by their bed, looking at her body, as though memorizing the rest of her this time, and not just her face, as he had done on previous occasions. Before he went toward the washstand, he gave her nether hair a gentle tug. "My goodness, Nana, just look at you," he teased.

She wrapped herself in the blankets and moved into the warm spot he had vacated. She dozed while he cleaned himself and then shaved, using water from the brass can that couldn't possibly still be warm. He took his time dressing, coming over to the bed to kiss her once or twice between smallclothes, shirt, breeches and waistcoat.

He was putting his watch in his pocket when she got up, retrieved her nightgown from the chair and pulled it on. She put her arms around him, stood on tiptoe and kissed him, willing herself not to cry before he walked out the door.

"Gran told me last night she'd have some pasties on the foyer table for me to take along," he told her, speaking into her hair now, his arms as tight around her as hers around him. "I don't want you to see me off."

"I'm not sure I could," she said, her voice small. "I love you, Oliver."

"I'm fully aware of that," he replied. "I love you, Nana. A man couldn't have a better wife. My Lord, I never thought I'd be saying that." He chuckled. "I'm about to benefit from one of the hitherto unexplored prerequisites of being a post captain, my dear. When the bosun pipes me aboard and I have a disgusting smile on my face, there's not a soul on board the *Tireless* who would dare risk a rude remark."

"You *are* pretty frightening," she teased in turn. "Which reminds me—if I had the nerve, I would go to the Drake today and tell Mrs. Fillion she was absolutely right."

He held her away for a good look. "Her advice to you? In the general commotion in this room last night, I forgot. Do tell."

In spite of their intimacy, Nana felt warmth rising up her

chest and into her face. "She said, 'Don't worry, Nana. Everything fits.'"

He was still laughing as he went down the stairs.

She cried herself back to sleep after the door closed behind him, waking an hour later when the sun was truly up. She rose again and went to the window, admiring the beautiful day, the street washed clean from the rain, the Cattewater far below a bright blue, with a hint of white chop. The weather vane on the house across the road swung south: fair winds to Spain.

A modest woman, she did something she had never done before: she took off her nightgown and stood in front of the full-length mirror by the washstand, looking herself over. She smiled to see red marks on her breasts and shoulders. Beyond that, she looked the same, even though nothing was the same about her. She had been initiated into the great mystery. *I wonder what is going on inside me right now,* she thought, resting both hands on her belly. *There might be a child growing.* Even if there was not, she knew it was only a matter of time, something they had so little of.

She dressed quickly and stripped the bed, not willing for Sal to remove the sheets. She took them to the washroom of the still-dark inn, then heated herself enough water for a bath in the tin tub. She sniffed her skin, wishing it smelled of brine, but breathing nothing beyond a musty fragrance—pungent but not unpleasant—and her own roses.

When she came into the kitchen, Gran was sitting at the table, just staring into space. She smiled at Nana, who came to her side, then knelt beside the chair and put her head in her grandmama's lap.

"Oh, Gran," she whispered. "I didn't know."

"No woman really does, until it happens," Gran said.

"He said he wants us to get another maid so I won't have

to clean the rooms anymore." Nana raised her head. "I said I would, but I think I won't. Gran, I need to keep really busy."

"He'll be back."

"I wish I knew when."

Nana feared the time would drag, but it did not, mainly because Gran saw to it that she had plenty to do, from daily visits to the grocers to hemming new sheets and towels, to learning how to keep the record of hotel expenses in the ledger.

The only real surprise happened the same day the *Tireless* sailed from Plymouth Sound. Mr. Lefebvre disappeared.

She had served him breakfast at the usual hour. He left, as usual, before nine o'clock, except this time he did not return. After the second day, she asked Pete to go into his room with her.

"Suppose he returned and we did not hear him, and he is lying ill," she said.

Pete did not seem as anxious as she thought he should, but he agreed, letting her into the room and standing in the doorway while she looked around.

"I hope he didn't owe any money," he commented. "I mean, we've been cheated before," he added, which sounded to Nana like it was tacked on for her benefit.

"No, he didn't," she replied, as she stacked his sketches into a neater pile on the table. "He was paid up through the end of January, so he has another two weeks."

That afternoon, Gran sent Nana and Sal to clean Mr. Lefebvre's room. It was empty now. Pete must have cleared out the Frenchman's possessions while she was at the fish market.

He put Lefebvre's effects in the storeroom off the kitchen, which contained other goods belonging to those who, in the past century and more, had skipped Plymouth without paying the landlord. When no one was around, she looked through Mr. Lefebvre's sketches, startled to see so many of her. She found a sketch of her husband, looking somewhat severe, and tucked it in her apron pocket. *You don't look that severe when you are loving me,* she thought.

At the end of the week, she returned to the storeroom to claim some of Mr. Lefebvre's pencils. There wasn't any sense in leaving something so useful to languish in a storeroom, she told herself, even as she looked around for paper, too. To her surprise, Mr. Lefebvre's sketchbook was on the shelf now, along with the wooden case of colored pencils and watercolors he always carried.

Where had they come from? She asked Pete about them that evening. He looked at her, as though wondering whether to say more, which only aroused her suspicions.

"Pete, you obviously know more than I do, and I won't be kept in the dark," she told him, trying to sound firm with a dear person who had known her since childhood.

He still didn't rush to an explanation, and when he did speak, she did not think he confessed everything.

"He was pressed."

"What?" she exclaimed. "Is the navy that desperate? I can't see him as a useful seaman."

"The navy is always desperate," he replied, with the ghost of a smile. "You know that. But I hear one of the East India ships nabbed him. The *Norfolk Revels* left the harbor right after the *Tireless.* He's on his way to Bombay, Nana."

She left it at that, because Pete did not look inclined to say more on the subject of a missing Frenchman. She did make a request, though. "Pete, I know you have a wealth of sources in the Barbican. Please keep me informed of what news you hear from Spain."

He did, bearing tales from lighters and hoys, and ships that came and went from Plymouth. Soult was still pursuing Sir John Moore and his little army to the edge of Spain. More small ships came and went.

Late one night when the inn was quiet, Captain Dennison of the *Goldfinch* brought her a letter. "Ow! Ooh! It's too hot to handle!" he teased as he gave it to her at the door, claimed a kiss on her cheek and ran back to the post chaise. "Exeter, Honiton, Axminster!" he called.

"Bridport, Dorchester, Milbourne," she whispered after him. "On to London, my friend."

She got no farther than the foyer before the letter was open, read and in her lap.

> *Beloved, this is too short to convey even a tenth of my regard and admiration. I'd be more eloquent, but suppose it fell into French hands? Can't have them suspect for a moment that the British are human, can we? But I am, and I miss you. Prospects are grim here, but you still keep me company on my watches. Hope this finds you well and thinking of me now and then. All my love, my heart, my lights and liver, Oliver.*

A day later, the ships began to straggle into the Sound. By noon, all Plymouth knew the scope of the disaster: the army had been forced off Spain at Corunna, Sir John Moore was dead and soldiers were being conveyed to England by every means possible, from victuallers and water hoys to ships of the line.

Without waiting for Nana to ask, Pete went down to the Barbican to find out what he could. He brought back news, along with officers—some wounded, all exhausted—who were part of the overflow from Barbican hotels and Stonehouse itself, the naval hospital near the Davenport docks. They filled the rooms upstairs and arranged pallets in the dining room and sitting room for the rest.

The demand was for food and tea, then, and hot water, the first any of the men had seen in weeks, after their 250-mile retreat from Burgos to the coast through Spain's snowy mountains, dogged by the French. Nana subdued her own fears as she ran up and down stairs, carrying towels and water, and then stew made of anything Gran could find. Tired smiles from men too weary to say much were enough reward.

One of the second lieutenants reminded Nana of her husband, with his thin lips and alert air, despite weariness that seemed to come off his body in waves. When everyone had been attended to, she pulled up a chair to his pallet in the dining room.

"What of the ships?" she asked. "Did you see or hear of the *Tireless?*"

"Your man on board?" the lieutenant asked.

She nodded.

He shook his head. "I'm no salt. I can't tell ships by their numbers, but you should have seen the flags signaling up and down! I do know the frigates were darting in as close to shore as they dared, to bombard the Frogs just behind us on the heights."

That would be Oliver, she thought. That would be any of them, she amended, feeling pride in the men who called Plymouth their seaport. "That's what they do," she said simply.

There wasn't an answer. The lieutenant, leaning against the wall on his pallet, had fallen asleep with a piece of bread in his hand.

By midnight, everyone was settled down, although some of the raggedy men were already crying out from nightmares.

Nana wanted to stuff cotton in her ears and run down into the cellar, but she stayed with Gran in the kitchen, preparing pots of porridge for breakfast and calmly discussing plans for the noon meal.

"Thank God for Captain Worthy's income," Gran said as she mixed dry amounts into pots. "I'm not certain that the Mulberry, even on her best days, could afford to feed the five thousand on our two loaves and fishes."

These were not the best days, to be sure. At three in the morning, one of the captains came to her room downstairs and begged her to sit with one of his dying lieutenants. Terrified, she followed him upstairs to the room she and Oliver had used for their wedding night. A young man, his face swollen and deformed by killing frostbite, was begging for his mother.

"Just hold his hand," the captain ordered. She did more; she held him in her arms until he died.

After three days of this, she was as tired as the soldiers. On the fourth day, most were able to travel toward their regimental homes, only to be replaced by others, as more ships came into the Sound. She learned from Pete's hurried visits to the harbor that the guildhall and churches were full of rank-and-file soldiers. Some attempt was made first to put them in the unmasted ships bobbing in the Hamoaze, but even that comparatively calm pitch and yaw was too much for landlubbers. Some were then forced to lie on the docks under canvas in raw January wind, until actual room could be found.

Captain Dennison stopped briefly, on his return from Admiralty House, only to tell her he was heading back to Spain. "He'll be along soon, Mrs. Worthy," he told her, after he drank some soup but waved away more time-consuming meat and cheese. "Tell you what, though—if something happens to

Oliver, I promise to take good care of you! There now, that's better. I'll wager you haven't smiled in a week."

He was right, absurd man. He looked at the post chaise waiting in front of the Mulberry to take him to his sloop. "My second home these days," he muttered, then chucked her under the chin. "Buck up, Nana. The soldiers coming in now are those who formed the rearguard of the retreat. Like as not, the *Tireless* was the last to pull away, too. You know your man."

Dennison was right again. In the middle of the afternoon, Oliver walked up the front steps and into her arms. She looked around him, willing the post chaise to disappear, but it did not. After a kiss that seared right through her loins, and another hug, he turned around and walked back to the waiting conveyance, all without a word spoken.

He returned five nights later, more tired than she had ever seen him. She put her arm around him and helped him into the kitchen, where he shook his head at food.

"Just a bed that doesn't move, Nana love," he told her.

She took him into her little room, helping him off with his clothes.

"I stink," he told her as she removed his shoes. "Haven't changed clothes in three weeks. Sorry."

He was asleep as soon as he lay down. She sat on her bed and watched him, relieved he was alive.

Pete and Gran were still moving about in the kitchen, talking in whispers.

"You needn't whisper," Nana said. "Nothing short of a volcanic eruption would wake Oliver right now. He's so worn down."

"He just needs some sleep." Gran put her hands on Nana's shoulders. "So do you. We've done every earthly thing we can. Go to bed, Nana."

She did as Gran ordered, dropping her clothes by the bed and squeezing herself into the small space, happy to settle in close behind her husband and hold him. He jerked awake once toward morning, but she shushed him and he slept again without a murmur.

She was dragged out of sleep an hour later by the terrible sound of her husband weeping. The raw keen sent a chill across her shoulders. *I don't know what to do,* she thought, as she did the only thing she could do, wrapping an arm and leg across his body as he cried as though his heart would break.

"Please tell me what's wrong," she whispered, when his tears subsided.

He shook his head violently, like a two-year-old asked to do something completely against his will. "I couldn't possibly burden you with this."

"What?"

"You heard me."

His voice was cold as wind off the Cattewater. He started to cry again.

Then she was angry with him, maybe angrier than she had ever been with anyone in her life, except her father, who had richly earned her dislike. She tugged at Oliver's shoulder, but he refused to turn and look at her.

Without a word, she climbed over her bed and knelt beside it, her hands tight around his face so he could not turn away.

"Captain Worthy, you listen to me," she ordered. "You came to the Mulberry and immediately started bearing all of my burdens, sick as you were. You even told me you loved me. Well, prove it! Let me really be your wife." She shook him again. "I know everything is bad right now, but something is worse, isn't it? You'd better tell me right now."

Or what? she thought miserably. *I'll hit you? I'll leave you? I'll stop loving you?* "Oliver, I didn't mean to call you captain," she said as she wiped his eyes with the sheet. "That was unkind."

He opened his eyes at that, and managed a half smile. "That *was* unkind."

She could have swooned with relief. She kissed his lips and then his cheeks and forehead, her arms tight around his neck now.

He was silent for the longest time. "Do you mean it, Nana?"

"Most emphatically. I was listening when the vicar spoke, and he said something about marrying for 'mutual society, help and comfort.'" To her own ears, she sounded as if she were babbling, but at least he was listening. "I'm just a woman. I can't fight your war. I wouldn't be brave enough. But I can listen, and by God, Oliver Worthy, I'll be damned if you have to cry alone! Don't you dare dismiss me again!"

She had never spoken with so much energy to anyone before. The last thing in the world she wanted to do was injure this man she loved more than her own body, and here she was in the early hours, speaking with such vehemence. *What have I done?* she asked herself miserably.

It must have been the right thing, because Oliver shifted backward a little on the narrow bed and held up the bed-clothes so she could get in. "I still stink," he said.

She hitched up her nightgown and put her leg over him. She pulled herself close until they were breast-to-breast. Oliver tried several times to speak, but couldn't. Finally, he closed his eyes and breathed slowly and carefully until he had calmed himself sufficiently, all the while she stroked his face.

He took a deep breath. "Mr. Proudy is dead."

Chapter Sixteen

"My darling, what happened?"

It spilled out of him. At one time she had to urge him to slow down.

"We were the last frigate away from Corunna. Major General Beresford brought up the rear, and he was on board. We took off all the rest of the wounded," he added, and there was no mistaking the pride in his voice.

She kissed his forehead. "I'm not surprised."

"Nana, the Channel was terrible. Even some of my best men were seasick, and that's rare." He sniffed her. "You smell so good."

"Of course I do. I'm just a Plymouth layabout."

"That's not what I've been hearing from others." Then he was back in the Channel again. "It was getting dark. We were having one squall after another, and the rigging had started to freeze."

He looked around the room. "I should be on my way. We have to sail as soon…"

Nana pressed her fingers to his lips. "Not now. Tell me."

Dutifully, he continued. "Christopher Quayle was in the

crosstrees on the mainmast. Mr. Proudy shouted for him to come down, but he couldn't move."

"Was he hurt?"

"No. Just afraid. It happens to the best of seamen, especially when the ship is pitching about. You can imagine."

She could. Just thinking about it made her heart race faster.

"Mr. Proudy started up the ratlines with a rope to retrieve Quayle."

"What was he going to do?"

"Lash Quayle to his back and carry him down. I've done it before. Had it done to me once, when I was a young gentleman. Not very dignified, when you're trying to convince yourself you're a sailor."

"Couldn't he just have stayed there until he got the nerve to come down?"

"Ordinarily, yes, but it was so cold he would have died up there. I was in my cabin when all this was going on. Mr. Brittle came to tell me what had happened, so I ran on deck, hollering to Mr. Proudy to stop."

"Why?"

"He's not a good climber, Nana. Some men just aren't, even the best officers." Oliver brought his other arm around her. "He always obeys me but he didn't this time. Damn the man! Why did Will not obey?"

That was the first time he had said Mr. Proudy's Christian name. Nana closed her eyes, grateful through her whole body that she would probably never command anything more than children, and maybe a handful of servants, if that.

"Will was almost to the crosstrees when he fell," Oliver said, his voice dogged now, as if determined to get through this nightmare. "To make it worse, he landed on the carpenter's mate and killed him. Will suffered for another day and a half in the worst agony. He kept asking for Sarah, his wife," Oliver sobbed. "Over and over! And damn me, I kept thinking. what if that had been me? Nana, what have we done?"

"We fell in love and married, just as the Proudys did," she murmured, tears in her eyes. "Even the navy can't stop that. Oliver. What happened to the man on lookout?"

"I carried him down," Oliver said. "I climbed barefoot. I wish to God Will had at least taken off his shoes! Sometimes it's easier that way." He sighed. "And then when Quayle was still on my back and crying, too, I had to stand in front of the whole crew and tell them if any of them blamed Quayle for what happened, I would personally flog them with two hundred stripes each." He burrowed his face into her shoulder "I sat with Will until he died, asking for Sarah and broken-hearted because she would not come."

There wasn't anything she could say, so she didn't try. She rubbed her hands across his back, pressing hard against his flesh To her relief, he slept again, his face more peaceful this time.

She couldn't sleep. She heard Sal and then Gran moving about in the kitchen. She tried to ease herself out of Oliver's close embrace, but his arms only tightened around her. "Don't leave me," he ordered, and it was in no way a suggestion.

"Aye, sir," she whispered. She had no urge to leave, beyond the need to help in the kitchen. Gran knew her grandson-in-law was here, so would never disturb them.

Nana watched her husband, seeing agitation cross his expressive face now and then as he slept, as though he had no relief from responsibility, not even in his new wife's bed Loving him, fearing for him, she put her hand gently around his neck, rubbing her thumb against the nape of it, where his hair was getting long again.

Her action seemed to serve as a trigger, because Oliver woke, managed a half smile that never reached his eyes and began to run his hand down her bare hip.

Almost before she knew it, they were making love: not gentle love, but something borne more of desperation and longing, of acute pain, even, as Oliver used her body to comfort himself for the loss of a valued first mate, maybe even a friend.

As new as she was to this marriage business, Nana understood, and gave herself to him gladly, thinking how puny her own contribution to his solace must be, realizing it was more powerful than she ever could have dreamed a mere month ago.

There was her own pleasure to consider, too. In all his own needs, her husband was mindful of hers in a way that touched her almost as much as their climax. If it were possible to banish care, relieve pain and renew hope for the future, they did exactly that, on a narrow bed in a small room off a kitchen in a shabby inn beloved by some and unknown by more.

Coming to know her body now, thanks to him, she would have wished him to continue, once they were both so satisfied, but she knew better this time. He was still tired right down to the soles of his feet. For all she knew, duty was a strumpet, blowing in his ear, teasing him in other ways she had no control over. So be it. If this was the cross of the wife of a captain in the Channel Fleet, then it was hers to bear. God willing, there would be other times, better ones.

"Nana, you're a remedy," he said finally, echoing what she thought he might be feeling. "Should I feel like a churl?"

"No. I don't mean this to sound frivolous, but there may come a day when I have burned the dinner, the children are misbehaving and the servants have cheated us, that you will be called on to service me."

He laughed out loud, and it was the healthiest sound. "Fair is fair," he told her, pinching her rump. "By God, you have a nice shape."

"I think it's pretty typical of females," she informed him.

He sat up, and she did, too. He took her on his lap, even as she blushed and tried to cover herself.

"You amaze me," he said, as he tugged up the sheet to cover them both. "Here we were, making love with sincere abandon, and now you're shy because you're naked."

"I hope you feel better," she said simply.

"How could I not?" he answered. His eyes clouded then. "I stopped in Salisbury to offer my condolences to Mrs. Proudy."

"Did she…"

"Already know? Yes. Virgil Dennison had dropped my letter off on his trip the week before. I stopped to give her the necessary papers allowing her access to her husband's prize money. I added more. She'll want for nothing."

"Except a husband," Nana said, not thinking.

Oliver winced. He put his finger over her lips when she opened them to apologize. "That's the tragedy of this bad business, Eleanor. She's not feeling any kindness toward the Royal Navy right now."

"I could go see her, but I'm not so sure she'd welcome a visit."

"No?"

She told him about standing at the Hoe with Mrs. Brittle, and how Mrs. Proudy had so pointedly avoided them. "She thinks I am too common, as the granddaughter of an innkeeper. We should be relieved she does not know of my unsavory lineage."

He tightened his arms around her.

"Just as long as you don't ever have cause to feel that way," she said. "I don't want to feel…unworthy."

"No, wife, you're very much a Worthy." He slid back down into the bed, keeping her on top of him. "In fact, be gentle with me again, in my weakened condition, Mrs. Ever-so-worthy."

She made herself comfortable—content with the ease he entered her—but couldn't help saying, "Now this is a new prospect. Does it change the rhythm? Oh, apparently not."

"I really have to leave now," Oliver said, after what seemed like only minutes later.

"A bath first," she insisted, getting up decisively this time. "Then back to duty."

"Indeed," he agreed, as he rose, too, and pulled on his shirt and trousers. "I'll spare your blushes and go ask Pete and Sal to carry some water into the washroom." He put his hand on the doorknob. "But only if you'll scrub my back."

She scrubbed his back, kissing it, too, until he told her she'd better stop. She could tell he was joking, but the edge of command was returning to his voice. She knew he was thinking about what lay ahead, and not his own pleasure any longer.

"Back to patrol?" she asked, pouring warm water on his back.

"More than that. We have to land Rogelio Rodriguez back onshore below Corunna. He came off with us, and now he has to return to find out what he can in the interior." He flicked some water on her. "Then we have to rendezvous in a few weeks, so I can take back the latest news."

"I like to think you send someone ashore to do that for you," she said, doubt in her voice.

"Alas, no. I wouldn't dream of putting my crew in that kind of danger," he said. "There. I didn't want to say it, but you need to know the risks I run. Some of them."

He left a short time later, after waiting patiently for Gran to fuss over him and fix another wheat poultice for his neck and ears.

"I meant to give you this last time," she told him gruffly, even as Nana watched her wink back tears.

He stuffed it in his duffel bag. "I just warm it?"

Gran had turned away to dab at her eyes, so Nana took his arm and led him along the corridor. "Warm it, but not too hot or you will probably tempt the ship's rats."

"Now that's a note to leave on," he said. He squared his shoulders as she opened the door. "Still, it's a better note than the one I came in on."

He pulled her into his embrace again, the feel of him so familiar to her now as to make her wonder how she ever managed before he came to the Mulberry.

"I almost forgot," he told her hair. "According to her husband, Mrs. Brittle is wanting a visit from you. Find a day to go to Torquay and drink tea with a lady who has not a qualm about you—her and most of the Channel Fleet, I might add."

She kept talking, not wanting to end the embrace he also seemed reluctant to discontinue. "How could the Channel Fleet know anything about me?"

"You'd be amazed at the gossip between ships, Nana. Those signal flags don't always dwell on business, I assure you." He cleared his throat. "I hear there were wagers on whether O. Worthy would ever get spliced. Apparently significant quid changed hands."

She remembered news of her own, and walked him to the gate. "I forgot something, too. Mr. Lefebvre vanished. Pete says he was pressed onto a merchantman bound for India."

"Imagine that" was all her quixotic husband said as he blew her a kiss and started down the street toward the harbor.

* * *

Nana knew a week was too soon for a letter from her husband. He told her that it usually took five days for the *Tireless* to reach Ferrol Station. Return trips could be the same length, or longer, depending on the winds, as always. Still, she looked for a letter delivered by Captain Dennison, who seemed to alternate his return voyages with Oliver's.

Beyond her own longings for a letter to be delivered at supernatural speed, Pete kept her posted on fleet news.

"The scuttlebutt seems to be the government is trying to decide when and where to send more troops, Nana," he said. "There's talk of Sir Arthur Wellesley commanding them."

"Who?"

"He's a Sepoy General, late from India." Pete shrugged. "One can hope."

Indeed one could. Unwilling to just wait for a letter, Nana forced herself to plan with her grandmother to paint the Mulberry when spring came, and refurbish the rooms.

Then she had something else to concentrate on besides refurbishment. Perhaps she could discuss it with Mrs. Brittle, when she visited soon. She was too shy to mention the issue with Gran.

She had noticed it the first ten days after her husband returned to sea: a headache that wouldn't go away, followed by real tenderness in her breasts. They even appeared to be enlarging, though she could easily credit her healthy eating. *Maybe I should be cutting back slightly,* she thought, the morning she dressed to visit Mrs. Brittle. *Oliver may want additional poundage, but I doubt he wants a whale for a wife. Maybe a little less cream in my porridge.*

She had promised Mrs. Brittle a little visit. What better time than now, when she had questions.

Mrs. Brittle lived in a tidy house overlooking Tor Bay, where several ships were riding at anchor.

"Sometimes they run in here instead of Plymouth," she said as she dispensed with the formality of a curtsey and hugged Nana. "The winds, you know. Always the wind."

Over tea and excellent ginger cake, Mrs. Brittle shared what news she had of the fleet, most of it from her oldest child, married these four years to a sailing master like her father, and based in Portsmouth. Her son was a Royal Navy surgeon, tending fever cases in the West Indies.

"My other two are around here somewhere," she said, as she held out the plate for another slice of cake.

Nana shook her head. "I think I'm finally starting to put on more weight than even Captain Worthy could want," she said, wondering how to segue from that harmless comment to what was going on inside her. She decided there was no sense in being missish: a spade, after all, would always be a spade to her, no matter how many years she studied under Miss Pym's refined tutelage. Hardly able to look at her kind hostess, Nana described her symptoms. "I hope it's not some malignancy from the fleet, or those soldiers we cared for, Mrs. Brittle," she concluded.

Mrs. Brittle smiled. "Well, let me think—has it been two weeks since the captain was in port?"

"Nearly so."

"My dear, let me assure you that what you have probably isn't a malignancy." She leaned a little closer and looked around to make sure her children hadn't wandered into the room. "Any urge to vomit?"

Nana shook her head.

"Have you noticed your friend is late in visiting you this month?"

Nana shook her head again. "Not yet. I have a few more

days." She opened her eyes wide. "Mrs. Brittle, you don't think…"

"I do, that is, assuming the captain…er…took advantage of the refreshment generally available only in port."

He did indeed, Nana thought. Several times, in fact. *I'm surprised I don't still have the mattress ticking imprinted on my rump.* She couldn't help herself. She laughed and looked her hostess square in the eye.

"Gran warned me about sailors."

"And you didn't listen!" Mrs. Brittle teased. She held out the ginger cake and Nana took another slice. "If it's any comfort, I never did, either, dearie. You're not contagious."

They laughed together as the February sleet angled in sideways around the snug house and the wind howled like a banshee, ruffling the surface of Tor Bay.

She spent the night with the Brittles, then left in good spirits in the morning. She was only a mile or two out of Torquay when she had to beg the coachman to stop. She let the step down herself and hurried to the edge of the road, where she tossed up a marvelous breakfast of porridge, eggs, toast and black pudding.

The coachman was solicitous, but she assured him she would be fine in a few minutes. More like a few months, she thought, accepting a glass of watered-down wine he had poured for her from a flask. She looked at the liquid, shook her head and handed it back, just in time to turn away and retch a little more.

She regained her equanimity soon enough and let him hand her back into the chaise. She leaned back and rested her hands gently on her stomach. She wasn't totally sure how this went—Mrs. Brittle was going to get another visit soon—but she knew it would be several months before anything showed. Still, she had company.

She patted her belly. "Baby, I do believe we have something of interest to include in my next letter to your father," she whispered. "I doubt he'll be surprised."

Chapter Seventeen

Nana didn't say anything to anyone, not even after several days passed and there was no evidence of her monthly flow, generally so reliable. She suddenly had much larger concerns.

A sloop of war—not Captain Dennison's—and a battered frigate rode at anchor in the Cattewater at the end of the week. When Pete returned from the harbor after his usual round of news gathering, and he asked her to sit down, she knew the news was bad.

"Tell me, Pete," she said quietly.

Her lips tight together, Gran came into the kitchen. She sat by Nana and grasped her hand.

Even then, she wasn't prepared. *Is anyone?* she wondered, as Pete, looking her directly in the eyes, told her Oliver was missing.

"It has something to do with going ashore south of Corunna."

"He said he was depositing a Spaniard onshore to ferret out troop movements and the like," she said, when she could speak. *I managed that,* she thought, surprised at herself. "He was supposed to retrieve him later or at least, the news."

Pete nodded, and she saw the relief on his face, which put

heart into her body. "That would make sense. Maybe the French captured him."

She closed her eyes, unable to bear his scrutiny. "What do we do now?"

Gran placed her hand firmly on Nana's shoulder. "We wait."

They waited. She didn't have the heart to say anything about her baby; there was enough to gnaw over. If she looked a little paler than usual, Gran would put it down to the terrible news. She woke early enough—did she even sleep?—to vomit into her waste can and discard the evidence before anyone was up. There was time to cry, early in the morning.

She derived more comfort than she could have suspected from her unborn child. "We won't think the worst yet, my love," she told her baby. "Your father would never want me to do that. Grow, please. We may need each other even more than I imagine now."

She found herself watching for Captain Dennison, clinging to the irrational knowledge that he would have news where no one else seemed to. *He would never leave me dangling,* she thought, as the days passed.

He didn't. With no fanfare, Virgil Dennison arrived on her doorstep one morning, just shortly after the poulterer deposited two fat hens and two dozen eggs.

Nearly overwhelmed by relief at seeing his familiar face, Nana couldn't help notice how his eyes followed the basket of eggs Sal carried into the pantry.

"Gran, could you scramble a half dozen of those for the captain, and cook some bacon?"

"Only if you sit here so I can listen, Captain," Gran said. When Dennison nodded, she began to slice large slabs of bacon into a pan already on the Rumford.

Dennison sat down at the table, not even taking off his

cloak, until Nana shyly suggested that he make himself at home. Without even glancing outside, she knew there had to be a post chaise waiting.

"Sal, could you take porridge and toast out to the coachman?" she said, calming herself with mundane conversation. "Ask how he likes his tea."

Then she gave Dennison her attention, not even trying to stop the tears that welled up in her eyes. "Please tell me something," she begged, "even if it's bad news."

He dabbed at her eyes with a napkin. "It could be worse, Mrs. Worthy," he assured her. "Believe me."

"Then tell me now! I know something of what he was doing on the coast."

After Dennison drank an entire quart of water, the story came out. "He had returned with a jolly boat to a beach below Corunna, near a fishing village called Corcubion. Apparently the French were waiting. The sailors said troops opened fire. One of their number was killed, and so was the Spaniard Oliver was to meet."

"But not Oliver."

"No." Dennison looked up as Gran set the bacon and eggs in front of him. "Mrs. Massie, you're a wonder."

"Keep talking," the woman demanded.

Dennison busied himself with a slice of bacon and a forkful of eggs, speaking around them. "The French took them to the garrison in Corcubion and they were incarcerated for a week. Then the commandant released the sailors with the boat and a letter from Marshal Soult to King George himself."

"But not my husband."

He shook his head. "I was to take that letter to Admiral Lord Wharton on the *Agamemnon*. Thank God he read it in my presence." He gestured with his fork. "What I tell you now must never leave this room."

"You know it won't," Nana said.

"Soult wants to exchange your husband for a French general who was captured a year ago at Benevente. Plus twenty-thousand pounds."

Nana gasped at the enormity of the sum. "Will Whitehall even *consider* such a huge amount in exchange?"

"I don't know," Dennison said honestly. "The government has always been reluctant to stoop to extortion, and exchanges are few and far between. Lord Wharton has great faith in your husband's resourcefulness and endorsed the request. I have that letter, also. The action onshore went fast, but the sailors in the jolly boat think Oliver was able to retrieve some information from Rodriguez before he died on the beach." Dennison leaned forward. "Never repeat this—whether England commits more soldiers to the peninsula might depend on that message. That may carry the matter with Horse Guards."

Nana sat back and let Dennison wolf down his breakfast. After another quart of water, he rose to take his leave. Nana walked him to the post chaise, gathering strength from his arm around her.

"Is there anything I can do?" she asked, as he prepared to step inside the chaise.

He shook his head. "I won't tell you not to worry. He's been taken to La Estrella del Mar, a former convent south of Corunna, where some stragglers from the army who didn't escape a month ago have been gathered. That much we know. You know how resourceful he is." He couldn't help but smile at her. "He has every reason to want to return to you with a whole skin. Mrs. Worthy, you're far and away the best thing that has ever happened to a most deserving man."

He left before she could feel embarrassed. Nana stood at the gate and watched the post chaise until it disappeared from sight, and then turned her attention to the ships in the harbor. Almost without thinking, she turned until she was facing Spain, far distant, and stood there a long time, thinking.

By the time she entered the Mulberry again, she had made up her mind. Pete and Gran were still in the kitchen. Nana clasped her hands behind her back so they would not betray her with their trembling. "I am going to London tomorrow," she announced, not looking at either of the two people so dear to her. "I intend to speak to my father, Lord Ratliffe, and I intend to be on the *Goldfinch* when it sails. Thanks to my husband, I have the means to encourage my…uh…father to agree to the admiral's endorsement. Money talks with him." She held up her hand when Pete opened his mouth. "I will not be dissuaded." She turned on her heel and left the room.

Nana had ample time to change her mind, but she did not, despite Pete's protestations and Gran's tears. She grew more resolute as the hours passed, even though Pete assured her she would never be allowed on the sloop, and besides, what good could she do?

"I *will* be on that ship," she told him calmly.

She packed for the journey. When Pete stubbornly refused to make arrangements for the post chaise, she went to the harbor herself, asked around and accomplished the matter herself. A visit to her husband's solicitors secured a bank draft of sufficient proportions to grease any wheels with her father, if such was needed. She had no illusions about what fueled his interest.

"We'll stop for exchanges and food only," she told the coachman early the next morning, staring down his protests. *If my darling can do it, I can, too,* she thought. After a quick kiss and embrace with Gran, who had offered surprisingly little objection, she let the coachman help her into the chaise. She had hoped to see Pete before she left, and felt scorched by his disapproval. "I suppose it can't be helped," she murmured under her breath.

Suddenly there he was in the yard, his old navy ditty bag slung over his shoulder. "Wait," she told the coachman. "Let down the step, please."

Tears came to her eyes as she watched his rolling gait, knowing what pain his arthritis gave him, and humbled by his devotion to her. Relieved, too. She couldn't pretend to know what lay ahead in London.

"I haven't been to London in years" was all he said. "Seems like a good time for a visit."

She wisely made no comment.

Exhausted, but with even greater appreciation for the efforts of the men who also not only endured the blockade, but who carried messages to and from London, Nana arrived there forty hours later. She asked to be taken directly to Admiralty House.

Admission to the chambers of the naval administrators proved to be simplicity, partly because Dennison had kindly left her with a letter of recommendation, and partly because her father was curious to know who Mrs. Captain Oliver Worthy might be.

She had to reluctantly give Lord Ratliffe points for swallowing his astonishment to see her. He had changed but little in the five years since she had run from his London house, mortified at his suggestion that she was his chattel to dispose of to the highest bidder. He was fleshier around the face, but so were the other administrators. She was used to the always-hungry look of actual men at sea. These well-fleshed men surprised her, at first. She wondered if men like her father had any idea of the privations experienced by those who labored tirelessly to keep England safe from Napoleon.

Never mind. She would deal with her father, no matter how it revolted her. "I am Captain Worthy's wife, my lord," she said formally. The porter who had shown her and Pete into the office was still standing there, and she had no intention of admitting Lord Ratliffe was her father.

Lord Ratliffe dismissed the porter. When the door closed, he came around his desk toward her. She stepped out of his way and sat down in the chair.

"Sir, I insist upon knowing what is happening."

He could have refused her, but he didn't. She glanced at Pete and the look of pride on his face, and then she understood. *Could it be that* I *am in charge here?* she thought. "Well?" she asked, keeping her voice level.

His eyes on her, Lord Ratliffe sat down again. He told her substantially what Captain Dennison had said earlier. Nana schooled her impatience not to tell him she had already heard this, knowing such an admission would hang Dennison.

After exhibiting what she hoped was surprise and dismay, she allowed a decent interval to pass then asked, "Will the government pay the ransom?"

Lord Ratliffe looked everywhere but at her face. "The issue is money. Soult is demanding a ransom of thirty thousand pounds for his return, plus the release of a French officer here. Surely I needn't tell you how tight the treasury is right now, with the war on."

She had seen Soult's demand for £20,000. *Father, you play a deep game,* she thought in disgust. *You know how rich my husband is, and you are going to extort the extra from me, for your own purposes. Considering how badly you think I failed you before, so be it.*

She reached into her reticule. "I have a bank draft for ten thousand pounds. Inform Sir Spencer Perceval, please, and plead with the other lords of the Admiralty to add this to the ransom so Captain Worthy can be brought home safely."

As sure as she knew his character, she knew that £10,000 was headed directly into her father's own pockets. *I would pay ten times that for Oliver's release,* she thought, *but you will not hear that from me.*

"Who is to make the deal?" she demanded.

"I am," her father replied. "I will take the money and a letter from King George himself, since Soult's letter was addressed to him."

He hesitated, and a faint bell began to clang inside her head. He wasn't telling her something. She could not dampen the disquiet that began to spread over her, and involuntarily settled her hand against her belly to protect her child against so much evil.

Lord Ratliffe continued. "Captain Worthy will be released. When he returns to England, I will then escort the French general back to Spain."

"I will come with you for the first exchange," she said, her voice quiet, but allowing no room for argument.

He surprised her then. She expected an outright refusal and got none. After a momentary pause, as though he were factoring some new detail into the equation, he nodded. "I would have it no other way, Eleanor. You deserve the opportunity." He smiled at her, which only made her shiver. "In fact, when I arrive at La Estrella with the captain's young wife, the French will certainly know we are serious. Good of you to think of this, Eleanor."

The bells clanged louder, but she ignored them. "There are no lengths I would not go, to help my husband," she told him, meaning every word.

"We are agreed, then," Lord Ratliffe said. He finally returned his gaze to her face, where it remained only a second before darting off, as though he had not the courage for her scrutiny.

He stood. "I will be in Plymouth aboard the *Goldfinch* in five days. Captain Dennison will take us to the *Tireless,* which is standing off the coast of Corunna."

"I will be there, my lord," she said, standing and handing him the bank draft. He bowed; she curtseyed.

"Eleanor, am I correct that you have told no one I am your father?" he asked as she and Pete crossed the room.

"No one," she said, biting off the words. "Not ever."

"That's a relief," he replied.

"For me, too," she responded, refusing to be shamed by his cut.

On the return to Plymouth, Pete tried to dissuade her from taking passage to Spain on the *Goldfinch.* "As much as I distrust your father, he'll have to carry through with the exchange. Ye don't have to be there."

She couldn't explain her own fears to Pete, the ones that had set off such alarms as she listened to her father. "I have to see this whole exchange with my own eyes, Pete," she told him.

He looked at her then, with a gaze almost fatherly. Suddenly, she knew he knew.

"You know there is another reason I wish ye wouldn't go," he began. "Nana…"

"Does Gran know?" she asked quietly.

He shook his head. "I only discovered it on this fast trip to London, with you trying to keep down your meals." He smiled at her. "Whether ye know it or not, ye look a little different, too. Ye have a kind of rosy glow, in spite of all the misery around us at present."

"I was going to tell you both when I returned from Mrs. Brittle, but then all the bad news came, and we had enough on our plate. Don't tell Gran," she begged.

"It's not like ye can keep it a deep, dark secret, Nana," he said, a teasing note in his voice now, which reassured her that he would do as she asked.

"Just this little while, Pete. When I come back from Spain with Oliver, we'll tell her." She sighed. "I can't have her thinking I am a repetition of my mother."

"Remember this— Gran loved your mother, and from what she tells me, Rachel was as sweet and biddable as you are." It was his turn to sigh. "It's just that she loved the wrong man. You didn't make that mistake."

She kissed his cheek, then turned her gaze to the highway, as the chaise passed Staines, then Bagshot, to be followed by Hartford Bridge, Basingstone and Whitchurch, on the long road from London to Plymouth.

The trip to Ferrol Station took five days, where the *Goldfinch* rendezvoused with the *Tireless*. Nana's morning sickness went unnoticed; Lord Ratliffe was even sicker than she was, to everyone's gratification.

Wounded because Captain Dennison had insisted on relinquishing his tiny cabin to Nana and not himself, Lord Ratliffe demanded prerogatives impossible to meet on a ship as small as the *Goldfinch*. He sulked in the even-smaller cabin belonging to the sloop's only mate, who had been forced to sling his hammock with the sailing master. When winds and currents shot the *Goldfinch* from Plymouth Sound into the waters of the Channel like a cork from a bottle, he had succumbed to seasickness that incapacitated him through four of the five days.

"How did he ever manage to serve on a ship of the line?" Nana asked Dennison one afternoon as she sat in a canvas chair he had ordered placed on the deck.

The wind blew raw, but the deck was more pleasant than the stench of bilge water, tar, revisited food and seldom-washed bodies belowdecks. With a wool scarf wrapped tight, one of Gran's wheat poultices to protect her ears and her own boat cloak, Nana was content to stare into the distance, impatient to see Spain.

Dennison stood by her chair, eyes constantly scanning the horizon, where grey water and grey sky joined. "I do not think Lord Ratliffe spent much time at sea" was all he said, and Nana could tell he chose his words carefully.

"I know little about him."

It was easy for her to say that, because it was the truth. For years he had educated her, requiring nothing more from her than a yearly letter, describing her progress, and then the miniature painting once she was twelve. Gran never spoke of him.

"He began a career at sea," Dennison said. He squatted on the deck beside her, undignified for a captain, but obviously not wanting his words to carry to the helmsman. "I hear there was scandal in the West Indies, where he and his ship showed a clean pair of heels in a fight, if I can so phrase it."

A coward, then; she was hardly surprised. "He still works for the Admiralty?"

Dennison made a face. "He still has influence, mainly because the king likes him. Oliver and I report to Lord Ratliffe, and he sifts through our messages and sends them— most of them, hopefully—to Lord Mulgrave."

She stared at him, then shifted her gaze so he would not

wonder. Oliver had never mentioned his connection with her father.

"Oliver doesn't trust him," Dennison said. "He told me I should deliver my messages to Lord Mulgrave."

Dennison returned to his duties then and Nana continued her contemplation of the horizon. She thanked God no one knew the viscount was her father. *He is a coward,* she thought. *I know he is a thief, because he took £10,000 from me. I wonder what else he is?*

She found out that night at dinner. The sloop's wardroom was tiny, and they sat even more elbow-to-elbow, because Lord Ratliffe had decided he felt well enough to join them. The viscount looked with some disfavor to see someone as common at Pete Carter at the table, but said nothing.

He seemed to have recovered from both his seasickness and his pique at being assigned a cabin far unworthy of him. He made no objection to the cask beef and hard bread on his plate, even choosing the occasion to reminisce on his few years at sea.

"I am certain they were glorious ones," Dennison commented dryly.

"Indeed they were," Lord Ratliffe replied.

Dennison made no comment, but merely glanced at Nana and winked.

"And now we go to release a real hero from his detainment," Dennison said a few minutes later.

True to the credo of all self-involved men, Lord Ratliffe either had no idea Dennison's comment was a gibe at his own less-than-stellar career with the fleet, or grandly chose to overlook it. "Indeed we do," he said, generously including himself in any honors that might appertain to springing Captain Worthy from prison.

Nana saw the disgust on Dennison's face as he returned his

attention to the wooden beef in front of him. She glanced at her father, who seemed unable to decide if Dennison had insulted him, or not.

She had thought to rush in with a comment of her own, to deflect attention from the captain, but Dennison's mate beat her to the punch.

"My Lord, who is it you are exchanging for Captain Worthy?"

"A real prize, which is probably why we had to further sweeten the pot with thirty thousand pounds," Lord Ratliffe replied. "A captain's only a captain, after all."

Well, that's a cut to me, Nana thought. *Oliver is worth a hundred times whatever paltry sum Whitehall is paying.*

"We are exchanging General Charles Lefebvre-Desnouettes."

Nana gasped. She could not help herself. A split second later, Pete Carter trod deliberately on her foot.

It was too late; all eyes were on her.

"Do *you* know him?" Lord Ratliffe condescended to ask, in a tone of voice that indicated nothing could be further from the realm of possibility.

Think, Nana, she ordered herself. She looked at her father with what she hoped was sufficient calm. "Oh, no, my lord." She managed a shiver. "A rat just ran across my foot."

The men around the table laughed. "That is more than likely, Mrs. Worthy," Dennison said. "Even the rats are crowded in a sloop of war. Tell us more, Lord Ratliffe."

Preening in the attention, he told them of Lefebvre-Desnoutte's capture at Benevente in 1808 and his parole to Cheltenham. "The emperor would like him back, naturally," Ratliffe concluded, "and we need whatever information Worthy might possess. After the captain returns to England, I am to escort the general to France under a flag of truce. Beyond that, I cannot say." He looked around, triumphant.

Nana finished her dinner in silence, but with a burning desire to speak to Pete as soon as she could decently leave the table and claim a turn on deck would do her good.

The moment came soon enough. Bells sounded and Dennison's mate rose, hoisted to his feet like a marionette by the sound. "My watch," he said cheerfully, bowing to Lord Ratliffe and Nana.

It was the signal for the dinner party—such as it was—to disperse. Nana escaped to the deck, after a fierce look at Pete.

He followed her to the rail, where she rounded on him. "I want to know what's going on, Pete," she demanded.

He put up his hands, as if to ward her off. "I'm as fair blinded as you by that news," he said. "How many Lefebvres can England support?"

"Do you think *our* Mr. Lefebvre was giving secrets to the Lefebvre in Cheltenham?" she asked. She thought a moment. "My word, there he was, sketching everything in Plymouth's harbors!" She looked at Pete, who was having trouble meeting her eyes. "You knew that, didn't you?"

His answer seemed to be extracted by pincers. "Not until your husband told me. Then we decided to have him pressed and put aboard that merchantman bound for India." It came out in a rush of words.

"You two might have trusted me" was all Nana could think of to say.

"Nana, it happened so fast."

"I suppose it did," she said grudgingly, after a pause long enough to restore some of her dignity. "I may have to give my husband a generous helping of my mind. And why did he never tell me he knew Lord Ratliffe?"

I'd rather give him a big kiss and a huge hug, she thought that night, as she swung lightly in Captain Dennison's sleeping cot. *All I really want is to know he is safe.* She rested her hands on her belly—something she always did now, as she composed herself for sleep—and closed her eyes.

Chapter Eighteen

Next morning, the *Goldfinch* hailed the *Tireless,* swinging at her anchor off Corunna like a puppy waiting for its master. The sea was calm, but Dennison was taking no chances with his cargo. He ordered his crew to rig a bosun's chair.

"Lord Ratliffe can drop in the water, for all I care," he told Nana, "but Oliver would tack my…um…ears to the deck if you even got your feet wet." He helped her into the canvas sling and secured her with a rope. He kissed her cheek. "Just hold tight to your bandbox and think of Oliver, Nana!"

And don't look down, she added to herself as the crew swung her overhead on the line secured aboard Oliver's frigate. She was let down on the deck of the *Tireless* as gently as an egg. Mr. Ramseur himself helped her out of the chair, which swung back to take her father, and then Pete.

Nana went to the rail and waved to Captain Dennison, who laughed and blew her a kiss. "He's a scoundrel," she told Mr. Ramseur, who grinned and turned predictably red.

Once all were on board, the *Goldfinch* stood off from the *Tireless,* then made enough sail to be safely distant, but not out of sight.

"He's going to watch here until Captain Worthy is back aboard," Mr. Ramseur told her, as he escorted her belowdecks himself, to her husband's cabin.

Lord Ratliffe threw the expected tantrum, demanding to know why he was not assigned to Oliver's cabin. Mr. Ramseur turned pale under his tirade, but lost none of his resolution. "My lord, you may take this up with Captain Worthy, when he returns," he said, his voice firm. "You will be in the late Mr. Proudy's cabin. Follow me, please."

Pete remained with Nana. "I'll have them make me a pallet in the main cabin," he told Nana, as he watched Lord Ratliffe's retreating form. "I don't trust the man at all."

She had no objections. A marine stood sentry duty outside Oliver's quarters, but having Pete close by was a reassurance. All she wanted to do now was lie down and hope this current wave of nausea would pass soon enough, as the others had.

The door to her husband's sleeping compartment opened inside the main cabin, which stretched across the stern of the *Tireless* and contained his chartroom and lavatory, as well: life in miniature aboard a warship.

With a sigh, she crawled into his sleeping cot and covered herself with a blanket that smelled of her husband and threatened to bring on tears. She probably could have resisted tears, if she had not turned onto her back and looked at the deck beams, where two sketches of her were tacked.

"Oh, my darling," she whispered, as she looked at the sketch Lefebvre had made of her on the guildhall steps. It was the other one that startled her, the one she remembered Lefebvre drawing when he drew Sal. Oliver must have asked for it before he sailed the first time.

She knew herself—and Oliver now—well enough to know that her husband loved her, but that additional sketch filled her eyes with tears, as she began to comprehend the depths of his devotion. Before he had even convinced himself that he would ever dare love her, he had wanted her with him.

"And there I will be, my love," she said, as she swung in the cot, cried and committed herself even more deeply to him than she ever could have thought possible. No matter how short or long their future together might be, she was his always.

Mr. Ramseur wasted no time in preparing to take Lord Ratliffe and the ransom ashore. He had not expected Nana's order that she accompany the frigate's little jolly boat to land.

No one had. Even Pete looked surprised, and ready to argue. She ignored him.

"I insist, Mr. Ramseur," she said. "There is nothing you can do that will dissuade me, not if you remonstrate and argue until you turn blue."

It was spoken quietly but plainly; she could hardly believe her own ears. Biddable, kind, gentle, self-effacing Nana politely stepped aside for Eleanor Massie Worthy, the wife of one of England's finest post captains, who would no more take no for an answer than the captain himself.

"Don't even try me, Mr. Ramseur," she added, digging her toes into the deck. She meant every word.

She found an ally from a surprising source.

"I say she goes, too," Lord Ratliffe said. "We have a white flag, and the colonel—or whoever commands the garrison— is expecting a considerable sum of money. Would you keep him waiting?"

Poor Mr. Ramseur. He hadn't a chance. She could see he was weighing his captain's displeasure at his wife in a small boat heading to an enemy shore against the odds that he might be greatly relieved to see her. And there was the glowering Admiralty officer to consider, as well.

"Aye, then, my lord," the acting first mate said, although he did not say it gladly. He turned to the rail and looked down into the jolly boat, where its crew rode the waves. He nodded to the men on deck, who had already hoisted the ransom chest toward the midship rail. "Lower away, and handsomely now!" he shouted.

The box went over the side, to be released by the men below into the center of the jolly boat. Pete went over the side next, assuring Mr. Ramseur that he still knew how to climb down main chains.

Mr. Ramseur had the bosun rig a knot for Nana to step into. He even brought her a length of rope to tie around her skirts. "No sense in giving anyone below a glimpse," he mumbled, as she voiced her appreciation.

"Hang on now," he said practically into her ear. "Sit straight and let the ropes do the work."

She took a deep breath and did as he said, as she rose first to clear the rail, and then dropped slowly and carefully into the jolly boat. Hands reached for her and released her from the ropes as efficiently as if they did that for captains' wives every day. She untied her skirts and Pete escorted her toward the rear of the jolly boat, where she wrapped her cloak tight around her.

She looked up, waiting for Lord Ratliffe to be swung below next. They all waited. Nothing happened. She and Pete were looking at each other when they heard "Jolly boat away!" in a loud voice that wasn't Mr. Ramseur's.

The men at their oars looked at each other, then back at her, but did not push away from the ship.

Then the rope tethering them to the *Tireless* shot down into the jolly boat. "Jolly boat now, Admiralty orders!" bellowed the voice again. "Disobey at peril of death!"

"My God," Pete said, as the crew still sat. "Ratliffe is a coward, too, and he must not care who knows it."

Still the men looked at Nana, as if waiting to hear what she said. *Thank God I am braver than my father,* she thought. She sat up straighter. "I won't have you risk death on my behalf," she told the crew. "Do as he says."

Did I just say that? she asked herself as the jolly boat swung away from the *Tireless*. The bosun's mate at the tiller couldn't help himself. "You're a rum one, Mrs. Worthy," he said, even though Pete glowered at him.

When the jolly boat was away from the ship, the oars were stowed and the sail went up, flying a white flag, with the Union Jack below. Nana forced herself to breathe in and out and swallow the gorge that rose in her, more from fear this time than morning sickness.

She looked back once at the *Tireless*. Mr. Ramseur stood on the quarterdeck, his telescope trained on them. She waved to him and he waved his hat at her. She could see no sign of Lord Ratliffe. *What a coward he is,* she thought. *He is even too afraid to conduct what must be a mundane piece of work. What country at war* wouldn't *want £20,000 with so little exertion?* Plus a general of cavalry who, for all she knew, would be carrying back sketches from Plymouth, drawn by another Lefebvre. *I will tell him what I think, when I see him again later this afternoon.*

"What a mess this is," she said to no one in particular, as the jolly boat raced along. The sailors sitting nearest to her laughed, which made her smile. She knew she was in good hands. As sure as they were in a mess, she knew these men would defend her to the death.

The jolly boat sailed into the small harbor, escorted by

a French cutter. Waiting onshore was an officer in full dress uniform.

The crewman in the bow of the *Tireless*'s jolly boat tossed the line to his French counterpart, who snugged it tight, and then snugged in the line from the stern. They were tight against the dock. As the crew waited, a French sailor, unable to hide his disbelief at seeing an Englishwoman, steadied Nana as she held out her hand to him, and helped her over the gunwale, and then up the steps. The crew followed her, with the ransom chest carried between them. Pete brought up the rear.

Now what? she thought. The colonel gaped at her, before recovering himself enough to bow. She curtseyed as calmly as though she spent every afternoon of the week landing on enemy territory with a fortune. To her amusement, the colonel unbent enough to stride to the dock and look down into the boat, as if expecting someone else to materialize.

"It's just us, sir," she said cheerfully. "I am Mrs. Oliver Worthy, and I believe my husband is your prisoner."

She knew her French was adequate. Maybe all those years at Miss Pym's would amount to something after all. "Sir? Is there something else we need to present to you?"

Pete handed her a canvas and tar-covered pouch, which had been lowered along with the chest. She gave it to the colonel, who still stared at her.

This will never do, Nana thought. "I insist on being taken to my husband at once, General." She didn't think he was a general, but enough years in Plymouth had taught her that elevating anyone's rank was a prime tool of flattery.

The French officer was no exception to the rule. He recovered himself and bowed again. "Madame Worthy, Colonel Jean Baptiste San Sauvir, at your service." He placed his hand over his heart. "I am yours to command."

I doubt that, she thought, as she returned his bow with an even better curtsey. She was grateful there was no way the colonel could see how her heart hammered against her rib cage.

San Sauvir offered his arm, and she took it. He paused for a few words with his soldiers, who appropriated the ransom chest, then ordered the crew and Pete to remain where they were.

"Oh, no," Nana said. "Monsieur Pete Carter stays with me. He is my husband's valet and I will not be dissuaded in this."

The colonel bowed again, and motioned Pete forward. "I would never wish to incur the wrath of Captain Worthy."

"I doubt you would," she said in English. "He's a tough customer."

The crew of the jolly boat laughed, stopping immediately when the bosun's mate glared at them. They sat down on the wharf, surrounded by French soldiers, as the colonel led Nana and Pete toward what had formerly been a convent, but which now bristled with cannon.

"This is a far cry from the Barbican," she told Pete, as they climbed the steps.

Pete grinned at her. "Nana, there appears to be more of the rascal in you than I ever knew."

"Maybe my mother would be pleased," she said.

The muskets leaning up against a statue of the Virgin Mary seemed strangely out of place inside the convent, but so were the cannonballs stacked inside the chapel, she noticed as they passed. Rows of tents lined the interior courtyard. Someone less reverent than most had strung a clothesline from a cross to another statue opposite.

Her heart beat faster after they mounted another flight of stairs to what must have been the nun's cells, each with a sentry outside the door. The captain of the guard appeared, saluted and handed Colonel San Sauvir a set of keys.

He turned a key in the lock, swung open the door and bowed. "Do go in, Mrs. Worthy," he said, gesturing. She heard a chair turn over in the cell, as though someone had leaped up. "You, too, Mr. Carter. I'll allow you a few minutes and then I will return." He ushered them in and closed the door behind him.

"Nana!"

Oliver, bearded and shaggy, grabbed her. She clung to him, trying to hold as much of him at once as she could, even as he buried his face in her hair and then kissed her neck.

"What on earth are you doing here?" he murmured, then made an answer impossible when he kissed her.

If she had planned to scold him about not telling her the truth of Lefebvre's disappearance, she forgot, in the simple pleasure of embracing the man who had her heart and was the father of her baby. She held him off from her then, assessing him. Other than appearing shaggy, he looked none the worse for wear.

"I'm well enough," he said, answering her unspoken question. "The colonel likes to have a fourth at cards. I am quick to pick up games, even if I detest them. Pete, why the devil is she here?"

Pete scratched his head. "Captain, please believe me when I tell you I had no idea of this stubborn streak. She wouldn't hear of anything else."

Oliver led them to his cot and they sat down. "I had thought some member of the Admiralty or representative from Whitehall would deliver the ransom," he said. "You do have the ransom."

"Yes, sir," Pete said, and then was unable to keep the disgust from his voice. "Lord Rat himself is even now on the *Tireless,* too cowardly to get into the jolly boat with us, for this transaction."

Oliver must have decided she wasn't close enough, because he pulled her onto his lap. "I can't say I am surprised, Nana." She settled against him and he rested his chin on her head. "He'll get more than a shaking down from me, when we're back on the *Tireless*." He looked at Pete then. "How does my ship look?"

"Fine, sor, as orderly as you please. The crew says Mr. Ramseur is doing a capital job."

"That's a relief." Oliver looked at the door. "Now we need to get our little colonel back, so we can return to my ship. It may not need me, but I miss it."

He set Nana on the cot and went to the door, just as a key rattled in the lock and it swung open. Colonel San Sauvir entered the cell, this time holding the papers that had accompanied the ransom. The sentry came with him.

Colonel San Sauvir bowed and sat in the only chair in the room.

"Colonel, is the ransom amount as Marshal Soult dictated?" Oliver asked, returning to his perch on the cot.

"Indeed it is," he replied. "Twenty thousand good English pounds." He looked at the paper in his hand. "There is one difficulty, though."

"Surely nothing we cannot solve right here," Oliver said. "I have a ship that needs a commander, and my wife really isn't accustomed to captivity." He spoke lightly.

The colonel shook his head. "As to that, Captain, perhaps you need to look over this letter. It's from your government, I might add."

Oliver rose and took the letter, scanning it quickly. As Nana watched, his face paled. He read it again, then handed it back. There was no mistaking the tremor in his hand.

"You can't mean this."

The colonel shrugged. "These are the terms, Captain Worthy. Who am I to argue with the Emperor Napoleon *and* our government? I am no fool." He looked at the letter, then directly at Nana.

"Madame Worthy, perhaps you did not know—the ransom is here, yes, but since you must be representing the government, you must be detained until your husband returns to England and then General Lefebvre-Desnouettes is escorted to France." He smiled at her. "Once this is done, and barring any further difficulty, you should be eligible for release in a few months. It might be longer. Who can say?"

Nana stared at him, then at her husband, who was shaking his head in disbelief.

The colonel did not meet either gaze, but returned his attention to the document. "It appears a Lord Ratliffe was to have been the hostage. How kind of you to come in his place, Mrs. Worthy."

Chapter Nineteen

Stunned, Oliver stared at the colonel. "You would *do* that?"

The colonel only shrugged again and held out the letter. "I am only following the orders of your government. Surely you can ask no more of an enemy combatant."

"No, I cannot," Oliver agreed. "I refuse to leave without my wife, though, so it appears that both of us will be your guests. There will be no exchange for Lefebvre-Desnouettes."

The colonel gestured with the letter again. "You would go against the express wishes of your own government?" He shook his head sadly. "I know what the penalty for treason is in France. Zip! One slice of Dr. Guillotine's remarkable engine. Tell me, do the English still hang, draw and quarter treasonous offenders?"

"They do indeed," Oliver said. "That is why I appeal to your humanity. I cannot leave my wife behind, but I know I must do my duty."

"Then, sir, I would say you have a dilemma," the colonel said serenely.

Nana had heard enough. She didn't look at Oliver

Colonel, I will consider this opportunity in your custody as way to improve my French."

"Nana!"

She put a hand on her husband's arm. "Oliver, I think we hould discuss this in private. Colonel, would you mind ithdrawing?"

Colonel San Sauvir was happy to go. In fact, he sprang up ith the alacrity of one half his age and bulk. "With pleasure!" e went to the small barred window. "I fear this discussion as already gone on too long. I would not dream of releasing ou, Captain Worthy, with night approaching so fast."

"I'm certain you wouldn't," Oliver said sarcastically.

"Now, dear," Nana said, increasing the pressure on his arm.

"Very well, Colonel," Oliver said at last. "Please see that y men are housed and fed tonight."

"I would never consider anything else, Captain. Do excuse e now, so I can make arrangements."

"This is a fine how-de-do," Oliver said when the door osed. He put his arm around her.

"I'm sorry," she said. "If I had known any of the conditions, never would have made it so convenient for my…for Lord atliffe…to jump ship."

She was relieved that her husband preferred philosophy ver anger. "I have to wonder if he ever would have sum- oned up the courage to get into the jolly boat, even if you adn't offered him such a useful substitute," he mused.

"Captain Dennison did mention rumors about his early aval career," she said.

"More than rumors, Nana love," Oliver said. He glanced Pete. "You've heard them, too, I suppose."

"How he took his ship out of a fight in the West Indies and ft the *Resolve* to its fate? More than rumors, Nana," Pete said.

"And now he's done the same to us, damn his eyes," Olive said. He settled back against the wall and gathered her close "I can't leave you here, Nana."

"You must." She relaxed against him, but roused hersel again. "By the way, why did you and Pete keep such a deep dark secret about Henri Lefebvre? Couldn't you trust me?"

To their credit, Oliver and Pete looked at each othe abashed. "Oh, it doesn't matter," she told them.

"It does, Nana," Oliver replied.

She watched his discomfort and thought he would say m more. He held her more firmly. "I wasn't going to tell you thi but there is an odd connection between Henri Lefebvre an your father."

Nana listened, amazed, and then ashamed, as he told finding a drawing of her by Lefebvre on Ratliffe's desk i Admiralty House.

"Then they had a connection," she said and put her han to her mouth as she took the next leap. "Is my father a *spy* Oh, Oliver!"

"I think, at the very least, that he served as a conduit fo both Lefebvres to exchange information. Now that we kno it is Lefebvre-Desnouettes who is to be exchanged, it must n take place. Perhaps it's just as well that your father showe the white feather so this can't go forward," Oliver told he "And then there is the matter of information I gleaned fro Señor Rodriguez."

"No one knows in England if ye learned anything, sor Pete commented, from his perch on the end of the cot.

"I did."

He kept his voice soft, as though the room was packed wi agents of the French. "Before he died in my arms, he hande

ne a sheet of paper—information directly from Marshal Soult
imself—that Rodriguez intercepted."

Nana turned to look at him. "They didn't find it?"

"No, thanks to Gran."

She stared at him. "You're quizzing me."

"Not at all. Remember when I left? Gran gave me another
wheat poultice for my ears. They'd been bothering me, so I
wore it ashore around my neck when we came to fetch off
Rodriguez. When he handed me the sheet, I rolled it up quicker
han you can say Jack Robinson and slid it into the poultice."

"My word," Nana said. She looked at the table, where the
poultice lay. "No one suspected?"

"No. Not that they didn't strip me and check all my body
openings." He winced. "Yet another reason to detest the
French. I didn't say anything, of course." He touched his face.
The bruises are gone, but I did lose a tooth in the service of
King George. I may send a bill to Bonaparte."

She hugged him and eyed the poultice again. "You
ust…just leave it there?"

"Sometimes the best place to hide things is in plain sight.
I even talked our friend Le Colonel into letting his cook set
it in the warming oven, when my ears ache."

"Well, I'm fair gobsmacked," Nana said, which made her
usband laugh and make some remark about Miss Pym
putting her in the corner of a room and leaving her there for
half a day, if she had said that ten years ago.

She was serious soon enough. "So you can leave, and
probably Pete, but not me?"

"It sounds that way. You heard him. He's a bureaucrat at
heart and stickler with that damned piece of paper. It states I
alone am to be exchanged for Lefebvre-Desnouettes, with a
surety left behind." He tightened his grip on her. "I'm not

leaving without you. What kind of man would abandon his wife to a French prison?"

"The kind who follows orders," she reminded him.

"Nana, don't," he said, and she saw how that tack pained him.

"Several months here, sor?" Pete interjected. He looked at Nana with an expression she remembered from years ago when she was small and caught in some misdeed. "Nana, ye need to take ye're own advice about sharing information."

"Nana, are you in some sort of trouble?" Oliver asked.

"I-I'm not certain I would put it quite that way," she said, stalling.

"Nana, you're already surprising me by even *being* here in Spain," Oliver said. "I thought I had spliced myself to a calm and biddable wife."

"Ordinarily I am precisely that," she said. "My bigger problem is that I love you."

She had hoped he might laugh at that, but he only sighed and pulled her closer. He kissed her ear. "Told you it wasn't a good idea."

"Nana. If you don't tell him, I will," Pete warned.

"Oh, very well," she said, and lowered her voice. "That last visit of yours. Well…" She paused, suddenly shy. There Oliver was, looking at her with a frown, and there was Pete. "Some months in Spain might be cutting it a little close." She paused again, wishing her husband wasn't so dense. "You'd probably prefer your son or daughter to be born on English soil, wouldn't you?"

He stared at her. "Well, damn me, *I'm* fair gobsmacked this time," he said softly. He turned his face into her shoulder.

They sat that way until Pete cleared his throat. "I have an idea," he said.

"That's a good thing," Oliver said frankly, "because I'm all ut of them." He tightened his grip on her. "I won't leave Nana."

"Maybe you don't have to." Pete looked at her, as if sizing er up. "Nana, we're about the same height. Wrapped in my loak, and if it's dark enough, who'd be the wiser if you left nstead of me?"

She could think of all kinds of reasons to object, but something in Pete's eyes told her to save her breath.

"I could put on your dress and cloak, and you could cover ne up in the cot there," Pete said, looking at Oliver for obection. He shrugged. "I suppose there are better plans, but I an't think of any."

"Nor I," Oliver agreed. "Damn, but it chafes me Lord Ratliffe isn't brave enough to do his own work!" He considred the matter. "After Nana and I leave, anyone looking in vould think you were Nana, distraught and unable to rise."

"Hopefully long enough for you to get back to the *ireless*," Pete said.

"What would the French do to you, Pete?" Nana asked. "I ouldn't bear it if something happened."

Pete sidestepped her question and addressed Oliver. "You now the colonel. How close would he look?"

Oliver considered the matter. He had rested his hands on er belly, just as she did. The warmth of his fingers put the eart back in her

"Maybe not close at all."

"But what would he do to Pete when he discovered the deeption?" she asked again. "I don't want something terrible n my conscience. I couldn't live with it."

"It might not be your decision," Pete replied.

"Let's ratchet up some guilt for the colonel," Oliver said

finally. "I think he will be back. Could you work up some tears, Nana love? Really gusty ones?"

She didn't think it would be hard at all, considering the way she felt at that moment, and told him so.

"I can tell him that I realize I must leave my wife behind as repugnant as that is. All the time, you can be crying as loud as you please, Nana. I'll beg him to let Pete and me leave just at sunrise. The sooner we're away, the sooner the matter will be resolved. Don't most men find a woman's tears unnerving?"

"We don't have many other weapons," Nana admitted.

"I can almost wager he'll be so upset he'll send his aide—a real slow-top—to see us away. If we can clear the beach before anyone notices, we have a chance." Oliver looked at Pete. "What will happen to Pete is an unknown, and we cannot change that."

"Bravo," Pete said softly. "Get Nana to the *Tireless* and stop Lord Rat from any more mischief."

Oliver put his hand on the old man's shoulder. "Isn't this where you're supposed to tell me you are no longer subject to navy requirements and remind me you can do as you please?"

"Maybe I was wrong, sor. You know I'd do anything for Nana."

"So would I, Pete. Thank you from the bottom of my heart."

The plan didn't require much strategy beyond listening for the colonel's footsteps and working up an ocean of tears. Just the sound of footsteps in the corridor—never mind if it was the colonel or not—was enough to start her tears bubbling up from that part of her brain where terror was firmly in charge.

When Oliver stood up and nodded to her, she threw herself into his arms, clinging to him and wailing as though the Four Horsemen of the Apocalypse were stamping impatiently outside the door, instead of one overweight French colonel.

He sidled into the cell and stared at her, uncertain, as she cried and then sagged against her husband, who picked her up and deposited her on the cot.

"Keep it up, love," he whispered.

She curled into a ball and continued to weep.

"Should I send for a physician?" the colonel asked, his voice quavering. Nana could barely hear him over her own racket.

"What good would that do, since you will not allow her to leave with me?" Oliver said, sounding more weary than ten men with hysterical wives.

"I have my orders," Colonel San Sauvir said feebly.

"As one officer to another, I do not dispute that. Do one thing for me, at least—let me and Pete leave as soon as it's light. The sooner we're away, the sooner this matter will be resolved."

"*Oui,* certainly."

Oliver sat down heavily beside her. "Colonel San Sauvir, I depend upon your word as a gentleman that she will be treated with the utmost care."

"You have that, Captain Worthy."

Nana heard him open the door and speak to someone in the corridor. In a moment, there was the smell of food in the room.

"Is there anything else I can do for you? I will have a pallet brought here for Monsieur Carter. Some smelling salts for your wife? Can I warm that poultice?"

"No, you've done all you can," Oliver replied, his voice so mournful that she had to remind herself to continue her own charade.

"There is one more thing," her husband said. "Pass the word to my men on the beach to be ready to receive me and Pete at first light."

"I will do that now, Captain." There was a long pause, then

San Sauvir said, "Do give your charming wife my sympathies." The door clanged shut behind him.

With a laugh, Oliver leaned back against her hip. "Nana,
you're amazing."

She sat up, wiping her eyes with her sleeve. "It wasn't hard,
Oliver. I'm scared to death."

He handed her his handkerchief. "I wish we had a better
plan. Unless Lord Nelson himself rises from the dead and
suddenly appears on the horizon with the whole Royal Navy,
I can't imagine what it would be."

Exhausted by the events of the day, and even more by the
weariness that seemed to be her lot since finding herself with
child, Nana slept soundly in her husband's arms. She vaguely
heard him conversing in low tones with Pete, but was too
tired to care.

When it was still dark, Oliver woke her by unbuttoning her
dress. She stood up dutifully; shivering, she stepped out of her
dress. She untied her petticoat and let it drop, but kept on her
chemise. In another moment, Oliver handed her Pete's
clothing, which she put on quickly.

"Too big around the waist," she whispered, holding the
waistband away from her.

"Savor the moment, Nana," Oliver teased, as he handed her
Pete's belt. "It'll pass in a month or two, eh?"

She jabbed him with her elbow and he kissed her neck in
return.

"Can ye button me the back, sor?" Pete asked, which made
her laugh out loud, then cover her mouth.

"I'll do it, Pete," she said. "Did you already tie on my
petticoat?"

He muttered something which she took for a yes.

When she finished, Oliver grinned at him. "Twirl around, Pete. Let's see how captivating you are."

Pete said something that made her gasp and then giggle.

Pete's shoes were too large, but Oliver tore off a length of her petticoat that Pete wore, and stuffed the toes so she could at least keep them on. Wrapping Pete's boat cloak around her, she lay down on the pallet he had vacated, and he replaced her beside Oliver on the cot.

"You're not nearly so soft, my love," Oliver told him.

"Mind your manners," Pete growled. "You know buggery's a hanging offense in the fleet."

"Stop it, you two," Nana said.

Wide-awake, they lay still. The room began to lighten slowly, as dawn came. When she could see outlines in the cell, Nana got up.

Oliver rose, too, and stood peering out of the small window. "Perfect," he said. "It's raining. Nobody will wonder at your hood up over your face, Nana."

She heard footsteps in the hall and took a deep breath. "Pete, I love you," she whispered. "If it's a boy, we're naming him after you."

"Ye'd better, Nana." Pete laughed softly, and tucked the blanket high around him, turning toward the wall.

She heard the key turn in the lock and a high voice proclaiming, "Get up! Get up!" in French.

"Thank the Lord. It's Lieutenant DuPuy, the dumbest man on the continent," Oliver whispered. He gave her a quick kiss and made sure her hood was hanging over her face.

The door opened. She stood behind Oliver, letting him shield her from the lantern light.

"Get out now!"

She could see Oliver securing the thin wheat poultice

around his neck. "Cold morning," he said in French. "One moment, Lieutenant."

He went back to the cot, leaned over it and kissed Pete. "I'll send someone for you as soon as I can, my love," he said. He stood up and clapped Nana on the shoulder, pushing her forward roughly. "Come on, Pete. Let's get this over with before she starts to cry again."

On cue, Pete began to wail in a high falsetto, which made the French lieutenant gasp and then giggle nervously. He couldn't leave the cell fast enough.

With her husband's hand on her shoulder, Nana began Pete's rolling, arthritic walk. Tears started in her eyes as she walked along the corridor, remembering the time Gran had punished her with no dinner when she had imitated Pete's walk for her little Plymouth friends.

She nearly lost Pete's shoes on the stairs, but they were out of the convent soon enough. When the door closed behind them, her husband could not hold back an audible sigh of relief.

Following the French lieutenant and his bobbing lantern, they walked through the convent's gates and down to the beach. The sun was up now, but it was raining. The grey of the sky met the grey of the sea and she thanked God for the bluster and the rain that kept the French sentries crouched by their fires.

Oliver steadied her as they went carefully down the slippery steps of the quay toward the *Tireless*'s jolly boat. She could barely make out the sailors, sitting there, ready to row. Oliver pushed her forward into the boat. "Hurry up, Pete," he said gruffly. "We haven't got all day, damn ye."

She stumbled toward the stern of the jolly boat. The bosun's mate sitting there looked her in the eyes. To his ever-lasting credit, he caught on immediately and shoved her down beside him, forcing her low in the jolly boat and out of sight of the French soldiers standing by to cast off the lines that bound them to Spain.

Hurry, hurry, my love, Nana thought as she watched her husband standing so casually on the dock, talking to the lieutenant.

"You and your colonel had better make sure my wife is treated with all respect, or by God, I will bring the whole fleet down upon your head," Oliver said, biting off each word.

The lieutenant pulled himself up tall and bowed. "Sir! We are Frenchmen! We do not make war on females! Leave now!"

"With pleasure," Oliver said, with a stiff nod of his head.

He took his time getting into the boat, pausing to look back at the lieutenant and glare at him. "I'm trusting you with my heart's delight," he told the Frenchman.

"Sir! Please! Go!" the lieutenant snapped. He turned on his heel and left the wharf, after ordering the soldiers to release the lines.

Oliver sat down in the bow.

"The Frogs took the sail," the bosun's mate said in a low voice.

"Then row, lads," Oliver ordered, "handsomely now!"

Chapter Twenty

Oliver sat in the bow, watching his wife crouched in the stern, her eyes fastened upon him, her terror obvious. He wanted to move back and reassure her, but he couldn't risk upsetting the boat. They were moving slowly out to sea, under guns that bristled from the convent's parapet. An alarm raised now would blow them from the water.

Call him a fool, but he could not help the relief he felt, just in being on the water again. After all these years, it was his native element, and would remain so, no matter how much he loved his wife, and all the children that would probably follow, provided they survived to reach the *Tireless*. As he kept his unwavering gaze upon the creature dearest to him in all the universe, he hoped she would understand this dual nature of his. He thought she did, which made her even more beloved, if that were humanly possible.

After ten minutes of energetic rowing, the *Tireless* came into view through the mist. He didn't know when he had seen a more welcome sight, unless it was Nana, her arms open wide, come to greet him at the door of the Mulberry, these past few times.

It didn't come as a surprise to him that Nana was carrying

his child. Their few couplings had been fervid and intense, almost a mirror of his—and now their—knowledge that the clock was always ticking every second he spent on land. He wondered what it would be like to someday make a baby in leisure. He looked at the receding coastline. A tranquil love life would depend entirely on Boney, he thought.

As he watched the convent, he felt the rumble even before he saw the flash. Maybe DuPuy wasn't the fool he had thought. Or maybe Colonel San Sauvir felt remorse at his suffering wife in the cell. Pete had obviously been discovered, and San Sauvir must have not been amused by an arthritic sailor in a dress.

Nana cried out in terror as the cannonball splashed into the water some yards behind the jolly boat. Her scream of "Pete!" drilled right into his brain. *I've got to get to her,* he thought, even as he knew better than to move. The last thing they needed was for him to be pitched into the sea, and the note, snatched from Rodriguez at terrible cost, to be soaked. He stayed where he was, and was gratified a second later to see the bosun's mate put his arm around Nana, and speak to her. His wife nodded, and set her lips firmly together.

I must see that Riley is promoted as soon as possible, Oliver thought.

"Row, lads!" the bosun's mate shouted.

They needed no encouragement. Still, the pace seemed desperately slow. He pressed his own lips in a firm line as the next cannonball landed in front of the jolly boat. *Oh God, we're bracketed now,* he thought.

"Nana, can you swim?" he shouted.

She nodded, telling him with her eyes how much she loved him. Her hand was pressed involuntarily to her belly, protecting their child against the next barrage that would probably take them out of the water.

It never came. The *Tireless*'s starboard gunports opened and hurled an answering barrage. He watched his frigate, commanded ably by Mr. Ramseur, leave its anchorage as though on springs and swoop toward the coast. Mr. Ramseur wore the ship expertly and the guns on the port side belched fire. The sailors in the jolly boat rowed for all they were worth.

The bosun's mate had pushed Nana down between the thwarts, where she huddled, her hands over her ears.

The French gunners fired again, but their target was the *Tireless* now. Oliver yearned with all his heart for the next fifteen minutes to pass quickly. They could haul Nana aboard, he could regain his own quarterdeck and they would make all sail for England. He had to trust his acting first mate to do what his captain would do.

Mr. Ramseur did not disappoint. Like a mother eagle swooping to defend her chicks, the *Tireless* sailed as close to the wind as she dared, then backed her sails. In a blessed few minutes, the bosun's mate—God bless the man—was holding Nana up to the chains and she was clambering up. Willing hands reached for her and swung her over the rail. Oliver closed his eyes in relief, and turned his attention to the shore, where the guns still fired.

The target wasn't the *Tireless* this time, but the *Goldfinch,* teasing the French gunners like a strumpet, diverting their attention from larger prey.

"Your turn, sir," the bosun's mate said.

He gave the man's shoulder a squeeze as he passed him, then threw himself against the chains for his own climb to the deck. He looked down as the sailors secured the jolly boat to the *Tireless,* then made their own ascent, none the worse for wear.

Nana stood there, shivering, but his attention had to be on the quarterdeck where Mr. Ramseur stood, his eyes boring ahead at the coastline. He looked down at his captain, and Oliver saw the familiar Ramseur again, a little unsure.

Oliver cupped his hands to his mouth. "Mr. Ramseur, take us out of here. I'm tired of an enemy shore!"

The gunners in the ship's waist cheered as the acting first mate shouted, "You heard him!" then cheered again as Oliver grabbed his wife in a monumental embrace that threatened to topple her.

He couldn't overlook the tears on her face. "We'll get Pete out," he assured her. "I have an idea. It might even be a good one."

His arm around her, he walked her to the quarterdeck and up the short ladder. Mr. Ramseur immediately took the lee side of the deck, but Oliver went to him and shook his hand.

"Mr. Ramseur, you are no longer acting first mate. You're my number one now. I can't thank you enough."

Mr. Ramseur blushed and stammered his thanks.

"I'm taking Nana below," he said. "The deck's yours." He looked around. "Where is Lord Ratliffe?"

Ramseur nodded toward the *Goldfinch,* which was retiring now, too. "He said he had important work at Admiralty. We transferred him late last night at his request."

"I can well imagine," Oliver said dryly. "Have the signal-man run up this message—'Captain Worthy boarding.'"

"Aye aye, sir," Mr. Ramseur said.

Oliver helped Nana belowdecks and into his cabin. He was startled to see her bandbox in his sleeping cabin, then remembered she had been on his ship only a day ago. Even still wrapped in Pete's cloak, she shivered. As she watched, he opened her bandbox and took out her nightgown. Without a word, he took off Pete's cloak as she unbuckled the belt. The trousers hit the floor next, followed by the shirt. Without saying a word, she raised her arms and he dropped her nightgown over her.

He picked her up, holding her close, then put her in his

sleeping cot, which swung from the overhead deck beams. He found another blanket and tucked it around her as she burrowed into his bed.

"Don't leave me yet," she asked.

He needed no more invitation. With a sigh, he took off his shoes and then his uniform jacket and lay down beside her, careful not to set the cot rocking too vigorously. He put his arm around her and she tucked herself close to him, one leg thrown over him, in that way he had come to like so well.

"I've never been so frightened," she admitted. "I don't know how any of you face that, week in and week out."

"Maybe we do it so our wives and children can rest easy in their own English beds," he replied. Maybe that was the truth. It seemed far simpler than any proclamations from politicians, but he felt that way now.

Her head was resting on his chest, so he kissed her hair. He held her close until she stopped shivering and began to relax, her breasts heavy and warm against his side.

"I didn't know you had asked Mr. Lefebvre for a sketch of me before you left that first time," she said, her voice sleepy.

He looked up at the two pictures of her on the overhead deck beam. "It seemed like a good idea. And then you so brazenly sent me a picture of your own."

"Rag manners on my part," she admitted. "I didn't want you to forget me, because I knew I was going to remember you forever, even if I never saw you again."

Her words were as honest as everything else about her. He knew it was time for another confession.

"Nana, I never really told you why I came to the Mulberry in the first place."

He thought she was asleep, because it took her a moment to answer him.

"I assumed you saw one of those flyers I put up at the Drake."

"Not at all. I had already dropped my luggage there because I always stayed at the Drake. When I was at Admiralty House, reporting on my latest mission to your father, he told me what turned out to be a cock-and-bull story about you rejecting all his attempts to help you."

His answer was an unladylike snort from his wife.

"He asked me to stay at the Mulberry and make a report on how things were."

"We were at our last prayers."

"I know. When I learned how things really were, I wrote him what I thought was a real taradiddle about how times were tough, but the Mulberry was doing well. I can only surmise he didn't believe me."

"And what about Mr. Lefebvre?"

He felt his eyes grow heavy as his wife's body heat reminded him how tired he was. "Nana, Lefebvre sketched picture after picture of the harbor and what came and went. They're hidden in his sketchbook, at least those he didn't send on to your father, or to Colonel Lefebvre-Desnouttes, who is supposed to be the object of this exchange, probably engineered by Lord Ratliffe."

She sat up and leaned on her elbow to look him in the face. "Can you prove this?"

"Maybe not, but I can bluff your father." He sat up and kissed her, then pushed her down and wrapped the blanket around her. "Keep that spot warm. I'll be back."

She wouldn't release his hand, so he stayed a few more minutes at her side until she fell asleep.

He gained the deck again to see the *Goldfinch* alongside. "It's still yours, Mr. Ramseur," he said as he took off his shoes and stockings for stability and walked the sloping plank between the ships.

Dennison saluted as he came aboard. "Well done, indeed, sir," he said.

Leaning against the rail, Oliver acquainted the younger captain with the details of their escape. "So you see, a good man is a prisoner there now, and I want him back." He looked around. "Where's that blasted Lord Ratliffe?"

Dennison made a face. "Lord, what a chowderhead! If we were to make a pact and drop him overboard, not one man on either ship would tell."

"I have a better idea. Let's send him ashore for another exchange. I owe Napoleon an Admiralty officer. Where is he now?"

"In my mate's cabin."

Oliver went belowdecks and in another moment was perched on the sleeping cot across from his father-in-law, who crouched on a stool, unable to hide the terror on his face.

Oliver just looked at him, sizing him up and down in silence until Ratliffe raised his hands, as if surrendering. He tried to speak, but no words came out.

Oliver kept his tone affable. "I'm sorry to stare, my lord, but I've been wondering what a man looks like who is so willing to sacrifice his daughter for his own safety. Like you, eh?"

Lord Ratliffe paled. "I have important work to do at Admiralty House. I…" His voice trailed away.

"Your work was to be a surety for General Lefebvre-Desnouettes' release," Oliver said, snapping off his words. "I have no doubt that Colonel San Sauvir would have treated you better than his own mother!"

He couldn't help himself. The terror in Nana's face, and Pete's calm acceptance of his fate, swam before his eyes. No wonder his voice rose; they could probably hear him on the *Tireless*.

"And there's this matter of both Lefebvres—one a favorite of Napoleon, and the other a spy. Uh, that would be the one you sent to Plymouth and lodged at the Mulberry. The same one who ever-so-carefully sketched every ship coming and going and sent them to you, and through you, to the general in Cheltenham. Shame on you, Lord Ratliffe, for betraying your country."

He said the last quietly, his eyes boring into Lord Ratliffe, who refused to look at him.

"I have disposed of Henri Lefebvre."

Lord Ratliffe raised terrified eyes to him. "My God, how?" he croaked.

"He's on a long voyage to India, on an East India merchantman. Poor man found himself impressed and thrown aboard at the last minute."

To his credit, Lord Ratliffe did attempt to mount a defense. "You can't connect me to him!"

"I can," Oliver said, crossing his fingers behind his back. "It seems Henri left a letter with your name on it. I suppose he didn't trust you, either. Smart of him." Never taking his eyes from the viscount, Oliver stretched out on the sleeping cot. "The Crown still hangs, draws and quarters traitors, Lord Ratliffe. It probably won't be your best day."

The next sound then was urine running down the viscount's leg and onto the deck. *What a weakling you are,* Oliver thought, as he watched in disgust. *I'm so glad Nana has none of your traits.*

Oliver put his hands behind his head. "You can still be a hero."

"H-how?" the man asked, quaking, as he stared in horror at his puddle on the deck.

"We can put you in Captain Dennison's gig with a white flag and exchange you for Pete Carter. It's not a fair exchange, though, because he's a far better man than you. I doubt you'll be in Colonel San Sauvir's custody very long." Oliver frowned. "Well, it might be a while, because I can assure you we will not exchange Lefebvre-Desnouettes now. Thanks to you, he probably knows too much."

"What makes you think Napoleon will ever release me then, if there is no exchange?"

Oliver swung his feet over the edge of the cot. It took every bit of strength he possessed not to grab his father-in-law and shake him. "Because with or without traitors, we're going to defeat the French! In spite of you!"

He clapped his hands together, which made Lord Ratliffe jump. "That's the offer. If you go back to England now, you'll go in chains, and then you'll stare at your own intestines as they're spooled from your body. Or you can remain in a Spanish prison until we finally defeat Napoleon. You'll return a hero."

"You'll say nothing?" Something of that cagey look was coming back into Lord Ratliffe's eyes.

"Not a word, as long as you resign immediately from all duties at Admiralty House and retire to your country estate. If there is ever a peep from you, I'll be at Whitehall with all my evidence." Oliver stood. "I'm being overly generous. What say you?"

"What choice do I have?" the viscount snapped.

"None, really," Oliver said serenely. "Hurry up. I want to get Nana back to Plymouth."

"I can't believe you married a bastard," the viscount said, goading him, the last attempt of a weak man.

Steady, Oliver, he told himself, even as his hand balled into a fist. *Take a deep breath.* "Smartest thing I ever did," he replied finally.

"A bastard with a barely literate grandmother. You're probably already the laughingstock of the fleet."

Oliver opened the door, and made an elaborate bow. "After you, my lord. Before you go, let me thank you from the bottom of my heart for never telling *anyone* that you are my wife's father. Now *that* would be hard to live down."

He turned a deaf ear to the viscount's demand that he at least be allowed to change his pantaloons, and ushered him on deck, where Captain Dennison had ordered the gig readied for a trip to Spain, flying a white flag.

Lord Ratliffe may have been rendered toothless of argument, but he did not go over the side without another shot.

"Eleanor is a most ungrateful child," he hissed, as he prepared to lower himself down the side. "She could have been mistress to an earl, at least, and now she's stuck with a sea captain."

"Poor thing," Oliver commiserated. "At least no one sold her to the highest bidder." He had a sudden thought, and it made his blood run cold. "Did you do this to any other of your by-blows? I assume there are more."

"One," the viscount said. The *Goldfinch* lurched, and he clung to the ship's rail as the watching sailors laughed. "She was biddable, at least."

Poor girl, Oliver thought. Poor girl. "Any more?" he asked casually.

He had to give Lord Ratliffe points for vindictiveness, even when he was clinging to the ship's rail in a most indecorous fashion. "One more," he gasped. "She'll be on the street in a wink, now that I'm headed to exile."

"No, she won't," Oliver said, as he itched to wrap his fingers around his father-in-law's throat. "At Miss Pym's?"

The viscount started down the chains. "Where else? Pym is *my* bastard sister."

"Care to name her?"

"Your problem, Worthy."

Oliver leaned over the rail, keeping his voice low. "We'll find her. That'll please Nana to have sisters. *Au revoir,* Lord Ratliffe. Good of you to exchange yourself for an old jack tar, with nothing to redeem him but courage and loyalty." He snapped off his best salute. "You're my hero."

Nana was dressed and on deck, sitting with Matthew, when Oliver returned from the *Goldfinch.* She refused to go below until hours later, when the gig deposited Pete Carter on the *Tireless.* His face was bruised, and he was missing two teeth, but he pirouetted around the deck in her dress, as the crew laughed, then gave him three cheers.

She didn't leave Pete's side until the surgeon had seen to his injuries, pronounced him able enough to eat and prescribed trousers and shirt again, because "it's a cold voyage to Plymouth, Carter."

Pete wouldn't accept Oliver's offer of Mr. Ramseur's cabin, now that his second mate had moved into the late Mr. Proudy's quarters. "No, sor, but thankee," he said. "I'd feel better swinging in a hammock by the guns."

Nana required no convincing to get back in her nightgown and return to his sleeping cot. After kissing her and telling her not to wait up, Oliver went back on deck. He stood on the quarterdeck as Mr. Ramseur turned the watch over to a midshipman, took one last look around, then joined him.

They watched the *Goldfinch* skimming ahead of them toward Ferrol Station. Their own course was Plymouth. Oliver knew he had another forty-hour post chaise journey to London ahead, and then a return to the Channel Fleet, but in between, there would always and everlastingly be Plymouth. It was more than port to him now; it was his home, and Nana's, and his child's, even now growing inside the dearest person he knew. He hoped it would always mystify him that someone with brown eyes, an affable air and—generally—a biddable demeanor could be his compass rose.

"Well, Mr. Ramseur, what's done is done," he said. "I'm going below. Tell Mr. Toplady there that I'm only to be disturbed if Napoleon himself rows out to meet us."

"I wouldn't dare tell him that, sir," Mr. Ramseur said. "He'd be petrified. I'll tell him to hail me."

He thought Nana was asleep, so Oliver undressed quietly and crawled into his sleeping cot to settle himself beside her. He was tugging down his nightshirt when she gathered him close.

"I love you, Oliver Worthy," she whispered in his ear. "Are you really going to retrieve a half sister of mine from Miss Pym's?"

"If she'll go. Let's both go to Bath and find her, shall we? I think I can convince Lord Mulgrave that I need a week's shore leave. If she won't leave, we'll at least make sure her tuition is paid until such time as she finishes her studies and finds employment."

Nana took his hand and kissed it, then tucked it against her breast. "Bless you," she said.

They swung silently in the cot.

"I have another confession."

He was already exploring her breast, but he stopped. "Should I be worried?"

"I…I convinced Brustein and Carter to let me have a draft of ten thousand pounds, to add to the Whitehall ransom. Lord Ratliffe claimed Whitehall was unhappy about paying twenty thousand, and I thought that would help."

"Whitehall paid twenty thousand pounds without complaint," he said. "That was the sum in the ransom chest." He threw his head back and laughed. "That old fox! He got ten thousand of my money!"

Nana looked at him anxiously. "I feel terrible about that."

He returned to his exploration of her breasts. "It'll go to his creditors, who deserve to be paid. I can stand the strain, Nana. Don't let that worry you. We'll just feed the Mulberry lodgers more porridge and less cod and leeks."

Nana seemed to be concentrating on his massage more than his words. "Do that easier," she asked, her breath coming a little faster. "I'm tender there. No, don't stop."

"How about this instead?" he asked, his lips on her breasts now, and his hand lower.

"That's…about prime," she said, then closed her eyes and sighed.

He shifted on the cot until she was under him. "If we do this carefully, we won't end up on the deck. A noise like that would bring the sentry outside my door running in here."

"We can't have that," she said. "My goodness, Captain Worthy."

He settled himself on her and her legs went around him. He smiled as she moved so carefully. "I think we're squared away in the center," he told her. "We can even take advantage of the ship's pitch and yaw."

"It's not physics," she murmured, kissing his shoulder.

"Geometry, then," he said.

"I'm busy. Hush."

He did. Afterward, he rested his hand on her belly. "When will you feel movement? Any idea?"

"I'll ask Mrs. Brittle," she said, putting her hand on his. "Maybe consult a physician."

"That would be best. I hope he doesn't tell you that…uh…geometry in a sleeping cot isn't a good idea."

"I won't listen, if he does," she said simply.

They swung gently.

"Mrs. Worthy, I have a suggestion."

She nodded.

"It might be a girl. What say we name her Rachel, after your mother?"

She caught her breath and said his name, which covered him like a benediction. She touched his face. When she spoke, she sounded hesitant, shy almost. "Oliver, am I worthy?"

"In deed, bone, blood and name." He kissed her fingers, and she twined them in his. "But you always were, Nana, always."

Author's Note

General Charles Lefebvre-Desnouettes, a cavalry officer and favorite of Napoleon, was captured in Spain in 1808. Paroled to Cheltenham, England, he was joined there by his wife, Stephanie. The two of them became favorites of the local gentry, attending many social events.

Alas, Lefebvre-Desnouettes was no gentleman, for he jumped his parole and escaped to France in 1811. He served again at Napoleon's side through the disastrous Russian Campaign, and at Waterloo in 1815.

The resourceful Lefebvre-Desnouettes fled next to the United States. He lived in Louisiana until 1821, when his ever-loyal Stephanie arranged passage to Amsterdam. Alas, again, the general's ship sank in a storm off the Irish coast and he drowned.

* * * * *

Celebrate 60 years of pure reading pleasure with Harlequin® Books!

Harlequin Romance® is celebrating by showering you with
DIAMOND BRIDES *in February 2009.*
Six stories that promise to bring a touch of sparkle to your life, with diamond proposals and dazzling weddings, sparkling brides and gorgeous grooms!

Enjoy a sneak peek at Caroline Anderson's
TWO LITTLE MIRACLES,
available February 2009 from Harlequin Romance®.

I've found her.'

Max froze.

It was what he'd been waiting for since June, but now—now he was almost afraid to voice the question. His heart stalling, he leaned slowly back in his chair and scoured the investigator's face for clues. 'Where?' he asked, and his voice sounded rough and unused, like a rusty hinge.

'In Suffolk. She's living in a cottage.'

Living. His heart crashed back to life, and he sucked in a long, slow breath. All these months he'd feared—

'Is she well?'

'Yes, she's well.'

He had to force himself to ask the next question. 'Alone?'

The man paused. 'No. The cottage belongs to a man called John Blake. He's working away at the moment, but he comes and goes.'

God. He felt sick. So sick he hardly registered the next few words, but then gradually they sank in. 'She's got *what?*'

'Babies. Twin girls. They're eight months old.'

'Eight—?' he echoed under his breath. 'They must be his.'

He was thinking out loud, but the P.I. heard and corrected him.

'Apparently not. I gather they're hers. She's been there since mid-January last year, and they were born during the summer—June, the woman in the post office thought. She was more than helpful. I think there's been a certain amount of speculation about their relationship.'

He'd just bet there had. God, he was going to kill her. Or Blake. Maybe both of them.

'Of course, looking at the dates, she was presumably pregnant when she left you, so they could be yours, or she could have been having an affair with this Blake character before…'

He glared at the unfortunate P.I. 'Just stick to your job. I can do the math,' he snapped, swallowing the unpalatable possibility that she'd been unfaithful to him before she'd left. 'Where is she? I want the address.'

'It's all in here,' the man said, sliding a large envelope across the desk to him. 'With my invoice.'

'I'll get it seen to. Thank you.'

'If there's anything else you need, Mr Gallagher, any further information—'

'I'll be in touch.'

'The woman in the post office told me Blake was away at the moment, if that helps,' he added quietly, and opened the door.

Max stared down at the envelope, hardly daring to open it, but when the door clicked softly shut behind the P.I., he eased up the flap, tipped it and felt his breath jam in his throat as the photos spilled out over the desk.

Oh, lord, she looked gorgeous. Different, though. It took him a moment to recognise her, because she'd grown her hair and it was tied back in a ponytail, making her look younger and somehow freer. The blond highlights were gone, and it was back to its natural soft golden-brown, with a little curl in the end of the ponytail that he wanted to thread his finger through and tug, just gently, to draw her back to him.

Crazy. She'd put on a little weight, but it suited her. She

ooked well and happy and beautiful, but oddly, considering
ow desperate he'd been for news of her for the past year—
ne year, three weeks and two days, to be exact—it wasn't
nly Julia who held his attention after the initial shock. It was
he babies sitting side by side in a supermarket trolley. Two
dentical and absolutely beautiful little girls.

* * * * *

*When Max Gallagher hires a P.I. to find his estranged
wife, Julia, he discovers she's not alone—she has twin
baby girls, and they might be his. Now workaholic Max
has just two weeks to prove that he can be a wonderful
husband and father to the family he wants to treasure.*

Look for TWO LITTLE MIRACLES *by
Caroline Anderson, available
February 2009 from Harlequin Romance®.*

HARLEQUIN *Romance*®

This February the Harlequin® Romance series
will feature six Diamond Brides stories featuring
diamond proposals and gorgeous grooms.

Share your dream wedding proposal and you could WIN!

The most romantic entry will win a diamond
necklace and will inspire a proposal in one of
our upcoming Diamond Grooms books in 2010.

In 100 words or less, tell us the most romantic
way that you dream of being proposed to.

For more information, and to enter
the Diamond Brides Proposal contest, please visit
www.DiamondBridesProposal.com

Or mail your entry to us at:

IN THE U.S.: 3010 Walden Ave., P.O. Box 9069, Buffalo, NY 14269-9069
IN CANADA: 225 Duncan Mill Road, Don Mills, ON M3B 3K9

REQUEST YOUR FREE BOOKS!

Harlequin® Historical
Historical Romantic Adventure!

2 FREE NOVELS PLUS 2 FREE GIFTS!

YES! Please send me 2 FREE Harlequin® Historical novels and my 2 FREE gifts (gifts are worth about $10). After receiving them, if I don't wish to receive any more books, I can return the shipping statement marked "cancel". If I don't cancel, I will receive 6 brand-new novels every month and be billed just $4.94 per book in the U.S. or $5.49 per book in Canada, plus 25¢ shipping and handling per book and applicable taxes, if any*. That's a savings of 20% off the cover price! I understand that accepting the 2 free books and gifts places me under no obligation to buy anything. I can always return a shipment and cancel at any time. Even if I never buy another book, the two free books and gifts are mine to keep forever.

246 HDN ERUM 349 HDN ERUA

Name	(PLEASE PRINT)	
Address		Apt. #
City	State/Prov.	Zip/Postal Code

Signature (if under 18, a parent or guardian must sign)

Mail to the **Harlequin Reader Service:**
IN U.S.A.: P.O. Box 1867, Buffalo, NY 14240-1867
IN CANADA: P.O. Box 609, Fort Erie, Ontario L2A 5X3

Not valid to current subscribers of Harlequin Historical books.

Want to try two free books from another line?
Call 1-800-873-8635 or visit www.morefreebooks.com.

* Terms and prices subject to change without notice. N.Y. residents add applicable sales tax. Canadian residents will be charged applicable provincial taxes and GST. Offer not valid in Quebec. This offer is limited to one order per household. All orders subject to approval. Credit or debit balances in a customer's account(s) may be offset by any other outstanding balance owed by or to the customer. Please allow 4 to 6 weeks for delivery. Offer available while quantities last.

Your Privacy: Harlequin Books is committed to protecting your privacy. Our Privacy Policy is available online at www.eHarlequin.com or upon request from the Reader Service. From time to time we make our lists of customers available to reputable third parties who may have a product or service of interest to you. If you would prefer we not share your name and address, please check here. ☐

You're invited to join our Tell Harlequin Reader Panel!

By joining our new reader panel you will:

- Receive Harlequin® books—they are FREE and yours to keep with no obligation to purchase anything!
- Participate in fun online surveys
- Exchange opinions and ideas with women just like you
- Have a say in our new book ideas and help us publish the best in women's fiction

In addition, you will have a chance to win great prizes and receive special gifts! See Web site for details. Some conditions apply. Space is limited.

To join, visit us at
www.TellHarlequin.com.

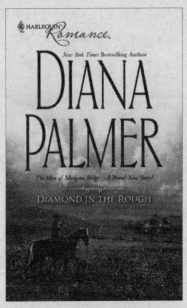

DIAMOND IN THE ROUGH

John Callister is a millionaire rancher, yet when he meets lovely Sassy Peale and she thinks he's a cowboy, he goes along with her misconception. He's had enough of gold diggers, and this is a chance to be valued for himself, not his money. But when Sassy finds out the truth, she feels John was merely playing with her. John will have to convince her that he's truly the man she fell in love with—a diamond in the rough.

THE MEN OF MEDICINE RIDGE—a brand-new miniseries set in the wilds of Montana!

Available April 2009 wherever you buy books.